ROCK & ROLL OVER

Edited By
ERIC SUMMERS

STARbooks PRESS
Herndon, VA

MW01671129

Copyright © 2010 by STARbooks Press

ISBN 10: 1-934187-81-X

ISBN 13: 978-1-934187-81-4

This book is a work of fiction. Names, characters, places, situations and incidents are the product of the authors' imaginations or are used fictitiously. Any resemblance to actual events, locales, or persons, living or dead, is purely coincidental. All rights reserved, including the right of reproduction in whole or in part in any form.

Published in the United States by STARbooks Press

PO Box 711612, Herndon, VA 20171

Many thanks to graphic artist John Nail for the cover design. Mr. Nail may be reached at: tojonail@bellsouth.net.

Printed in the United States

STARbooks PRESS

Herndon, VA

STARbooks Press Titles by Eric Summers

Muscle Worshipers

Love in a Lock-Up

Unmasked – Erotic Tales of Gay Superheroes

Don't Ask, Don't Tie Me Up

Ride Me Cowboy

Service with a Smile

Never Enough – The Lost Writings of John Patrick

Unwrapped – Erotic Holiday Tales

Can't Get Enough – More Erotica Written by John Patrick

Unmasked II – More Erotic Tales of Gay Superheroes

Teammates

Rock & Roll Over

CONTENTS

A WOUND TURNED TO LIGHT
By Stephen Osborne

Sometimes the words wouldn't come. Other times, the tune would elude Tommy. It was rare, however, when he couldn't sit down with his Martin guitar and nothing came to him.

Tommy let his mind wander. Occasionally, a song would come to him seemingly through the ether, and all he had to do was write it down. Soon his fingers were picking out a tune. Unfortunately, it didn't take Tommy long to realize that he was playing an old Bob Dylan song.

Face it, he told himself. *You're just not in the songwriting mood.*

He hadn't been for months, though, and the other guys in Sexual Napalm were counting on him to come up with several additional songs for their new album. The last album, *Bad Hotel*, had sold fairly well but had drawn mixed reviews. Part of the problem, as their bass player Andy had complained (often and loudly), was that *Bad Hotel* didn't have a hit song on it. "It's not that the album sucks," he had said one night when he and Tommy had tried to out-drink each other, "it's just that nothing pops on it. Not a single fucking song grabs you by the throat and makes you want to listen to it. I mean really listen to it."

And, he'd been right. Tommy had promised to come up with something really special for their next release. So far, though, nothing was coming to him.

Tommy finished picking out the Dylan tune and then just sat, cross legged on the floor, clutching the guitar and stared off into space. His cell phone chirped, waking him from his reverie.

He smiled when he saw who was calling. "Hey," he answered.

"How's my favorite rock star doing?" Hearing John's voice always made Tommy smile. Tommy had never known anyone so full of life and laughter. When they'd first met, a chance encounter at a book store, Tommy hadn't really considered John as a possible partner. The more he talked with him, though, the more he began to like John. They were a study in contrasts. Tommy was famous, had pinup boy good looks, long black hair that was kept spiked up in the front, and often forgot to eat, making him painfully thin. John on the other hand, while not overweight, certainly never let a meal go untouched. John kept his hair George Clooney-short and wouldn't even consider putting product in it. John, who was an assistant manager of an ice cream parlor, hadn't even heard of Sexual Napalm His musical tastes ran more to Verdi and Bizet. The most modern composer he enjoyed, prior to meeting Tommy, had been Andrew Lloyd Webber.

"He's fine. How's my favorite slinger of ice cream?"

John chuckled. "Bored. I'm bored and wanting my rock star boyfriend to take me out tonight."

Tommy gently set the guitar aside and stretched out his legs. "Well, it seems that my planned evening of songwriting is scratched in any case. Nothing is coming to me, so I might as well go out and get some air. What did you have in mind?"

The two debated back and forth over several scenarios and eventually decided that they'd enjoy a few drinks at the

Mongoose, a trendy bar owned by a famous actor. Although John agreed, Tommy thought he detected a slight note of discontent in his boyfriend's voice. "What? Don't feel like rubbing elbows with L.A.'s In-crowd? There's a great band playing there tonight. I know it's not exactly your type of music, but ..."

"I just thought we could hit Carol and Mark's party and then go to the Mongoose. You know. Just make an appearance."

"It's so far out of the way," Tommy complained. "We'd miss the first set."

There was a minuscule pause before John said, "Okay. You know I can't say no to you. We'll go to the Mongoose, and I'll tell Carol we'll make it the next time."

Tommy wondered briefly what excuse he'd come up with the next time John wanted to see some friends. While John seemed to accept the fact that Tommy was closeted, he often forgot just what that meant to their social life. Tommy couldn't take the chance and show up with another guy at a party. Someone might become suspicious, and before long, there would be stories in the tabloids questioning Tommy's sexuality. No one would question two guys showing up at the Mongoose, however. Randall Smith, the actor who owned the Mongoose, kept tight security on the place, and the doorman would never allow access to anyone he even suspected of being from the press. Tommy knew of many other closeted people in the entertainment industry who frequented the Mongoose, knowing it to be a safe haven.

"Great," Tommy said. "I'll pick you up in half an hour."

Due to Los Angeles traffic, it was more than forty-five minutes before Tommy's Corvette pulled up outside John's modest apartment building. Before getting out, Tommy pulled the hood of his sweatshirt up to hide his trademark spiked hair. There didn't seem to be anyone around, but one could never be too careful.

There was a grin on John's cherubic face when he opened the door. Seeing Tommy's hoodie, he smirked, "Are you coming to rob the place or take me out on a date?"

Tommy stepped inside, carefully lowering the hood. He hated to mess up his hair. "I thought we'd go on a date, but if you want to play 'Capture the Burglar' later, I'd be game for some role-playing."

John planted a kiss on Tommy's lips. The two entwined and continued kissing until, with a snort, Tommy gently pushed John away. "While I know it's customary not to show up too early at the Mongoose, I also don't want to get there right at last call. Come on. I really want to see the band playing there tonight. They say the drummer is so good he can make you weep."

They headed out to Tommy's car but not before Tommy put the hood back in place. Had it been his imagination or had John sighed when he'd covered his head again? Generally John was upbeat and cheery, but the last few times they'd been out, Tommy thought he detected something in John's eyes, as if something perturbed the young man. Tommy had assumed that he was projecting his own frustrations over his writer's block into John, but what if something were truly bothering his lover?

There was quite a line to get into the Mongoose. There was no point in trying to get ahead in the line by using his fame – too many celebrities partied at the Mongoose, and all were treated equal. Once inside, however, there was a private bar where, if the rich and famous wanted, they could really let their hair down.

Tonight, however, Tommy wanted to stay in the main bar, so he could see Killer Storm, the band with the drummer who, if the critics were right, could bring about tears. John seemed happy enough while they waited to get in, and the two swapped stories about their day to pass the time. Tommy noticed a few people in line giving him the eye, but no one approached him. Such things just weren't done at the Mongoose.

The doorman recognized Tommy. "Well, if it isn't Mr. Sexual Napalm."

"One fifth of Sexual Napalm, anyway."

The doorman smiled. "The other guys in the group must be too good to frequent a dive like this. You're the only one that ever comes here."

"I hear Killer Storm is one hell of a band. Looking forward to hearing them."

"Better than that shit you guys put out," the doorman replied with a wink.

Tommy knew the guy was joking, but after their last album, the remark stung a little. "Catch ya later, my friend," he said as he and John slipped through the door.

The Mongoose was kept extremely dark, and it took several moments for their eyes to adjust. Getting his bearings, Tommy led the way to a small table not too far away from the stage. "This good for you?" he asked John.

John grinned. "Sure."

They sat. A pretty waitress with impossibly blue eyes came over to take their drink orders. "What can I get for ya, Tommy?" she asked. Waitresses at the Mongoose were used to celebrities. This one knew enough to acknowledge that she recognized him but was smart enough not to gush over him.

Not long after they got their drinks, beer for John and Jameson's for Tommy, the band started their first set. John, emboldened by the darkness of the place, slowly slid his foot across until it nudged against Tommy's. After a brief second, Tommy pulled his foot away.

"Sorry," John said, his tone saying he was anything but sorry.

Tommy leaned forward so that he could be heard over the music and gave John a pleading look. "Someone might see. Even here you've got to be careful."

John rolled his eyes. "My foot was barely touching yours. Hardly something that screams out, 'We're fucking!' It's not like we were blatantly playing footsie. In this light, no one could have possibly seen us."

"You never know," Tommy warned. He settled back to enjoy the music.

A brief look of anger crossed John's face, but Tommy was glad to see his lover eventually relax. John even seemed to enjoy the tunes being belted out by Killer Storm. During a break between songs, Tommy said, "They're good, aren't they? The drummer certainly lives up to his reputation."

John drained the rest of his beer. "They're not bad at all. I mean, they're no Rossini, but they're good. Not as good as Sexual Napalm, of course."

Tommy grinned. "Of course."

Tommy was pretty stoned by the time they got back to John's apartment. John himself was pleasantly tipsy, but unlike his partner, he could at least stand without swaying. They stood in the doorway to the bedroom, kissing and pulling at their clothes. Whiskey always made Tommy horny or at least he claimed it did, and John couldn't dispute the assertion. After much pawing and repeated wet, sloppy kisses, they got naked (more or less, one white sock remained on Tommy's left foot) and jumped into bed. Tommy tried to get on top of John, but to his surprise, John wrestled him around until Tommy was looking up into his boyfriend's eyes.

"What's up with you tonight?" Tommy asked, a little surprised. It wasn't like John to be that assertive.

"I thought I'd fuck you tonight for a change." There was a mischievous twinkle in John's eyes.

Tommy chuckled uneasily. "You're kidding, right?"

John grinned. "Do I look like I'm kidding?"

Swallowing hard, Tommy nodded slowly. Generally, Tommy was the pitcher and John the catcher, owing to Tommy's seeming inability to relax while being fucked. Still, he was nice and drunk and as relaxed as he was bound to get.

"Okay," he whispered. "Just go slow, okay?"

"I won't hurt you. I promise."

John broke out the condoms and lube. He used a generous amount of lube on the head of his dick and made sure that Tommy's hole was well-greased before he positioned himself between Tommy's legs. As he raised Tommy's legs to his shoulders John noticed the sock that they'd missed. He pulled it off and tossed it aside.

"Let me know if it starts to hurt at all," he said.

Tommy took a deep breath as he felt John enter him.

Wow, he thought. *This feels so much better than I remember. Maybe it's the Jameson's, but this doesn't hurt at all.*

Tommy moaned and writhed on the bed, tangling himself in John's sheets. John proceeded slowly, only increasing his thrusts at the urging of Tommy. Soon John was slamming his cock into Tommy's ass with a fury. The bed seemed to howl in protest as the two bucked and smacked against each other. The headboard began to sound out a beat against the wall.

"Oh, God," Tommy groaned. "Fuck me harder."

John could only grunt his response. Sensing his boyfriend was close to coming, Tommy began jacking his dick hard. Tommy wasn't sure the bed would hold out much longer, let alone him and John.

John came first, letting loose little squeals of pleasure as he pumped his cock hard into Tommy's butt. Before John's cock ceased throbbing within him, Tommy came himself, sending a stream of goo up onto his stomach, chest, and even onto the pillow next to his head.

After they'd cleaned up, they lay on the bed, snuggling. Tommy was exhausted and wanted nothing more than to fall asleep in John's arms, but he wanted to satisfy his nagging doubt before giving himself over to the Sandman. Even now, there was something in the way that John was holding him that just didn't feel right, as if John was lost in troubles.

"Are you okay?" Tommy asked.

It was several moments before John answered. "I'm fine," he said.

"You don't sound it."

John ran a hand through Tommy's long hair. "Go to sleep," he said.

Tommy awoke sometime in the night, knowing that something was wrong. He sat up and saw John sitting, naked, on the side of the bed with his head in his hands. John sniffed and ran a hand across his face when he realized Tommy was awake.

"I didn't mean to disturb you," he said.

Tommy reached over and placed a hand on John's back. He was getting a sinking feeling in the pit of his stomach, and he knew that, despite his protests, John wasn't happy. "What's wrong?"

"I think I know why you don't like to get fucked," John said.

Tommy tried to laugh. "I certainly liked getting fucked earlier. We'll have to switch up more often. I'm okay with that. I guess I just had to be drunk enough ..."

"You're afraid to let anyone in. Physically and mentally. You close yourself off."

The air in the room suddenly felt very hot to Tommy. He breathed out slowly. "If this is because of what happened at the Mongoose, I don't know, maybe I overreacted, but you've got to understand that in the rock world I come from, there's no way ..."

"That you could come out of the closet. Yes, I know. You've said that hundreds of times to me. And I can't tell you what to do. All I know is that I can't have a boyfriend that I can't touch whenever I want to. I can't only go to places where *you* feel safe. It's just not me. I'm not asking you to come out of the closet. I'm just saying that I'm not sure I can live this way anymore."

"So ... what are you saying?" Tommy's heart felt ready to burst. "Are you breaking up with me?"

John bit his knuckle. "I think maybe you'd better go home. Back to your place."

Tommy kept hoping that John would laugh and say it was all a joke. He dressed as slowly as he could, but John just cried softly and said nothing. When Tommy had everything on, John accompanied him to the door, avoiding looking into Tommy's eyes.

"Don't forget to put your hoodie up," he said. "Wouldn't want one of my neighbors to recognize you as you leave."

John gave Tommy a kiss at the door, something Tommy wished he hadn't done. It was too final. As he got into his car, the tears began to flow.

Tommy sat cross-legged on the floor, holding his precious Martin guitar. He didn't figure he could write anything, not the way he felt. He strummed softly, not really playing anything and wondered if there was anything he could do to get John back.

And then, the song came. It wrote itself. It filled Tommy's soul and flowed out of his fingers as they plucked the strings. It was the most honest, the most personal song Tommy had ever written. It would change Sexual Napalm; that was for sure, providing the other guys in the group would let him add it to the album. They would. Tommy would see to that.

There was no other title for the song, either, than "My Love for John."

BLESSED BY HER MAJESTY
By Derrick Della Giorgia

When you feel the black of the street all over your skin and clothes no matter how many wet tissues you've consumed, when you are stuck with the flavor of the breakfast you've had exactly twelve hours before because the only other calories that barely saved you from fainting came from an almost tasteless sugar bag, when your only desire is to survive the roaring mass of people behind you and be fast enough to secure first row in front of the stage, you don't think of yourself as sexy. Who is going to want you?

"Move in an orderly fashion, or the gate in front of you will never open!" Order, gate, never, open were the only four words that left a sediment in everybody's head once their meaning was deciphered through the French accent. At least four policemen were pushing us back and threatening us never to open the gate that separated us from Her.

Nobody was in front of me; that was the only consolation. I didn't even remember when I'd started the line, but I clearly recalled the gelid wind that had been piercing my face for eight hours after midnight and the scalding sun that had cooked my T-shirt over my shoulders from 11:00 am until 4:00 pm. Paris is a tough city if you dwell in the street, even in July. The sweet kiss of the Eiffel Tower, the fascinating mysteries of Notre Dame, the second-hand book stores along the Seine, the sinful chocolate bites at Fauchon ... all that had vanished after the first two hours in line. Now, my only concern was to find enough room to bend and stretch my backbone before my vertebrae crashed into each another.

"Excuse me." I turned behind and apologized for pushing my ass into his stomach. There wasn't space to breathe: a foul-smelling agglomerate of flesh in the back and a dangerously heavy metal barrier in the front. Thousands of people were in my same conditions, thousands of fans waiting to see Her, the only woman that was able to cause such a calamity. She was all over the news. Photographers, news people, curious tourists, helicopters controlling the situation from above; the *Palais Omnisports de Paris-Bercy* or simply Bercy burst with life and tension. I'd already been interviewed five times, in English, French, and Spanish. "What does this concert mean to you? When did you get here? How many times have you seen the concert so far? What's the point of seeing the same thing over and over again? Why is she worth this agonizing wait?" The questions never changed. People simply thought it was a sort of disease, a meaningless tour de force, *"C'est très stupid!"* – a French couple had commented after hearing why we were all there. Stupid fans. The part they unfortunately missed was that Her concerts were a concentrate of our society. Fashion, vocabulary, art, music, politics, spirituality were spun and spat out in your face for you to do what you thought best. The same way you go see a piece of art in a museum over and over again and every time you absorb something different, I attended Her concerts as many times as I could. And, it was never the same, always better. Enriching.

"I've seen you before. Were you also in Rome?" The Portuguese guy next to me asked me after catching his breath. He wasn't near me outside, but once the gate was open, nobody could control the river of lava expanding toward the stage. People flew, jumped, rolled, crawled and never stopped until they were as close to the stage as they could get. That was fosse debut for you, the standing area. If you wanted to see the concert without going through all that, you could get a seat. But, that is not the kind of animals we are talking about in this story.

"Yes, I was!" Of course, I was. I couldn't miss Her Majesty when she decided to honored my city with Her presence. Three more days of line and a much bloodier entrance.

"I saw your pictures on Facebook. Amazing!" Joao fruitlessly tried to rub a black mark off his chin. He had fallen face first into the shoe of the guy in front of him, but with a remarkable act of acrobatics, he'd managed to get back up and pass him, too.

"This time will be even better. I feel it." I could rest now. First row, center. In three hours – that was how much it took for all the technicalities to be in place and for Bercy to fill. She would be standing in front of me, charging me with Her potency. In the meantime, I could enjoy the second reason why the concert revived me so much every single time. I was in love with the sound-check guy. I guess after seeing the concert seven times, you really learn who everybody is and how they contribute to the show. I had met Her manager, head of security, Her make-up artist, the water guy (like clockwork, at the same point of the show the same guy handed Her water), and the sound-check guy. Steve was from New York, half Japanese, thick black glasses, massive tattoo on his right arm. He told me that he liked Rome, and he'd love to have time to visit it. That if he screwed up his job – that was in Madrid – half of the people probably wouldn't hear anything, and in Amsterdam, that I was quite cool to get first row all the time. To be honest, it took me some time to notice he was sexy; my mind is solely irrigated with fantasies about Her by the time I reach the stage. Most likely due to the Vatican fumes of love when he was checking the stage of the Olympic Stadium of Rome, his sapphire blue eyes landed on me, and we exchanged a smile. Since then, his role acquired more importance to me as his body was filed in a memory drawer of my mind. Not less significant, the sexy way he knelt at particular vital spots of the catwalk – carelessly allowing his jeans to go down on his ass as he emitted long sentences into the microphone. All in all, an excitingly hot package – especially when your crotch keeps rubbing a hard metal barrier in front of you under the pressure of the thousands of less fortunate – or less fast? – fans behind you.

Bercy, half full – one hour to go. Security was done; it was time for Steve to work his magic. And there he was, to my surprise, wearing a white tight tank top instead of his usual long sleeve black T-shirt. He started on the left side of the main stage and came down to me along the catwalk, his deltoids and biceps rhythmically inflating every time he pushed the mike into his lips.

"What's up, Steve?" I yelled at him before he could see me.

"Hi, there!" His shyness turned me on.

"Do you know that guy?" Joao immediately asked me. He'd only seen the concert three times.

"Yeah, I've seen him all the times." I replied without turning to look at him, hinting I wasn't going to answer any other questions.

Something was wrong with the audio right in the middle of the catwalk, which made Steve extremely busy and worried. "I did that!" He said. "I did that, too!" He was nervous. "I'll try that then." He walked back and forth and stopped in front of me. I looked up at him the way I would in an hour, at Her.

"Guys, you gotta make me room. I need to check something over there." He jumped off the stage, blinked at me and dove into the pool of fans where we were. "I apologize, but I have to do this."

He positioned himself right behind me and started his prayer into the microphone. "Right, checked, works perfectly from here, got it." If the litany of monosyllables made no sense to anybody, the same couldn't be said about the semicircular movements of his waist against my ass. Hotter than my boiling body in that inferno of energy, his crotch inflamed my senses to the point I would have fainted, and I would have missed the concert!

"You don't mind my arm, do you?" He mumbled away from the mike.

"I don't mind your arm nor your dick ..." I whispered into his ear.

"I'll see you get both then." He told me with the most serious expression on his face and nodding with his head as he jumped out of the fosse debut. I guess I can confirm Paris is the most romantic city in the world, even in the claustrophobic arena of Bercy.

The second the lights went off, Bercy trembled for twenty consecutive seconds. The darkness announced She was about to show up on stage; no more distractions, no more talking, no more waiting. The time had come.

The screens came to life accompanied by dozens of speakers. Colored rays of light started twirling from ceilings to floor, turning Bercy into a jewel box preserving the most precious stone. She emerged from below in all Her perfection, riding the notes of one of Her classics and singing Her right to be who She was. My clothes were wet again and slid on my skin as the possessed people around me morphed a dance. In those moments, I knew it had all been worth it, and I reconfirmed to myself I would do it all over again as soon as it was possible. She kept advancing toward me, consuming the air in my lungs with my heartbeat dangerously skyrocketing. To my relief, the sudden darkness wasn't my eyes being abandoned by my brain, but Steve's agile torso trying to squeeze among us again. He practically peeled Joao off me and inserted his hips in the middle, slowly pushing and pulling to get right behind me.

"I have some more checking to do over here." He spread all over my neck with his lips and delicately kissed me on my ear. Being that it was one of Her crew, whom I also happened to like a lot, I let him free to do whatever he wanted. The little detail he needed to realize though was that I was Hers and Hers only now; so he could only get me passively. All that reasoning wasn't explained to him; I was too concentrated not to miss Her glance down at me. She was so close I could touch Her if She decided to. Her legs were swirling right above me in a chaotic perfect sequence.

"You really like her, right?" Steve commented on my reactions as they were perceived by the rest of the world. "I think she likes you too, you are the only one she keeps staring at. Damn!" He gave voice to my most fragile thoughts, adding a sweet physical injection of pleasure with his crotch all along my back.

"You know you can do it!" I broke a couple of vocal cords when She turned and pointed at me. She came closer to the edge of the catwalk and blinked at me, finishing the song.

"I really think she likes you ... and so do I ..." Steve pushed his hands under my T-shirt and felt me all over; first he hugged me, then he caressed my chest delicately descending on my hips and adventuring his finger tips into my jeans. Not sure whether for him or Her, I was fully hard and in sweet pain as Saint Theresa of Avila described her being pierced by the long spear of gold.

Our bodies in the fosse were melted into one big flesh entity by the time we were half way through the show. Steve's was one with mine. His kisses accompanied me through the music, and his words intertwined with my fantasies. She was back on the main stage, too far away for me to plunge into the immense of Her eyes. But somebody was ready to plunge into me, according to the movements going on at waist level. Steve was so hard I wondered whether he'd stuck his big mike into his pants. I felt him so close; I felt it so close.

"Give it to me ..." The sound-check guy had the balls to tell me as he attempted to unbutton my jeans. "Please ..." The whole experience swallowed me in, depriving me of any control over my body or mind. Two were the likely causes of that situation. Her crawling toward me again and his using his hands in a way I wasn't physically able to interrupt. Steve didn't even unbutton my pants, he simply pulled them down – taking advantage of the lubrication provided by my extensive sweating – and left them hangin on my legs where they didn't bother his act.

"Feels good." It did feel good to push my ass against his hard cock. It felt so good I didn't even consider for a second that somebody could see that. But then again, who would look down when up on stage there was Her? I handed him my last bag of sun protection, convinced he wouldn't miss the point. With a delay not longer than ten seconds, I recognized the expensive lotion being smeared between my legs and Steve's hand making its way to find my secret button. The central screen got busy with sexy pictures of Her, and Steve moved closer to me, the only possible way to do that being for him to enter me. The transition was smooth. As a mechanic machine brought to maximum potency, my body was working hard not to break. Steve's lazy thrusting matched the unchangeable state of nirvana I was living. She was again inches away from me, this time much more aggressive. As I described it days later, that was my first – and last up to today – unlocalized orgasm. Usually, the pleasure starts in your groin and disseminates to your limbs losing intensity. What I felt that night was equally pleasurable in every part of my body.

"Her majesty is blessing you," Steve said when She looked down at me and yelled: "Yeah!" Perfectly synchronized with Steve's hot spurt invading my thighs and mine spraying the metal barrier I was squeezed against.

ROCK BATTLES COUNTRY
By Jay Starre

They say cheaters never prosper, but of course, sometimes they do. Slammer and Wade found that out as they battled to beat each other in the hottest new singing contest to hit the music scene.

The Canadian cable channel series, *Seattle's Singing Sensation*, claimed a fairly broad television audience. The West Coast city had a reputation for its independent music scene, and it was no surprise to anyone that the finalists included such a varied group of artists.

By the time those ten finalists were announced, it was already apparent two of the contestants were way out in front. Wade and Slammer couldn't have been more different. Both shaggy-haired and claiming awesome voices – that was it for their similarities.

One of the youngest singers at only nineteen, Wade was a pale, green-eyed blond with a short stocky frame. Big pink lips and a sweet smile between a strong nose and a dimpled chin, he was deadly cute. Quietly self-contained on stage and off, he exuded a sense of reserved power that belied his tender age.

At twenty-two, Slammer was older and believed himself wiser. Tall, dark and downright menacing on stage, Slammer belted out his tunes in a throaty shriek. Narrow features dominated by a sharp nose and a round mouth that pouted when he sang, he was scary handsome to the numerous fans he'd already accumulated. A dragon tattoo splashed over his right forearm. Accenting his dramatic dark looks, a large flat ivory plug stretched out each ear lobe.

The dark-haired rocker was wandering around the studio idling away the half hour before he was due to sing when he stumbled on a shocking scene. It involved Wade, his main competition, and one of the competition judges, Dan Green.

Slammer didn't really like Wade. A little jealous, he would admit, but mostly he just didn't like the sappy country flavor of his music, or his squeaky-clean attitude. Now, as he discovered the young blond down on his knees and engaged in a little judge fluffing, he liked him even less.

The pair had picked a pretty good spot for it, a darkened corner of a set for a TV series on hiatus for the summer. That set was a massive hanger with realistic-looking space fighter ships scattered about, which Slammer thought were cool. He went there whenever he had a chance.

Under the belly of one of the space ships, he first spotted their feet then heard their muffled conversation. Intrigued, he quietly made his way to the bulky rear of the ship and peered carefully around the corner.

Wade was on his knees. That sweet big smile of his hovered over a very fat cock rearing out of Dan Green's unzipped fly. Wade's dimpled chin was wet with drool and so were his pink lips. Obviously, he'd already been working on that stiff bone. He dived for more as Slammer hovered in the shadows and watched.

It was fascinating. Slammer had observed Wade sing with an envious fixation over the past month as they slogged their way through the preliminaries. He'd sensed from the beginning that the cute, somewhat chubby country singer would be the one to beat.

When he sang, his mouth opened generously above the microphone, as if he was about to swallow it. When he faced the audience, his bright lips glistened around straight white teeth. That smile opened wide for everyone watching, as if to welcome them into his big, sappy country heart.

At the moment, that generous mouth was busy enveloping the judge's slippery knob. One of those stubby, blunt cocks, it boasted a rammer head with an immense shank following. That gross size was no impediment for the kneeling country crooner. He slurped up the crown then dove for the judge's balls.

Slammer gawked with admiration as Wade deep-throated it all. The entire fat fuck-tube disappeared between his stretched pink lips. He made a low gurgling sound as the huge knob invaded his throat but didn't gag or choke. He let it slip out to reveal the vein-lined shaft wet with drool that dribbled onto his jutting chin.

He snorted for air then dove for balls again. Bobbing up and down, his mop of shaggy blond hair bobbed along with him. He made lots of noise, slurping and gurgling and smacking his lips, while the tall red-headed judge hovering over him mostly just moaned open-mouthed.

Green leaned back against the wall, hips thrust forward, and shook all over. "Fuck, Wade! Your hot mouth is going to make me come!"

Slammer grinned. If the audience had heard the saccharin-sweet judge swearing, they would have been totally shocked. Of course, if they could see him yanking his dick out of Wade's mouth and then blowing a big wad of dick-juice all over the place, they would have been pretty shocked, too.

He quickly slipped away before the pair could spot him. Grinning as he headed for their own stage, he contemplated what he'd just seen. The Judge, Dan Green, praised all the singers, even the most atrocious of them. Wade wasn't going to get ahead by sucking his cock. He was obviously just doing it because he wanted to.

That realization did more to unsettle him than any fear of cheating would have. The audience would never expect either cheating or cock-sucking from their cute blond country lad. No. But if Slammer had done either, no one would have been surprised. They probably would like him more.

Perhaps he could use his knowledge to get ahead himself. A little blackmail? He grinned at the thought. Or maybe, if he let the young and probably naïve country singer know he'd seen him on his knees with a judge's dick in his mouth, that alone might scare him enough, so he screwed up on stage.

Cheating certainly wasn't beyond him. He just wouldn't want to get caught and lose the competition because of it.

He went out and sang. Strutting the stage in his tight black jeans, he lunged with his crotch at the audience, and especially at a smiling Dan Green, while shaking his tight ass and caressing the microphone with his fingers. He shrieked out one of his pulse-pounding trademark tunes, which was no surprise to anyone.

But this time, he gave his show a little something extra. The secret knowledge he held and the tantalizing opportunity it presented had him unusually elated. Normally, his tone was dark. He'd pout and frown and glare at the audience, his body and voice thrusting angrily at them.

This time he grinned, he pranced, he even winked at a few trembling females in the front rows. He hit octaves that would put the others in the competition to shame. He held a piercing shrieked final note with warbling intensity as the audience screamed along with him.

Breathless and smirking, he listened to the judges' praise as they unanimously proclaimed this was his best performance yet. He bowed theatrically to Green as the judge waxed effusive about his "transformation." He was tempted to blow the judge a sarcastic kiss but wasn't quite ready to go that far.

A trio of unremarkable performances followed. All seemed intimidated by what he'd managed on stage before them. Then Wade appeared.

Slammer observed from the wings. The pleasure he'd been feeling as he watched the previous three crash and burn in contrast to his own stunning display quickly dissipated as Wade proceeded to offer his unhurried, sweet show.

The young country singer boasted a deep, controlled voice that went well with his subdued choices of song. His stocky frame, well-muscled but also padded with a pleasing layer of the remains of his baby fat, suited that voice, as did his understated blue jeans and plaid dress shirts. He rolled up his sleeves to reveal strong, smooth forearms and add a touch of casualness to his tidy appearance.

His shaggy blond locks were always squeaky clean and shiny. He'd worn a cowboy hat at his first few performances but had abandoned it on the advice of their wardrobe people. Slammer had overheard them telling the young singer his sexy hair and cute face were assets he should bet on rather than that rather ordinary cowboy hat.

As he sang, Slammer noted how the audience grew totally silent, breathlessly enthralled by his gentle innocence. He himself was surprised at how the song affected him. It was an emotional, but understated ballad, compared to his own high-octane shout at the world.

He stared at Wade's wide mouth, hovering over the microphone, and naturally, it reminded him of that same mouth hovering over Dan Green's fat stiff cock, only an hour earlier. His own cock swelled and stiffened in his tight jeans. Once he got that hard-on, it just wouldn't go away.

He found himself staring at Wade's round, chunky ass. He wondered if the blond singer would take cock up the ass as willingly as he'd taken it down the throat. He pondered what that sexy can would look like naked, how deep the crack was, how pink the tight asshole would be.

Slammer squirmed in the shadows backstage, his cock throbbing and his imagination running riot. It was so quiet in the studio as Wade crooned out his melancholy song, it was as if the whole world held its breath.

Fuck! It was a disaster! He rearranged his dick and squeezed it as he continued to watch the blond singer mesmerize the audience. If only they knew he was a hungry little cock-sucker!

Then it hit him.

He'd fuck that sweet mouth and that sweet ass! He'd fuck Wade good, then he'd somehow use it to vanquish his opponent, destroying his innocent reputation while enhancing his own well-deserved wicked one.

The audience was on their feet at the end of Wade's performance. Dan Green claimed he'd had tears in his eyes while listening. Slammer was disgusted, but still hard, as he slipped away to plot his opponent's downfall.

He'd made no effort to befriend Wade previously. In fact, he'd rebuffed every overture the young blond offered. He switched gears that very evening putting his new ploy into play.

The production was pretty cheap, and they had put up their contestants in a dormitory-type hotel just off the studio lot. The guys, five of them, all bunked together and shared a single large bathroom with a pair of common shower stalls and sinks.

As soon as he saw Wade heading for the shower, he followed.

"You did OK out there today, country boy."

Wade was already naked and making his way to one of the shower stalls. He turned to the voice behind him and beamed. "Thanks, Slammer. You were so awesome you inspired me to do my best."

He resisted a roll of his eyes but couldn't help blurting out an honest reply. "I didn't want to fucking inspire you, I wanted to scare the shit out of you."

Wade merely laughed and continued on into the shower. Slammer cursed himself. Pissing off the country singer was not the plan! But he'd been completely caught up in the sight of Wade's lush white butt, naked and jiggling as he padded his way to the stall. He'd reverted to his usual rude self!

His cock reared upward, reminding him of his goal. He'd certainly have no trouble when it came to fucking that round white butt; he just had to make it happen. He stripped hastily and moved into the stall next to Wade, fisting his cock to keep it hard as he quickly soaped up and rinsed off.

He stepped out and waited with towel in hand. A moment later, Wade appeared, wet and smiling as he came close to reach for a towel on the rack beside Slammer. The rocker let his own towel slip just in time.

His stiff dick grazed Wade's bare hip. The blond looked down, his green eyes big as he took in the length and girth of that boner. He remained calm, though, as he took his towel and stepped away.

"Sorry about the hard-on. I just get so fucking horny when I sing. I need to jerk-off or something." He grinned and winked as he continued drying off casually and making no effort to hide his stiff dick.

"Not too easy in these close quarters," Wade replied as he dried off himself. His eyes darted all over as he took in the sight of that big boner and Slammer's naked body.

Slammer took his time. Proud of his body, he had no qualms about wearing tight clothes on stage to show it off. Contrary to his bad boy image, he'd been an athlete in high school and college, a gymnast in fact, and had all the lean muscle to show for it. Tall for a gymnast, his long limbs were smooth and ivory-pale, contrasting with his dark hair and eyes.

The young blond appeared captivated by Slammer's casual flaunting and took his time drying off as well.

"Fuck yeah, not all that easy to beat your meat with all these other guys around. I've had to be creative. Some of the stages at the studio are empty, so there's that."

Wade's eyes darted up to meet his, then slid away. Slammer smiled. Let him wonder!

The two continued drying themselves until it was no longer possible to pretend there was anything left to dry off. Slammer toyed with the idea of instigating some play right then and there, but knew one of their fellow singers might burst in at any time so that was out. Instead, he finally tossed his towel over his shoulder, winked and left Wade there gawking as he strolled out bare-ass naked into their room to dress.

Over the next week, Slammer made regular visits to the abandoned spaceship set. He thought he might catch Wade sucking on some more judge cock, or just be there hanging around in case Wade decided to look for him – and look for his cock.

He made it his practice to follow Wade into the shower every evening. He did his best to chat up the young blond, and surprised himself how easy it became. The kid was so damn easy-going! He flashed his stiff cock regularly and noticed that Wade was springing wood, too. His dick was pretty nice in fact. A bit on the stubby side but thick, very hard and bright pink.

He finally scored just before their next on-air competition – back in the exact spot where he'd first caught Wade deep-throating Judge Green's fat cock.

"Hey, Slammer. Nervous before the show?"

The sweet smile and the deep voice startled him as Wade appeared from out of the gloom. There were only a few overheads illuminating the massive set, and behind the fake space ship there was barely enough light to distinguish the stocky figure approaching. White teeth glowed dimly as the blond moved in close.

"Nope. Just horny. Really fucking horny."

Despite his claim, he was nervous but not because of the show. His heart beat faster in his chest, and his cock stiffened and strained against his fly. He managed a sarcastic smile as he groped his crotch and that swelling cock.

He took a deep breath, and he made his play. "Want to help me out with this?"

They were face-to-face. It was Wade who'd moved in so close they almost touched. It was Wade who giggled easily as he dropped to his knees and buried his face in Slammer's crotch.

That huge mouth clamped over the stiff shaft of his dick. Only the material of his tight jeans and tighter underwear was between that rearing bone and those sweet pink lips. He emitted a groan as he felt his knees going slightly weak. Even though it seemed all was going according to plan, he wasn't exactly in control as he'd expected. That mouth!

Wade surprised him. He used his teeth to squeeze and nip at shaft and head through his jeans, a tantalizing pressure that had Slammer gasping out loud. Before he knew it, the kneeling singer had his jeans undone and yanked down around his thighs. His underwear followed as Wade practically tore them off.

He opened wide and swallowed. With shocking ease, the blond eased open his throat and sucked in the tapered crown, then the shaft until his smooth cheeks were pressing against Slammer's bare crotch. He'd swallowed it all!

The tall rocker almost lost it. That tight throat and the wet lips and a fat tongue bathing the base of his boner, it was hot and exciting and much, much more than he'd expected. He had to do something.

"Fuck yeah, wrap those pretty lips around my big hard cock ... uhhhhhh ... suck it! Show me how much you like to be on your knees with a cock in your mouth!"

He was a crude as possible in the hopes of humiliating the kneeling blond and restoring some control over the situation. But just in case that wasn't enough, he reached out and grabbed a hand full of Wade's thick blond locks. He yanked that head backwards and thrust with his hips into the wet mouth. Green eyes stared up at him, but the pink lips only seemed to be smiling around the pumping dick. Slammer began to drill that mouth as he gripped the singer's hair and berated him.

"Yeah! Open wide! Take my dick! You love it! You're nothing but a hungry little cock-sucker. You just can't get enough cock, can you? Can you?"

Wade actually nodded his head vigorously as he accepted Slammer's savage pounding effortlessly. His wet lips slurped and his tongue twirled. He didn't even gag as cock-head rammed past his tonsils.

The kneeling country crooner did more than that. He grabbed hold of Slammer's tight butt and pulled it against his face. When the rocker lunged, those hands added force to the slam of hips against face. His lengthy red dick drove in and out relentlessly, faster with every passing moment.

The constant wet friction had him on his tiptoes with his entire body shaking. An approaching climax seized him by the balls. He couldn't forestall it, not with that slurping mouth engulfing him to the balls.

He had to make the most of it. "Swallow my load! I know you want it! Drain me dry, you little jizz-sucker!"

He was shaking so much, his knees ready to buckle, that he didn't have enough strength to force Wade to swallow his suddenly spurting load – even with one hand tangled in the kneeling singer's blond locks.

It was Wade who once more took control. He wrapped his plump pink lips around the spurting head and sucked. He swallowed noisily as he guzzled down every juicy drop while gazing up at Slammer with those big green eyes.

Slammer could barely keep from sliding down the wall and onto his knees. It was as if his insides were being sucked out of him. Those lips, cheeks, and that tongue vacuumed him dry.

When there wasn't another drop left to swallow, the blond pulled off with a smack. With a grin and a giggle, he rose to his feet and shocked the shaking rocker by planting a sloppy, open-mouthed kiss on his lips. He tasted his own cum.

"We better go, Slammer. I'm up first tonight. I'll be singing just for you tonight!"

He was speechless. What was with this kid? Obviously not so innocent in the sexual arena, but did he really think Slammer was his pal and not his deadly competition?

"I'll be thinking of my load in your belly when I sing," he managed to bleat out. He hoped his crudity would shock the blond.

But, Wade was already disappearing around the corner of the space ship, and he wasn't sure he even heard him.

The country crooner surprised the audience with something different that night. Instead of his usual haunting rural ballads, he came out dancing, belting out a vivacious country ode to pick-up trucks, faithful dogs and good old Friday night partying. It was fun, and it was upbeat, and the audience were on their feet clapping and hooting along with him.

Slammer's cock reared up hard again as he watched from the sidelines. As he observed that sexy round ass jiggle and prance, he realized what his next move had to be if he was to regain control of the situation.

By the time his turn on the stage came, his wicked determination had returned. He had the lighting crew darken the stage, so only his lanky frame was visible. His sleeveless, dark purple tank top clung to his lean torso. The dragon tattoo on his forearm flamed while the ivory plugs in his ear lobes caught the light in a dull glow.

He offered a dark melody in a throaty growl, slow, steady and menacing. The light-hearted mood established by Wade and the other singers was extinguished within a few moments of his appearance. He hit them hard, clutching the microphone in a fierce grip, glaring out at the darkened audience and slowly raising his voice until the finale. He fell to his knees and shrieked out a bone-chilling climax.

It took a moment for the judges to recover after the lights came up and before the eviscerated audience could gather themselves for a roaring applause. Dan Green led the praise, declaring that, "Only one other contestant can hope to match you. And we all know who that is."

That reference to Wade soured his sense of victory enough that he decided he had to pull out all the stops in his quest to dominate the blond country lad. And soon.

He followed Wade into the bathroom the next evening. That night, the remaining five contestants would perform for the last time then the television audience would vote. It was now or never. The entire contest rested on his ability to vanquish this one final opponent.

Wade was naked and about to step into the shower. He turned and smiled.

Slammer's heart pounded. What the hell was the kid thinking to put on such an innocent grin? It was time to really give it to him. "Get in there and close the door. I'm coming in right after I find something slippery to lube your butt-hole with."

The nasty remark was meant to shock, but Wade's green eyes sparkled and his smile broadened. "OK, Slammer. I can't wait."

The rocker wondered about that as he stroked his lengthy tool into a full hard-on. It was a good ten inches, a real gut-reamer. Even though Wade had proved he could swallow dick like a champ, his asshole was bound to be quite a bit smaller and tighter than that big mouth of his!

He tossed his clothes to the floor and snatched up a bottle of moisturizing cream from the sink counter. With big boner in hand, he opened the shower stall door and discovered his prey leaning against the wall spread-eagled and already soaped up.

"I'm ready," he said brightly, his head craned around and his green eyes on Slammer's dark brown ones.

Slammer hesitated. Fuck! Broad shoulders and a hefty back led down to a big round butt and stocky thighs. Smooth, pink and soapy. His eyes zeroed in on the twin mounds of that gorgeous butt. The crack was deep and inviting. Suddenly he knew what he had to do first.

"Rinse off and spread your legs. I'm going to eat you out good!"

His powerful voice did not fail him. His demanding growl was followed by a resounding smack to one of those enticing butt globes. Wade's ass cheek jiggled and flamed pink where the open palm had landed before he quickly obeyed. Dunking himself under the shower head, all those suds washed away down his broad back and jutting butt.

He reached back and grabbed his own ass-cheeks and spread them wide. "Go ahead. It's all yours."

Slammer shuddered as he dropped to his knees behind that ivory-pale ass. With the cheeks spread open, he could see deep into the crack. Hairless and without any blemish at all, that milky skin flushed brightly where the puckered hole dominated the middle of the butt valley.

It looked tight, the lips clamped and pink even though Wade had both hands pulling his cheeks wide apart. Slammer grinned. He was going to fuck that hole good – after he sucked it inside out!

He crammed his face between the hefty butt-cheeks. His tongue came out, and he began his attack on the snug slot. Wade groaned and wriggled back into Slammer's face, then cried out when tongue began to dance over the tight entrance.

"Oh! Oh! That feels so good! Oh yeah! Please! Lick it!"

Music to his ears, Slammer probed with his tongue. He dug between the lips with the tip, then tickled and stroked the quaking entrance. He was rewarded with more vigorous squirming and more loud moaning, then with a slight pouting of those tight butt-lips.

He clamped his mouth over the hole and sucked. Wade heaved back into his face and bleated. "Yes! Oh yes! More! What are you doing to me? I love it!"

Slammer sucked, licked, tickled and probed. His drool coated the quivering hole and the distended lips. Spit ran down the pale crack toward the dangling balls. He smacked his lips loudly as he dined on cowboy singer hole and prepared it for his cock.

He pulled out and surveyed his handiwork. The hole was gooey and pink and pouting. The lips had curled outward and the center drooled. Still, it was a tight pucker. Wade was going to really feel it when his cock began to slide in.

"Time to fuck your hot little hole. You want a cock up the ass, don't you? I bet you love cock up the butt as much as you love sucking on it."

He rose as he spoke. The open bottle of moisturizing lotion was in one hand, and he squeezed it over his rearing boner then down into that spread ass-crack. The white cream oozed down over the pink hole and coated it. He smeared it over the length of his cock, then added more as he thrust the stiff tool between those big mounds.

"You want it? You want cock up the ass?"

"Yes! I want it!" Wade agreed, wriggling back against the slippery cock in his crack.

Slammer aimed the head and held it on target. It tapered nicely so that the tip easily settled between the snug butt-lips. It got bigger, and so did the shaft that followed, but it wasn't a fat cock, it was just extremely long.

He pushed, a little probe to test out the resistance. Wade grunted and jerked. His big butt jiggled, but he didn't pull away. Slammer could feel the sphincter stretching open, but not caving in.

He toyed with the idea of slamming home, wondering how loud Wade would squeal if he did, but that wasn't really what he wanted. He wanted to make Wade love it. He wanted Wade to love it so much he couldn't stop begging for more. Then he'd spring his trap.

So he probed again, a little deeper. The lips parted, yielded, then seized him. He pulled back just a little, then slowly began to push in. All that gooey cream definitely eased the way, and so did Wade's determination. He matched Slammer's forward pressure with a slow backwards push.

The head slid past those clamping lips and disappeared.

They both gasped. Even though the hole pulsed tightly around his buried head, Slammer knew it wasn't time to relent. He kept on pushing, ever so slowly. He stared down at that parted crack, the pink hole straining around his stiff shaft as it pushed deeper and deeper. Wade's hands clenched over his own beefy cheeks so fiercely they glowed red. He panted and moaned, but he met Slammer's slow feeding by arching his back and heaving into it.

The blond singer slowly swallowed it all.

Slammer's legs shook, and his heart pounded in his chest. The fuck tunnel remained tight as hell, encasing his slithering bone in muscle-clamping heat. The channel throbbed around his cock, massaging it relentlessly as it burrowed deeper and deeper – and finally all the way home.

"Fuck! You got it all. Your asshole loves cock!"

Wade panted and squirmed, his tongue out and licking at his pink lips. His eyes were closed, but he had a dreamy half-smile on his face that had Slammer shaking his head. He was loving it! Maybe too much.

His balls pressed up against Wade's smooth ass-crack. His cock was all the way up the blond's pulsing hole. It was time to fuck. He took a deep breath and began to withdraw. Cream eased the way as he pulled half-way out, stared down at his own stiff pole as it reappeared, then reversed direction and pumped it back in.

Wade squirmed and heaved. His head dropped, and his wet blond hair hung in thick strands around his face and over his strong neck. He grunted as that lengthy pole once more stuffed him full. He pressed his face flat against the shower stall, his mouth wide open and tongue lolling out, hands behind him holding his own ass-cheeks apart.

His submission was total. Slammer should have felt victorious, but he only felt greed for more. He grunted himself as he began to fuck in earnest. He pulled all the way out, aimed, and stabbed balls-deep. Cream squished and spurted. He buried his cock in that tight hole, twisted it around, probed with it, pumped savagely, withdrew, and then teased the snug lips with stabs of the head.

Wade took it all, his flushed ass jiggling, his own cock, fat and stiff, rearing up between his thighs. Slammer fucked and fucked, intent on massaging and teasing and savaging that hole as long as possible, but all too soon realizing he was fucking himself to orgasm.

He wasn't going to give in to a climax though before he wrenched one out of his squirming prey. He reached around Wade's writhing hips and seized his swaying cock. With cream-slippery fingers, he pumped it at the same rapid pace he pumped his cock into the country singer's asshole. Pumped from in front and from behind, Wade groaned and wriggled as he began to ride cock and fingers in a wild dance.

"I'm going to shoot!"

Thank god, Slammer said to himself. All that violent squirming was taking its toll on him, too. It only got more wild as Wade fucked himself to orgasm, humping and whimpering as his cock erupted in a violent squirting that splattered the shower wall in front of them.

The husky body in his arms tensed and flailed as cum escaped the fat cock in a flurry of spurts. The tight asshole convulsed crazily around Slammer's buried dick, and he had to yank it out before the clamping anal muscles bruised it!

As soon as he pulled out, he shot, too. Cum sprayed all over Wade's flushed big ass-cheek. It dribbled down the hefty curve and onto the stall floor. Slammer was light-headed and shaking when Wade turned around and pulled him into an embrace.

They were kissing before the rocker knew it. And not just a thank-you little kiss. No, Wade was practically devouring his mouth and tongue. The kid had loved that wild fuck. Really loved it!

He pulled away with a smack of lips and a gasp. Time to pounce.

"That was cool, kid. But it's time I set you straight. I plan on winning this competition, and I don't give a fuck how I do it. I saw you sucking Green's cock last week. I'm going to spill the beans, tell everyone about it, if you don't either purposely blow tonight's performance, or bow out. I'm not fucking around. I mean it."

Wade wasn't smiling now. He looked up into Slammer's eyes with a serious look on his face. The rocker steeled himself and didn't look away. "Well?"

"I just have one question. Was all this sex stuff just a way to manipulate me? You don't want to do it again?"

Slammer blinked. He wasn't sure what Wade was asking. He'd just threatened him with blackmail, and the kid wanted to know if they were going to fuck again!

"Grow up. It didn't mean anything. I just want to win. I don't care if I ever fuck you again."

Wade pushed him away, although not roughly. "I don't really care all that much if I win or not. But mostly I don't want to get Dan in any trouble. I'll quit tonight."

He didn't look at Slammer as he stepped out of the shower. The rocker was left to himself as he rinsed off and contemplated his victory. It didn't seem real yet, though. He only hoped Wade would do what he said. What choice did he have? It seemed a sure thing.

Still, there wasn't the sense of elation he'd anticipated. Sure, he felt a little guilty for the way he was treating Wade, but the kid needed to learn a lesson. Don't trust people so much. Don't be a sap.

On stage an hour later, the blond cowboy faced the audience with his trademark smile in place, but only fleetingly as he made his announcement. "I am bowing out of the competition due to some personal issues. This is my last song. I offer it to all of you as a goodbye, and especially to one person who taught me a valuable lesson."

Slammer watched from the wings. The stunned audience had let out a moan of disbelief before he cut it off with his song. Of course it was a sappy country ballad about love lost and love betrayed, and he sang it with all his usual talent, plus some.

There was outright weeping, and there was a standing ovation as he exited the stage without even waiting for the judges to speak. He walked past Slammer who was up next and nodded.

To the rocker's surprise, he was actually smiling as he leaned in and whispered in his ear. "Now you have what you want. Good for you. You certainly worked for it."

Then he gently shoved Slammer out onto the stage.

The rocker looked back, totally unsure if that was supposed to be sarcasm, but Wade only smiled and nodded again.

The crowd was buzzing when he reached center stage. The kid had really gone out with a bang! Damn him. Now it was up to Slammer to win them back. He faced them defiantly, as the music began.

His magnificent voice lashed out, silencing them and seizing their attention. He stepped up to the very edge of the stage and leaned out, threatening them as he shrieked another few lines. A pair of warbling and defiant ululations grabbed them by the throats and mesmerized them.

But then his voice failed. He stopped abruptly, frozen in place.

Suddenly, he didn't give a fuck about the competition. Or the audience. It had seemed so important to win, but now it seemed totally unimportant.

The music had continued, but he raised his hand and waved it off. The band stopped, the audience were on the edge of their seats again. What now?

"I'm quitting, too. Personal issues."

Gasps of disbelief, groans from the frustrated judges, but no weeping. Slammer grinned at that, then spun around and stalked toward the wings. As the crowd buzzed behind him, he turned and faced them one more time.

It wouldn't have been like him to go out without a final bit of wickedness.

"My boyfriend, Wade, and I don't need your fucking competition when we've got each other!"

Laughing hysterically, he met Wade in the wings and fell into his arms. They couldn't stop laughing as they shoved their way through the other stunned contestants and the open-mouthed back stage crew. They were still laughing when they escaped out the back door.

"Cheaters never prosper," Wade scolded his friend as they fled down the street toward their hotel.

Slammer couldn't let that pass. "Say that again when my cock is up your tight ass later tonight!"

Wade's smile only grew bigger. Uncharacteristically and with surprising ease, Slammer found himself smiling back.

THE BIGGEST FAN
By Rob Rosen

I'd been following his career since I was a pimply-faced teenager. Heck, he wasn't much older than I when he stormed onto the scene, that velvet voice of his flowing like honey from the radio, the family gathered around, Mom and Dad on the couch, we kids sprawled out on the floor, I, already eighteen and preparing for college. They'd listen, absent-mindedly, Mom knitting, Dad reading his paper, my sisters fighting, and then I, with my front row seat. Man, oh man, I'd just sit there, staring at that big box made of oak wood and chrome dials, my eyes and ears glued, hearing nothing but that rich baritone of his swirling around my head, a noticeable stirring in my shorts, my mind wandering to less-than-wholesome thoughts.

Of course, back then, I bought all the star rags; Silky Sal they called him. I'd cut them up and secretly stash them beneath my bed when he was featured. He was tall, dreamy, big-eyed, with an etched jaw and impossibly thick lips, all in shades of glossy black and white. Handsome as he was talented. There was this one shot, him on the beach, snug bathing trunks and sleeveless top, a tuft of chest hair poking out, muscular thighs, well-worked calves. A star, a real, honest to goodness star.

I often snuck that picture into the bathroom and locked the door behind me, dropping my pajama bottoms to the tiled floor, cock in hand, stroking rapid fast, the shower running to hide the noise, my eyes on his hairy legs and chest, the cum building up and spewing out, my moans muffled, eyelids fluttering, imagining what I'd do if I ever got the chance to meet him.

Unaware that this dream would someday come true; though so many years later; and not at all how I expected.

Time flew by. College came and went. A big job. A nice salary. Comfortable, if not slightly lonely. Silky Sal still played on my record player, but not so much on the radio anymore; my career skyrocketed while his did a nose-dive. The crooners were fast disappearing, rock and roll the latest craze. The star rags were now in color. No pictures of Sal, bathing suit or otherwise. But I was still out there, listening, waiting for a comeback that was probably never to happen.

See, rumors had always spread about him. Single guy. Confirmed bachelor. Lots of whispering. Not much good for a star's reputation. But hey, that only added to my fascination, that black and white of him now framed on my nightstand, my jacking no longer confined to the bathroom.

I spotted the ad over breakfast one day. Small nightclub, some fifty miles away. Silky Sal, one night only. Small band, barely even a cover charge. Sad for him, happy for yours truly. Probably my last chance, I figured. Maybe his, too. Where does an idol's career go after he appears in small nightclubs?

I dressed up, all spiffy-like. Nice suit and tie, haircut, shaved and beaming as I pulled up in my sedan. Place was packed. Guess I wasn't the only one still hanging on. Lots of women, all in their thirties, dressed to the nines. I, the only male going solo, seated in front, a table for one with a dry martini dead center, watching, waiting, breathlessly.

The band came out first, strumming the intro to one of his hits, my heart pounding out a mad samba in my chest, a bead of sweat trickling down my forehead. And then, there he was, waving as he walked on stage, much shorter in person than in the magazines, still lean, still handsome, the voice just as spectacular. Smooth, silky like his name implied, pitch perfect. Heavenly. The women screamed. I stared in rapt delight, his baritone vibrato twanging at my heartstrings, filling me up from stem to stern, and, of course, swelling my cock.

Midway through his first song, he stared down at me, a wink and a smile, the voice rolling over me like a cool wave on a hot summer's day. I smiled, nervously, toasting him with my glass held up high. He looked away, continuing on with his set, returning to me from time to time, blue eyes dazzling, twinkling like the stars in the heavens, setting my tummy rumbling each and every time. Was he cruising me? Hard to say. Still, worth checking out.

The crowd emptied fast when he was through. Not a neighborhood to find yourself in too much after dark. I went backstage, no one noticing me, or caring. Star on the door, faded gold, cracked paint. I knocked, waited. He creaked the door open, looked out and up, smile growing big and bright. "Front row, right?" he boomed, the door swinging open, him in a thin robe, the suit hanging behind him.

"Oh, uh, yes, Mister Jenson. Front row." My heart pounded now, chest swelling, ears ringing.

"Sal," he corrected. "You a fan or a tax collector?"

"Oh, a fan, sir. The biggest." I beamed.

"Then come on in," he made way, arms outstretched, and shut the door behind us. Click. Small room, dimly lit. Little couch, dressing table, a sink, not much else.

"I'm, uh, Jeff, sir. Jeff Halloway." I reached out my hand, sweaty, flesh on flesh, a spark traveling up my spine that spread like wildfire.

"Again, just call me Sal, Jeff," he laughed. "No sirs. I can't be more than a couple of years older than you, I mean."

I chuckled, nervously. "No, sir. I mean, Sal. Three years, two months, six days older, to be exact."

He nodded. "Ah, you really are a big fan, huh?" Again the laugh. "Not many left these days. Glad for the few die-hards." He stretched out the last word, hard, locking eyes with me, a tilt to his head. Bingo.

"There's always comebacks," I replied, emphasis on the come. "Especially with a voice like yours."

He sighed. "Not about the voices anymore, Jeff."

He turned and sat down, flopping onto the couch, legs splayed, hairy, just like in my picture. I stifled a moan, gazing down at him. Weird. Like a beautiful dream. I went for broke. "All about the looks these days," I opened with. "And you still have those, Sal."

He paused, weighing his options. Dangerous waters. For him, more than me. "Think so?" The voice had an edge to it now, gravelly.

"I have this picture of you. On the beach. Sun spilling down on you, all smiles, happy as a clam."

He laughed. "Took a half day to get that shot. Fucking freezing out there, pardon my French. Balls shrunk to chestnuts."

I coughed, a flush of red rising up my neck, splashing across my cheeks. "Hard to tell. You looked, um, okay, down there, I mean," I stammered, my cock swelling, stretching my briefs to their limits. "I mean, not that I'd know, never, um, having seen them before." My own voice went reedy, almost in a whisper.

He reached for the robe's belt, opening it up, slowly, his chest coming into view, densely matted in black curly hair, nipples thick, pink, hard muscles, sinewy. The robe opened further. Belly exposed, flat, etched, covered in down. Further still, a gulp from me, a sigh from him. A black bush, the base of a shaft, the robe completely opened now, Sal naked, framed in white cotton, his cock arcing up and out, swelling for me, low hanging balls, haloed in ebony hair. "How about now, Jeff? Bigger than chestnuts?"

I coughed, knees trembling. "I, um, I see your point."

His laugh returned, his hand on his prick, a gentle stroke, raising it to full mast. "Strange to see me like this, Jeff? Your idol, naked, hard?" He paused, watching me, intently. "I'd imagine it would be. Me, I don't have idols anymore. Everyone's just people now. Know what I mean? Except the fans. The fans I love. Would do anything for them."

I moved in an inch, two. "Anything, Sal?"

He stroked faster, balls rising. "Oh yeah, anything. I'm nothing without the fans, Jeff. Nothing without you."

I scratched my head, my mind racing, remembering all my fantasies, now seemingly within hand's reach. "Well, Sal, that beach shot. It was from the front. And, I, um …"

He chuckled, stood, his thick cock pointing at me, robe dropping to the floor, eyes lit up like fireflies. "You want to know what the backside looks like, Jeff?"

I nodded. "Thought about it." About a million times.

He reached over and locked the door, then turned around and got on all fours, his ass beckoning. "How's this?"

I sunk down, Indian style, pushing his legs apart, his heavy balls hanging low, hairy asshole winking out at me. I ran my index finger around the ring. "Real nice," I replied, reverently. "Now I see where you get the name Silky."

He reached behind and spread his cheeks apart for me. "Ever suck a star's asshole before, Jeff?"

I bent in, took a deep whiff, the smell of musk and sweat wafting joyously up my nose. "Not yet," I replied, my tongue darting out, running circles around it, zooming around and a around before delving inside. He moaned, bucking his ass into my face, pushing his cock between his legs, so he could whack the head beneath my chin. I backed an inch away, my tongue replaced by a spit-slick finger, my mouth now around his dick, salty as it pulsed inside. My finger slid in and back, his cock sinking down my throat, all in one easy glide, my free hand caressing his hairy legs and ass. Man, all that hair, all that muscle, sent my cock into overdrive.

I popped his prick out. "Hey, Sal, you ever suck a star's asshole before?"

He laughed. "Well now, Jeff, actually, I have. More than a few."

I laughed in return, spanking a cheek, then the other, a moan coming from his end. "Ever taste your own?"

He turned around, got Indian style with me, face to handsome face, eyes drawing me in, voice thick as molasses. "Not yet." He bent forward, a tentative kiss, a volt running down my back, exploding out my still-tethered cock. Our lips soon met, parted, his tongue snaking and coiling its way inside my mouth, the kiss hard, insistent, eager. He pulled back an inch, mouth smacking. "I taste pretty good, if I do say so myself."

"Agreed." I smiled, stroking his cock, the shaft throbbing in my grip, copious amounts of precum dripping over the head.

"Though maybe I should have something to compare it to."

I took the hint and hopped up, shucking off the suit as he leered up, naked in no time flat, cock jutting out above his head, his pointing up at me like a divining rod. I spread my legs apart and crouched down a bit. He slid beneath me, face up, my knees bending the rest of the way. "Here you go," I rasped. My asshole pressed down onto his lips, his tongue parting me, his hand stroking my dick, the feeling indescribable. "How's it taste?" I panted, yanking on my nipples, my balls bouncing hard against his chin.

"Like heaven," he replied, in between hungry sucks and slurps. "I could write a song about it."

I laughed. "Jeff's ass tastes like heaven. Catchy. But I don't think it would get much air-play."

He reached his hand between my legs. "How about finger play then?" He slid his index finger inside my ass, joining it with its partner, my breath sucking in, my ass tightening around them for the briefest of seconds before giving in, pleasure and pain mixed as one, the former soon outdistancing the latter by miles. "Any other fan requests?"

I stood back up, his fingers retracting in an audible pop. I reached down and helped him to his feet, his naked body pressed up vice-tight to mine, my arms wrapped around him, his face on my chest, my hands on his hairy ass, his on my smooth one. "Sing to me, Sal," I whispered in his ear, taking a tender lobe in between my teeth. "Sing to me while I fuck you."

That laugh of his, like pebbles washed up at the shore. "An inspired request, Jeff," he groaned. "That a dream come true then?"

My laugh echoed his, my fingers splaying his cheeks, prodding at his tight hole. "A recurring one, yes." I paused, a chill running down my back at the realization. "But what will I have once it actually does come true?"

He looked up, smiled, winked, a tender kiss placed on my lips, perfect. "Come up with a new one, Jeff. A better one." He lay on the floor, pulling me down on top of him. "But for now, let's make this one a reality."

My body ground into his, his arms over his head, hands in my hands. Mine, all mine. Soon enough, I pushed off, got on my knees, his feet up, ankles on my shoulders, the first song starting, a classic, one of my favorites. "How did you know," I asked, slicking lube from the bottle he somehow managed to grab from his garment bag, around his hole, his cock, my cock.

"It's the one they all ask for, Jeff. Though never quite like this." He smirked, eyelids temporarily closing as I gently pushed my way inside, the song starting up again, slow and steady, slow and steady, beautiful as a lullaby, my heart bursting at the seams as I filled his hole, inch by steely inch.

The beat picked up steam, as did my cock, ramming inside of him while I stroked his cock, his moans punctuating the melody, his hands playing the drums across his hirsute chest and belly. All the way in now, balls banging up against ass, that song melding into another one, about love, about happiness, perfect songs for a perfect evening.

"Close," I hummed, my lips above his, the lyrics swirling in my head.

"Let me see you come, Jeff," he panted, the last song reaching its crescendo just as I was reaching mine.

I pulled out, my balls lapping against his as I beat my dick, Sal reaching down to match my rhythm stroke for stroke, both of us gasping now, moans and groans bouncing around the small backstage room, my eyes locked on to his dick, his to mine, both of us shooting at the exact same moment, his cock spewing ounce after ounce of molten hot cum, mine flying out over his belly and chest, a mess of white dousing all that fine matting of fur just before I collapsed on top of him, a big, sticky mess, writhing together, joined as one, fan and idol, man to man.

He smiled and stroked my hair. I closed my eyes, realizing how much better the reality turned out to be, how I could never have dreamed this up, no matter how hard I tried. Still, even realities have to come to an end. The club was closing. He had other stops along his journey, and I needed to get home. One final kiss. A warm, wet towel to clean each other off.

I left him as I found him, in his robe, with that wide smile of his, my business card pressed in his hand. "In case you make it back this way again," I told him, shutting the door behind me, thinking that would be the last I ever saw of him, save for the cherished photo by my bed.

Though it wasn't the last time, not by a long shot.

A few months later, my doorbell rang. I answered it, cracking the door open just a hair, and there he stood, same smile, the robe replaced by a casual suit. "Hello, good sir," he said, with a slight bow. "I'm going house to house, seeing if there are any fans left for Silky Sal. Do you happen to know of any?"

My smile mirrored his as I let him in. "Well now, as a matter of fact, I'm a fan of Silky Sal. The biggest, I'd imagine."

He shut the door behind us and reached his hand out to cup my already swelling crotch. "Yeah, that remains to be seen." He leaned in for a kiss and a hug, those eyes of his sparkling like sapphires, his steely cock poking at mine through his slacks.

"How'd you find me?" I thought to ask, just after I came up for air.

He grinned. "Seems like your secretary is a fan, too. I called last week. She gave me your address and swore she wouldn't tell you that I was dropping by." He reached inside his jacket and removed an autographed picture. "This is for her, by the way. Yours I'll sign in person."

I took the gift and led him to the bedroom, his smile growing even brighter when he saw my framed memento. I turned to him and yanked him on the bed, both our shoes kicked off, his lips again on mine, eager, familiar.

I held him tight to me, shocked at our sudden reunion. "But, um, what are you doing here?" I asked.

The grin grew sheepish now, followed by a deep chuckle. "See, Jeff, I thought I'd finally take my own advice." He paused, another tender kiss planted on my waiting lips. "Remember when you asked me what would you do once your dream came true?"

I remembered. In fact, it was all I could think about since we parted. "You told me to come up with a new one. A better one."

A red flush spread across his cheeks, eyes boring right on through to my very soul, his hand sliding into my shorts. "All my dreams have come true, Jeff," he told me. "So I thought of a better one." He gripped my thick cock in his mitt, giving it a gentle squeeze. "Care for a new dream yourself, Jeff? A better one? A bigger one?"

I laughed, my own hand sliding down his slacks, cock in hand. "The biggest," I amended. "Always go for the biggest, Sal."

"Amen to that, Jeff," he whispered, his lips once more pressed to mine. "Amen to that."

SMOOTH & GROOVE
R. Talent

"I'll fuck you 'til you love me, faggot!" Roscoe, the tenor saxophone player, screeched from the stage of the café lounge with a handful of band mates holding him back.

Homer, a bass player, who wasn't performing that night and sitting next to me on the far end of the room, jumped to his feet, causing his chair to fly from under him back toward the window, and shouted back, "Don't mistake me for your daddy, you dick-sucking horn blower!"

"C'mon, then, bring it, motherfucker!"

"Guess what, motherfucker – fuck you!" Homer howled, shooting Roscoe the bird.

"You're mama."

"Fuck you and your 'ho-ass mama and your bottle-sucking daddy, you reformed prison bitch! Is it true what they say? It's like drug rehab – one less dick at a time?"

Roscoe tried his best to come off the stage in spite of the crowd holding him back. Homer tried storming the stage with an emerging crowd trying to hold him back. I was left shaking my head, trying to find the quickest way out of the building.

How did I end up at a jazz lounge with two mediocre jazz musicians fighting over me? The simple answer would be my interest in jazz. The truth, however, was that I fell into a heap of shit that started long before I stepped foot into this world.

A short time after my twentieth birthday, I came to the painstaking revelation that I knew the world about hip-hop and rap and nothing about any other kinds of music. After dealing with this embarrassing awareness publicly, I took it upon myself to whet my musical palette. I was pretty much floating around when my size thirteen feet led me to this Latin Jazz Festival downtown. I liked what I heard, but then again I didn't. I loved the beat. It was sick. It was just the lack of vocals to the instrumentals that began to wear on me. It seemed sort of sad that there wasn't somebody singing, in any language, to various crescendos.

Toward the end of night, it all started to make sense. The music was so good and so pure in its own right that any sort of lyrics would have tainted it. I was so lost in euphoria with this revelation that I didn't even bother to see the man stumbling toward me until it was far too late.

He was obviously a bit tipsy, but far from tore up and drunk. It was obvious that he was the kind of man that best operated on the excuse of liquid courage with a protruding bulge from his windbreakers pants.

"This shit ain't no real jazz," he said in a deep resonating voice that reeked of alcohol.

He was a tall man. The same shade of black as I was with a similar thickset frame. The differences ended there, however. I had a full head of hair with a clean-shaven face, and he had a clean-shaved head with a full gruffly beard. People would call me a pretty boy, and he was simply attractive in a masculine way.

"What did you say?" I asked.

"I said this shit here ain't no jazz. I don't know what the fuck kind of music this is. But it ain't jazz." He spat.

I knew if I did the subtle thing and slowly moved away, he would have followed me. If I manned up and told him to back off, he probably would have caused a commotion throwing off some of the musicians on stage. I was too far deep into it to let that to happen. So I stood there, and let him talk.

He didn't get loud like I thought he would. He just talked it out, talking to me about what real jazz was, and that he played with the last of the great giants as some sort of musical protégé. It wasn't until he started talking about his music career that I saw the shiny saxophone in his hands. He then told me that his name was Roscoe, and that he was tore up on the inside. Down the street, his visiting band played real jazz and barely got a spittle of an audience. He came down here to find that everybody and their families were supporting, in his words, a poor imitation of his craft.

He carried on about it for about a good five minutes before he told me that he could play some real jazz for me. He gave me his business card and everything. He then started talking about this club that I never even heard of and its popularity down in New Orleans. He quickly caught on that he wasn't in New Orleans and that his band was only in town for one night, offering to play me a set in his hotel room.

I knew what was up before he even started talking. He just simply verified it for me then with his invitation. I was quite sure that Roscoe heard that my city was good for picking up men that messed around that weren't so easy to clock. Roscoe had to have been a good twenty years older than I, a bit mature for my taste. Looking at his hands, however, and his big feet and what I had only heard about musicians and their whorish ways, I figured why not? More to the point,

I had spent the entire day listening to good music that had put me in the mood to get laid.

We got back to the hotel, which was about a couple of blocks up and across the street from the festival. If I wasn't so pumped with hormones, anticipating what was about to go down, I would have otherwise been at awe at the boutique hotel that he and his band mates were staying. It was the kind of hotel that the young hip people with money hung out. That just only added to my energy, and I thought it was doing the same for him.

When we got back to the room, he took off his shirt as if we were about to get to it, and he started moping about his wife leaving him and that this certain "friend" left him as well. It took him about a good three hours for him to finally admit that his "friend" was his lover, and that his lover was a man that happened to be a crack fiend that took him to the cleaners during their three-year relationship.

The next morning, I woke up next to Roscoe and his sour alcoholic-stained breath on the sofa. Nothing happened. And in spite of the horrifying stuff that Roscoe told me the night before about his past, my dick was still backed up and hard from what I thought was about to go down the night before. Without waking ol' boy up, I snuck off into the bathroom. I didn't just come all the way up here for nothing, I thought. The least I could do was make some sort of claim to fame to the luxurious hotel, by jumping in the shower for a quick jerk-off.

My hand found my dick, hard and ready to go. I had just begun to settle into a nice stroking rhythm under the running shower head when I saw the tattooed forearm wrap around my body. Roscoe was pressed close behind me. Warm breath roll off of my neck, and his sleeping dick slowly arising against the top of my crack, with his moving hand pressed firmly against my hard stomach. I was feeling it. I was feeling him. I wasn't in the mood to have sex with him then. We just simply made out in the shower and jerked each other off until our nuts washed down the drain.

I got dressed and left shortly afterwards, feeling seriously cheated out of a good night. My energy was soon renewed when I got off the elevator and locked eyes with this phyne Creole dude in the lobby. Though, sadly, I just went about my day.

About six months later, I found myself down in New Orleans (attending of all things a jazz festival) with one of the venues being the club Roscoe said that he infamously played. And not knowing anybody in his neck of the woods, I called him up wanting to get the hook up on some of the hot spots in town. Roscoe obliged, looking extremely good. Why didn't I have sex with him before? I was just about to make my move on him by the second day when he introduced me to his former crack fiend boyfriend.

I wasn't even mad. I was mildly relieved that I was spared from the yolk that could've been on my face. Without much choice, I decided to spend most of the festival as a tagalong to several different groups. On my last night in town, I joined these strangers for dinner, and lo and behold the phyne Creole dude that I saw in the lobby way that day. I knew it was he because there are very few people in this world that can genuinely be called yellow and sporting a weird five o'clock shadow that somehow worked.

We didn't talk much through dinner and dessert. When we did find a way to have a conversation, as he walked me back to my hotel, it was pretty much where he thought he knew me from somewhere. He gave me his name, which was Homer, hoping that it would jog some kind of memory. I could've easily spared him the torment and told him where he knew me from, but it was sort of fun to watch him childishly put the pieces of the puzzle together. He never did – that night. He instead promised to figure that out. In the meantime, however, he enjoyed my company, and we exchanged cell phone numbers to stay in contact.

Homer played it absolutely cool for the first three weeks. He kept the conversation going without it going there. He soon gave away his master plan by hitting me up everyday, and then with a few lines to bait me, to see if I was down, he pulled the reel, promising after another couple of months that he was going to come to my city to visit me. I told him about a sweet hotel he could stay at, and then he remembered where he saw me. He asked me, if I always knew. I came forward with the truth. He then asked why I didn't tell him before. The only answer I could give to that was, "If I did, we probably wouldn't be here."

Once he came up, I already made up my mind that we weren't going to have sex for awhile. I figured he come up here, I go down there. We do a few trips like that and then take it from there. He was on the same plane, which made dinner more delectable and dessert much sweeter. The biggest surprise to come of that night was Homer was older than Roscoe. At a glance, Homer barely looked out of his twenties. As I zoomed in closer, I could see possibly at a stretch thirty-seven or thirty-eight but not forty-three. I guess old dick was in season, I laughed in my head as I walked him back over to his hotel.

He went in, and I left.

I was about a good two blocks down before I decided that if anything was going to happen between us it needed to go down that night. Homer was an incredible guy. He was somebody I could see myself kicking it with. The problem was he lived down there, and I lived up here, and I wasn't about to go through the hassle of a long-distance relationship knowing that I had a very high sex drive. With the help of the valet and the concierge, who saw me walk him to his hotel, I was able to go up to his room.

He looked at me. I looked at him. Like a magnetic draw, we grabbed each other and started kissing fiendishly. We went from one side of the room to the other before finding ourselves naked on the bed with him kissing the hard contours of my body. I decided that with him between my legs sucking my nipples down my stomach to my groin that I should be the one to suck him off.

Homer sat on the edge of the bed with me crawling between his thin yellow legs spread wide open. He didn't possess a long cock. It looked more like an engorged softball. Nevertheless, I cupped the fat stubby monster in my hands, pulling the skin back from the head and began licking up and down along the shaft and lime-sized balls. The head was a beast to get into my mouth without bringing in my teeth into the fray. He tried assisting me by gently seizing the back of my head and giving me a direct line to his most sensitive spots.

He moaned with delight, stroking his balls against my chin. I got tired of that and started on them. I had the same problem with them as I did his dickhead, trying hard not to get the teeth in anyway involved.

"I guess somebody ain't a virgin," he mumbled. "C'mon up here, son."

I worked my mouth on his dick a bit longer, tasting everything New Orleans had to offer, and slowly made my way up his slender body where he held me captive in soulful kisses. He had me so open that I didn't remember when I found my way on my back. He was sucking, licking, kissing and eating me out ferociously that I was fighting being turned out and bitched out at the same time while grinding my ass into his face.

Homer slowed the breaks down by slipping in a finger or two, stretching me open. I was so ready by then I could've taken his sweet dick as is. It was easier said than done, working that huge sheathed head into my willing hole. I felt like pussy giving birth except the head was going back in.

"Open up for big daddy, son," he huskily whispered.

"Oh, man!" I moaned, not wanting to give in but found myself doing it anyway as I gasped in some strange falsetto.

Like I said, he didn't have a long dick but it filled every nook and cranny it needed to beyond satisfaction. It felt even better than some of the men that could have easily dug out my intestines. He started fucking me in ways and positions that I wasn't going to leave this world without remembering who was putting it down on me like that. He was bouncing me around from piston fuck to soulful lovemaking, with me giving in more with every other stroke.

I was being conquered. I was holding down the fort and surrendering all at the same time, feeling these constant waves of pleasure. I was panting. He was grunting, and before long, I was in a frenzy rotating my thighs against him and shot off this simmering pearly white jet of paste that came pouring back onto my stomach. He obviously wasn't far behind, letting out a ferocious grunt and sighing as he came in the condom in my ass.

That too should have been the end of my story except that after we had sex, we grew stronger. We became a long distance couple with the two of us wearing the hell out of the highway between our cities and the states in between.

We were going strong for about a couple of years before Homer made the proposal that I move down to New Orleans to be with him. I had no problem with it except for the fact that Homer wasn't out at home. Meaning – could be taken good or bad – that I would have to maintain a separate place and a separate life in a new city that didn't interfere with his established life. He then suddenly aborted that idea and started fixing me up on dates with various beautiful women. It was eventually revealed that he was pushing me to get married so that his wife wouldn't suspect anything out of the ordinary now that his jazz band was slowly losing jobs on the road.

I was blindsided by his marriage and his set up that while I wanted to call it quits, I couldn't. I was too deep into it to just cut him off. Then, as luck would have it, I ran into Roscoe again at his club. He still looked physically better than the day that I met him. The only difference was he was walking around with a gray cloud over his shoulders. When I caught up with him to ask him what was up, he told me that his boy went back to drugs and cleaned him out for the last time.

We talked again over a cup of coffee in some random parking lot in some random park in his SUV. I listened to him talk. I mean really listened. Maybe it was my sour mood at the time or maybe it was his or the memory where it led us the first time, but my hand found its way to his crotch. He was helping me undo it for him. We both helped pull out his growing long black cock, smelling the sex that only he could produce and my mouth quickly followed into his lap. He took it to a whole other level when he started up his vehicle and started driving around, telling me he didn't want to get caught up and caught out there. He claimed that I sucked him off so long that we took a nice little lap around Lake Pontchartrain ahead of any inkling of milk he was destined to shoot in my mouth.

Once again, I should've headed back home. That should've been the end of the story. Of course, it wasn't.

Roscoe and I started hanging tight giving me a reason to come back to New Orleans. With Roscoe, the icing on the cake was that Roscoe was single and out at home, not giving a flip about who knew or not. He just wasn't out in his professional circles. He often told me that with so many whores in the music industry that if everybody started to define who did what in the bedroom, it would throw everything off. Then, too, nobody was man enough to ask him to head up because he had four failed marriages under his belt and was a known ladies' man, so the rumor mill didn't spin too far.

After a few twists and tweaks, it almost perfectly began to shape up like this: Homer would come up to visit me still, and I would go down there to kick it with Roscoe back in New Orleans. And since neither man was looking for a commitment at that time, I thought everything was working itself out just fine. Without a doubt, there was drama approaching on the horizon. Homer got cold busted when he came back home to his wife with the hickeys I left around his neck and his dick. He decided that he needed a change; he wanted a serious relationship with me as we talked about many times before, and without many options he came up here to live with me to give it a try.

It was fine for a few months. It soon grew into the same tired story. I was angry with Homer after I thought he was trying to reconcile with his wife. I rebutted by jumping back into bed with Roscoe. It was only after I hooked up with Roscoe at a nearby hotel up here that I came back to the crib to find Homer waiting on me, to tell me that he went back down there to tell his wife everything about us. She sent a handwritten note that if I wanted him that I could have him, but I shouldn't expect that she would divorce him being that she wasn't going to turn him over like that.

I was so caught off guard and so turned on by his renewed lust that I let him fuck me just a couple of hours after I sent Roscoe back home after he fucked me. I was still tight. I was just unusually wet and slippery slick with the lube that was still inside of me. I could tell by the look in his eyes that he knew something was up, but he was so caught up in getting his that he just let it go thinking that it was only in his head.

The first time I did that was the worst, if not the scariest time. After that, it sort of became an adrenaline rush of fucking both men on the same day, narrowing the margin sometimes by only a half-hour, with one using the cum of the other as lube without even knowing it.

I was sort of coming to the end of the road having my fun with either one of them, seeing that the three of us was getting older. The three of us wanted something a bit more stable, a bit more drama-free. The thing was while Roscoe and Homer were looking at me for a long-term relationship, I was slowly looking to bow out of the complicated situation unscathed.

My successful run started to come unhinged when I decided to expand my musical diversity by listening to a CD that Roscoe passed onto me. I didn't think nothing of it until Homer came home one day, looked at me crooked and asked where did I get the music? I told him, thinking nothing of it. He happened to tell me that it was the accompanying music set that he and his newly formed jazz group were going to sell once they hit the road, playing a pure double bass medley for me.

Homer confronts Roscoe, and thankfully Roscoe didn't rat me out putting the pieces of the puzzle together. Roscoe instead started digging his heels convincing me that I should kick Homer and his crusty ass to the curb and relocate with him back to New Orleans. The ironic thing was that after

Roscoe found out about Homer and me, it really turned him on. But, Roscoe really got off on the idea that a young masculine bottom kat like myself was wearing the hell out of two old jazz dicks.

I was on the verge of shutting down the production that was my three way when I invited Roscoe over. I decided the best way to cut my losses was to break up with Roscoe first. And when my lease was up on my apartment, I was going to cut my losses with Homer as well. When Roscoe came over, he was ready for sex. He won.

The next thing I know, I wake up to Homer standing over my naked body wondering what the fuck happened. Of course, I altered the truth a bit, telling him that Roscoe came over asking my opinion of the music he gave me. I got us something to drink, which was part of the truth. The part that I lied about was that I said I stepped away to the bathroom and after taking a few sips of my drink, I woke up to him looking at me feeling like I got the dick down of my life.

This threw a wrench in my plans because Homer wanted to be my man even more, thinking that his friend had possibly done something to me. So a couple of weeks later, he decide to take me out to a jazz club, only to find out that Roscoe, his band mate, was moonlighting as a solo artist visiting from New Orleans.

One thing led to another and the jazz lounge erupted with the two men about to go at it while I snuck outside, never to look back again.

The story should've ended there. It didn't.

I was sound asleep when I woke up in the middle of the night with two pairs of eyes staring back at me, naked and unclothed, belonging to Roscoe and Homer cupping their engorged tubesteaks.

"Why didn't you just say so? Musicians get down any way we can with our muses."

PIECE
R. Talent

For a split second, the sight of his dick excited me. The saliva in my mouth went from a soaking wet rainstorm in a rainforest to cottonmouth dry in the second I thought about it a bit more. He was very big, yes – FREAKSHOW CIRCUS BIG – more inches and girth than I could have ever dreamed about in a millions years. The fact that he was real and it was real and in front of me with that thing made the whole thing even more surreal.

I grew up with Mathis. We weren't the best of friends even though we had our moments in the sun throughout the seasons. We happened to live our lives and go our separate ways after graduation, and I went without him ever crossing my mind again. We were no longer connected to the same neighborhood, no longer a part of the same fabric. Even when I went back home, I never inquired about him. He didn't even come into my mind.

Then, one day, as I was flipping the alternative paper, *The Grunge*, featuring the artists and creative freaks of the city, there he was with a third of a column discussing his tumultuous musical career. The reports were that he joined a local band, an eclectic hip-hop ensemble. It did okay, nothing big time just a few local dives around the city. I tried to find them, to check them out at one of the spots they were rumored to have played. But to no avail. Apparently there was a serious lag time between when the article was written and the article was published because by the time it went to print, the group had disbanded. Mathis changed into some funky clothes and branched off into a solo singing career. But that never got far either. He was signed to a major record company, but his career was not catered by the label as it should have been. When he found out the real reason why, that the label was more focused on their platinum rap artists than their R&B subsidiaries, rather than beat them at their own game, he instead chose to join them by touring behind his popular label mate, infiltrating his entourage until he became a part of the top brass.

That was where I found him finally, sitting alone at a bar inside of a very trendy hotel drowning his day away. He was still the youthful-looking nerdy-looking black Clark Kent I remembered from back in the day. He tired to tell the world that he changed from that boy into a man by sporting what can otherwise be described as a trimmed bush around his mouth. Even so, to me, he still looked like the same old same old, except with a bit of money lining his pockets that came off with more of a brash confidence than chic arrogance. Once he saw who I was, even that took away his Superman powers.

We talked for about a couple of hours, with him leading the discussions telling me everything I just told you. We exchanged numbers and parted ways, knowing that our conversation wasn't going to go beyond our last gin and tonic.

Six months later, maybe ten, Mathis surprised me with a phone call. He claimed that it was by accident, that he must've programmed his new phone with my number under his other friend's name. After apologizing for the mistake, he was telling me that he was trying to call his friend to ask him he wanted some tickets to the concert that night featuring his label mate, Cyclone, the rapper. I guess that was my cue to ask for the tickets. But failing to see the perks of knowing someone who knew somebody famous and phyne like Cyclone, at the time, I thought I had a better chance of being with him by jacking off to a magazine picture featuring his ripped tatted-up body.

"Not a fan, huh," Mathis said right off the bat, after long breaks of silence.

"Sure," I said, grabbing my dick thinking about Cyclone. "I thought you were trying to call your friend to give him the tickets."

"I can give you the tickets just the same as I can him," Mathis said.

"Then, cool," I said, letting him trail off the conversation with the intricate details about how I was to obtain them.

The concert was off the chain! It was like wrestling and soft-core porn rolled into one with gorgeous well-sculpted men drenched in sweat hopping around on stage rapping about all sort of suggestive things made every man, gay or straight, sport a proud hard-on in that arena.

Afterwards, I was ready to hit the club and find a man to unleash my lustful desires. If not, disappointingly start what would be the first of many jack-off sessions to this wonderful event. But, as I was practically dry humping this man with an incredibly firm and high booty next to his so-called girlfriend, as we tried to crowd out of the building, Mathis cupped me by the shoulder and led me around backstage.

The security alone kept my dick on brick. I could have fucked all of them beefy bastards and still left hornier than what I came in with, just thinking about them. If that wasn't enough, there were scores of other gorgeous men coupled and caressed by beautiful women, obviously groupies. I engaged in a few conversations with the some of the mean-mugged bouncers, scoring a couple of numbers on the sly. I was making full use of the food spread when Mathis introduced me to Cyclone in passing. Cyclone looked me up and down with his phyne barely shirtless self, mentioned that Mathis had told him about me, growing up and all sorts of shit that I forgot. Cyclone then asked if I was tagging along with them.

I didn't know what that meant, and didn't have time to ask as I was being ushered into one of five Hummer limos taking us to various clubs, scoring free drinks. I was sort of getting into the groove of this club-hopping business when we ended back up at their hotel where scores of sophisticated groupies calmly scattered throughout the lobby waiting on the star. While Cyclone and some of his crew members headed off to their suites with a handful of them, Mathis and I sloshed down the other end of the hall back to his room.

He too had a luxury suite, equipped with a sofa and a view of the city that were only shown in those high-end magazines. It was nice, extremely nice. I tried to thank him for the night. He tried being humble, saying that it was all the label's doing and that he was just a middleman between me and the night.

"Still," I smiled, sipping on more alcohol from the mini fridge on the sofa. "You made the shit happen."

"Yeah," he simpered. "I'm glad you enjoyed the night."

Without much thought, being that I was drunk, I started caressing my dick through my jeans telling him that it would be nice if we could finish off the beautiful night with something to smoke.

Like a soldier, he came through with some weed to smoke, claiming that it was some of the finest shit on the market. He claimed that it topped most of the stuff that came out of Amsterdam. It smoked smooth and was very good; taking me up on a high that was effortless and indulgent.

I was stroking my dick through my pants, feeling the honey drip slick my underwear.

“Damn, this shit is tight! I should've added getting some head to the mix.” I joked, seriously thinking about getting some head from one of the women downstairs.

Although, I was a man into men, I figured that a mouth was a mouth.

Then, out of nowhere, Mathis mumbled he could use some dick to toke on, too.

This put a huge smile on my face, not getting the faintest of vibes that he got down, too. I got more energy off of the security than I ever did him.

“Well, c'mon then, this could be our lucky day,” I said, undoing my jeans and sprawling my arms over behind to sofa.

“Damn, dick's already on brick,” he laughed nervously at my long seamless black dick arching out of my lap.

“Like the Washington Monument.” I said, sleepy-eyed. “Why don't you bring your mouth on over here and treat it like a lollipop!”

Mathis slowly descended to his knees, licking the underbelly and the head. With the night view before me, I got my tired ass up off the sofa and took the party over to the ceiling-to-floor windows. If I had been sober, I would've been scared at the open view or using my hand as a balance against it. But being drunk and high, neither of that bothered me, especially after he started sucking on my thinly-veined dick. He bobbed up and down as if he was going for apples, or in this case a banana. His mouth felt like heaven on my dick, wrapping his throat around my piece as he had my balls bouncing off of his pointy chin.

"Oh, shit," I mumbled. "Oh, no ... shit!"

I shot off like a cannon in his sweet mouth, unable to hold back or give any kind of warning with the slow response of overcoming the weed and alcohol.

"Shit," I sighed, recuperating from the ball-drainer and feeling good on an even higher cloud with his throat closing and opening to swallow my load.

Even when I was done, he was not, holding on to every last drop and then doing the courtesy of using his mouth to clean me up afterwards.

"Damn, that's some skills." I huffed, opening my eyes to find Mathis squatting on his knees, reaching between his legs and jacking off. "I can take care of that if you want."

"For real," Mathis said cool with the program.

"Yeah, I got to show my appreciation for everything." I smirked. Not knowing how I was going to keep my concentration on giving him head was going to work out with me being sleepy and intoxicated and sleepy so more.

"Cool." He said standing up.

I fell to my knees like a sack of potatoes, took control of his dick like it was nothing. He wasn't as big as me, but being that he was clean and cut made it worthwhile being that I had sometimes had cheese build up. I wasn't a fan of the taste like some foreskin lovers.

What got me though was my lack of abandon. Although we were on the fifty- or sixty- or seventy-something floor, I was still letting the city watch me suck off this dude. And while I was glad to do him this favor, other than for the night, the fan in me wanted to be down the hall giving head to the star. So I sucked Mathis like I would have sucked off that redbone Cyclone, if given the chance, and before Mathis could make the dramatic moans to orgasm, the door of his room was busted in by about fifteen or so men. They looked like they were cropped out of some unknown masculine black muscled porn with a couple of our brown brothers in the fray along with an incredibly ripped white guy and a tall yellow guy that also looked fresh out of the gym.

"What the fuck?" I said, with Mathis' dick dripping with my spit in face.

"Ah perk of being part of an entourage," Mathis said with a goofy smile, looking down at me.

"We're cool, bruh," one guy said.

"Yeah, we're just trying to join the party," the white guy said, in sort of corny fashion that reminded me of something straight out of a porno.

"Cool," I said. "Long as you brought plenty of condoms, we can party 'til the break of dawn."

"Of course, baby," the first guy said totting around a large clear bowl filled to the brim with black wrappers. "We got the condoms black and that good lube by the gallons."

"Shit, y'all came in here ready to do the damn thing," I mumbled.

"You're cool with?" Mathis asked.

"Shit, yeah," I said lowly. "I'm that kind of freak, and besides every one of those motherfuckers are a looker except for that one motherfucker, and I think he got a dick."

"You ain't never lied, bruh," Mathis grinned.

"Y'all just come out your clothes while I take care of my boy just like he took care of me," I said, mildly regretting that I wasted my first load on Mathis.

I sucked and damn near choked trying to suck Mathis off, getting taunts and cheers from the other guys in the room. A couple of guys daringly made there way over to us, so while I was sucking off Mathis, I had two other dicks I had to palm in front of the window.

After I got Mathis good to go, I took on one dick after another, inhaling the different kinds of man-funk that each of them had to offer. "Damn, you got that fire head."

"No doubt," I pulled off and responded favorably.

I sucked off the second guy but not the third. He was the one I really wanted to get with, but because my knees were killing me by then, I told him we had to move it on over somewhere else. He was cool with it, considering that it gave him the chance to literally be on my ass with his huge dick riding my crack.

He felt better than sex itself. His other friend, who was hairless except for around the eyes – not to be left out of the mix – grabbed me by my nipples and led me over to the king-sized bed. When they got me over there, another one of his friends started tonguing my nipples while another guy started sucking my renewed hard dick.

Before long, I was covered in hand and arms and other body parts that I could no longer see any part of my anatomy. I was being pushed and pulled. Pushed to the bed, and then pulled back up off it until these strong forceful hands pushed me down to the bed and brought my ass back up, pressing his dick under mine and his pubes into my hole just making it twitch and wet.

I wanted to look back to see whose doing this to me, but didn't, not wanting be intimidated by the number and size of men that I was destined to take care of. Yet, without even trying, I could make out the tight crowd men in the mirror above the bed and with my head being brought back so another man could position himself for some head from me, I got a quick glimpse of the man behind me in the mirrored headboard.

I recognized him. He was one of the cute bodyguards that I was talking to earlier, with the fluttering bulge in his pants.

His name was Antonio, I think?

Antonio started fingering my ass with cold lube as I suck off this random guy that was treating my throat like a masturbation sleeve with his thrust and hand holding the back of my head controlling the speed. I was snorting and gurgling and loving every minute of it, taking the time to get at his balls. Antonio pulled back for a minute and then started fingering my hole with both fingers as he announced that he got on a condom.

"Time for me to bust this cherry for the night," Antonio announced, bringing my ass back closer to him. He had me waiting in anticipation with the tip of his condom dancing across my anxious hole. "You ready pimp?"

"Yeah, dude," I managed to say after coming off dude for a second. "Do you?"

"Ain't like dude got much of a choice," the guy's whose dick I was sucking said, slapping my mouth back onto his genitalia.

"Ain't that the truth," Antonio laughed, grabbing me by my waist and tried throwing his dick up in me like it was nothing. "Damn, baby boy, you're tighter than a mug."

You thought otherwise, I thought, gripping my hole tighter against his invading dick hoping to embarrass him with his friends by coming so soon. I thought I had him, but it turned out he had me, jabbing me all proper like, having me squirm against that hard dick of his. I was fiendish for it before long, throwing my ass against him and everything as he grabbed me by my shoulder and had me bouncing off of his dick. It felt good, especially since this took any effort away from the dude I was sucking off, which meant that all he could do was aim his dick at my open mouth while Antonio did the rest.

"Ah, man," the guy in front of me screamed, holding on to the back of my head once again, and doing me the courtesy of spraying his nut on my afro and forehead.

This, or the idea of this, must have really done it for Antonio because he started pumping me hard and rough with the thick lube easing the brunt of what could have been a violent fuck. He was so in his own zone that nobody climbed in the bed in front of me, knowing that it would just be too much for me.

"I'm about to get that nut baby boy. Let me get that nut. Aw, damn!" He said shooting into my ass in his black condom.

Antonio was definitely the first to tag this ass that night, but certainly not the last as I engaged in a blur of acrobatics, with this position and that, sucking and fucking, getting eaten out and even in a couple of cases double penetration. That required a bit more weed to enjoy along with spine-tingling kisses up and down my sweaty body. The thing that took me over the edge was the constant "thank yous" I received from various men in the room every time some dude busted a nut and discarded a condom.

I had got hemmed by the whole room at least once, with several repeats including Antonio who had me on my back saying his name, calling him Daddy and Big Poppa at random, claiming my ass as his alone as one dude tried sucking me off. I tried getting him up off of me as I just gyrated my thighs bucking against Antonio, who didn't need an ounce of help doing his job.

"Aw, fuck me, man," I said beginning to lose my battle to a fourth orgasm to the large bucking bronco on top of me.

He was fucking me like it was his last day on earth, like he hadn't gotten off anytime that century with his dick swimming in my exposed hole and balls drumming against its door.

"Oh, c'mon, dawg," I screamed, noticing that my voice carried throughout the room as if we were the only two still left.

He grabbed my ankles to the air, and started fucking me nicer and harder until I had another load to get loose. I guess that was all it took because he started screaming and shouting, pulled out and pulled off his condom to show a small but sizeable load that he just rubbed against my inner thigh.

I was so tired that by the time he let go of my legs and they hit the bed, I feel asleep.

I don't know how long I was out, but I knew that the sun was out by the time I finished off Antonio, and it was still out when saw Cyclone in all his glorious nakedness standing above my cum-drenched body. With so many men in the room last night, it didn't even occur to me that the star of the show wasn't even there.

And there he was.

For a split second the sight of his dick excited me, in spite of the many I had already had before. Then the saliva in my mouth went from a soaking wet rainstorm in the wettest of rainforest to cottonmouth dry in the second I saw what I saw. He was very big, bigger than big. His dick was like freak show circus big with more inches and girth than I could have ever thought one human being could tote on one body, and the fact that he was real and it was realer than real was more than an idea that I could chew on.

"I know I got a big dick, son," Cyclone said with a sinister grin. "That's why I had my boys stretch you out, so I can take some of that good pussy."

I froze. I didn't mind the fucking. I just had a problem with the dick that I had to fuck. My mind instantly went back to an ad I saw in one of those fuck catalogs, advertising a massive black dong for novelty purposes only. It wasn't crazy enough to be fucked with unless somebody was crazy enough to fuck it. And even with the sea of dick I took, he was just too much.

"As much as I want to handle you just to say that I did, there is no way I can handle that lead pipe, partna," I said, exhausted and sore in the bed.

"Sure you can. Mind over matter, bruh, mind over matter."

He climbed over into the bed with his elephant hung dick leading the way.

"Talk to the mic, motherfucker," Cyclone growled, grabbing his dick and thumping it against my mouth like a hard slap.

While my mind said no, my whorish body was giving the go ahead as I barely got a fraction of the head passed my lips, which was a sore defeat coming from a man that was popping big dick in his mouth like a pill popper. Since I couldn't do much with the dick as a whole in my mouth, I focused strictly on the cumhole, licking the sweet honey that was steadily dripping from it.

It gave me new life, working over dick the best I could until I was lying on my side.

"Got that nice proper bubble ass," Cyclone said, slapping the side of my thigh and butt cheeks covered in dried crud.

I tried to ignore him, hoping that I could make him come with my mouth alone, making him forget about my ass.

"I know what you're trying to do," he said after about ten long minutes. "I'm still getting in that ass."

I tried to pull off, but he told me that it wasn't going to make much of a difference and that I needed to focus on one task at a time.

I did, nervously, thinking how in the hell was I going to pack all of this back there?

I was falling in love with sucking his dick when he announced that he was ready to get some ass. Knowing what he knew, he surprised me by bringing my knees back to my ears and eating me out like the last supper. He was tonguing it like it was going out of style, had me accidentally begging for it.

"Fuck me. Oh, fuck me, motherfucker!"

Without a beat, Cyclone had on a magnum and some of that thick lube worked up in my ass along with some of that anal desensitizer as a base. As he aimed that third leg against my hole, I felt even more betrayed by my body when it gobbled up and expanded around his slick dick. Even with the amount of dick I had already taken, I felt as if I was being stretched incredibly wide by this one. I only thought I was being split in two before. He didn't care, slowly building up to get his the way he wanted it. My hole and my body were shaking with every ramming thrust, and the surprising part was that it didn't hurt as I knew it should. It was so hot, and I was so turned on, that I couldn't believe that I was feeling another load stir. I was open, yet I felt stuffed, lusting for more of his dick to pound into me.

Cyclone looked down at me and smiled, knowing that he had me. He knew what he was doing and knew that he did it well, as my hole gave into each way of pleasure.

"Fuck me," I screamed with him taxing my ass for everything that it was worth. "Oh, gawd!"

"Yeah, son, yeah!" Cyclone shouted. "Give me some more of this good ass!"

It felt as if my hole was no longer my hole, just a tool for him use that I just happened to enjoy by chance as he looked at me looking back at him on top of me in the mirror. He was plowing and screwing, having me just lie there and take it.

"I'm about to come," he said very much in control, breathing huskily without an inkling that he was out of breath.

I was touching the sides of contracting abs, waiting on that moment, and before I knew it he shoved his dick all the way inside of me. And I automatically shot, a small pearl of a load, before he killed my ass over the next five minutes.

"Oh, shit," he bellowed. "I'm about there, pimp. I'm about there."

He sunk his dick back into me, deeper than he had ever gone before and collapsed on top of me, panting for dear life. After a minute or two, he came back up, still in side of me and kissed me on the side of my neck and jaw.

"Damn, baby boy, you a nice piece, got some ass on you, too." Cyclone smirked, after he pulled out of me.

There was a long silence between the two of us as he got off me and got his clothes back on, claiming that he was surprise that nobody called hotel security about the loud noise we had made.

"You should think about joining my entourage. It comes with a nice big perk."

"No doubt," I said rolling upright. "The biggest perk I ever had!"

UNDER COVER OF NIGHT
By Stephen Osborne

Taylor examined himself carefully in the bathroom mirror. His long blond locks were stuffed – convincingly, if he said so himself – under a wig of dark, curly hair. He'd darkened his eyebrows and put on a pair of horn-rimmed glasses. The lenses were just glass with no magnification, and the frames, while distinctive, weren't out of fashion. Taylor twisted his mouth, trying to decide if the disguise was effective. Would anyone recognize Taylor Moll under all the fakery?

He couldn't take any chances. There had already been too many rumors about him, too many stories in the press and on the Internet. Just months ago AfterElton.com had run a story about him, speculating about his sexuality. One of the tabloids had printed a grainy photograph of him on a hotel balcony, lip-locked with a hot Latino with muscles to die for. Luckily, the picture was so poor that few took any notice of it. The majority of the fans of his group, Witchcraft, simply couldn't believe that the heart-throb lead singer of the band could be homosexual. The group was just too gritty, despite their good looks. Too rockin'. Too butch.

Taylor sighed and adjusted the wig slightly. Maybe it would be better to just forget going out tonight. Maybe he should just stay home and jerk off, thinking of Witchcraft's lead guitarist, Ricky Yarnell. Ever since they'd started playing together four years ago, Taylor had secretly yearned for the tall, lanky Yarnell. He didn't normally go for skinny guys, but something about the way the guitarist moved pushed every single one of Taylor's buttons. He was so cocky, so confidant. Ricky swaggered when he walked, which made Taylor just want to tackle him and yank all his clothes off.

Too bad he was straight.

Taylor bit his lip. He shouldn't have thought about Ricky. Now he was getting horny, and there was no question about whether to stay at his hotel room alone or go out to find some hot guy to fuck. Nope, tonight his right hand just wouldn't do. Taylor needed to hear someone other than himself moan for a change.

Taylor stood back from the mirror a few feet, keeping an eye on his reflection. The clothes were just right. Some tight, generic jeans and a shirt from the Gap. Nothing flashy. Nothing that Taylor would normally wear. Even the tennis shoes on his feet were scuffed and worn. Taylor kept his "going out clothes," along with his wigs, packed in a special suitcase and made sure that none of his band mates ever got a peek inside. Not that it really mattered. He could always say he liked to go out every now and then without being recognized. Hell, some rock stars were masters of disguise. Hadn't George Harrison always gone out under the *nom de plume* of Mr. Hughes? And Michael Jackson had been known to not only disguise himself – he disguised his kids as well!

Grabbing the wallet with his fake ID and his key card for the hotel, Taylor headed for the door. Before he reached it, though, the telephone rang. He stopped, wondering if he should ignore it. Witchcraft was in Indianapolis for several days to do a shoot for their new video, and by now, some journalists might have figured out where they were staying and what names they were using. On the other hand, maybe it was Ricky, requesting his presence for a night out on the town. Well, he could dream ...

Taylor shoved the wallet into his back pocket and slowly walked over to the phone. When he finally picked up, he was pleasantly shocked to hear Carl's voice on the line. Carl was their drummer, and like many a drummer before him, he was, in a word, exuberant. In spirit, he was an odd mixture of Keith Moon and Levon Helm. Carl was a wild party animal, but he had Helm's country boy charm about him. The charm worked well with the ladies, and it was a rare night that Carl didn't have at least one woman to share his bed. The animal part made Carl a terror to hotel managers and bartenders everywhere.

"I figger'd you'd be out getting you some poon by now," Carl said, chuckling loudly.

Taylor was never quite sure how much of Carl's speech was an affectation and how much was genuinely him. "I was just about out the door," Taylor answered.

"Got plans? I thought we'd go out and have us a time. You know, get to know the locals."

The last thing Taylor wanted was to go out with Carl. "Sorry. Previous plans. I thought you and Ricky were going out tonight."

"Ricky rang me just a few minutes ago. He's got him a big ol' headache. Gonna stay in tonight. Not me. Carl's Junior is hearing the call of the wild."

Carl's Junior was the drummer's pet name for his schlong. There were rumors and stories about the size of Carl's cock, which was reported to be mind-bogglingly huge. Taylor could confirm the rumors. He had once walked backstage after a show to find Carl getting head from a groupie. The young blonde woman was gagging on the monster meat Carl was feeding her. The sight had given Taylor a new respect for the drummer. While Taylor wasn't particularly attracted to Carl, he did speculate about the fun that could be had with such an enormous tool.

"You're on your own, I'm afraid," Taylor said. "Maybe we can do something tomorrow night."

"I might just hold ya to that," Carl drawled. "We don't spend near enough time together nowadays. One might think you were avoiding us on purpose, like you had some big secret or something."

Carl spoke in a joking tone, but it still sent alarm bells ringing in Taylor's head. He didn't want his band mates speculating about him. "I promise we'll hit the town tomorrow night," Taylor said. "You don't need me or Ricky to have fun, my friend. You're a party all your own."

"Ain't that the truth!"

"Just remember we've got the photo shoot tomorrow afternoon. Try to be sober for that."

Carl laughed. "I ain't making no promises. I'll be there, and I'll be standing on my own two feet, but sober is asking a hell of a lot."

Taylor stayed on the line a few more minutes, talking small talk with Carl. While he was anxious to get out to some of the gay bars he'd Googled earlier, Taylor wanted to make sure that Carl wasn't really suspicious. The subject didn't come up again, and Carl's joking manner finally put Taylor at ease. No one in the band suspected. Thank, God. Taylor said goodbye to the drummer and hung up.

The hotel they were staying in was right in the heart of downtown Indianapolis and was one of the oldest (and swankiest) establishments in the city. The nearest gay bar, however, was blocks away, and Taylor didn't feel like walking. He managed to slink out the main doors without the doorman giving him much attention, but he decided not to take any chances with the taxis waiting nearby. Instead, he walked down the block to another hotel and hailed one of the cabs there.

"Talbott Street," he told the cabbie.

The driver glanced in the rear view mirror and nodded.

He doesn't recognize me, Taylor thought. *How could he, under all this crap?* Taylor sighed. He hadn't realized how tense he'd been. Luckily people tend to look at the obvious – hair color, clothes, eyes. Few ever checked the things that are hard to disguise, such as body type and the ears. Ears were hard to change, especially the earlobes, and Taylor had very distinctive earlobes that gave his ears a nearly webbed look. So far, though, no one had noticed that the guy with the dark, curly hair had the same ears as rock star Taylor Moll.

Taylor was fairly impressed with the bar he'd chosen. It had two levels, with a large dance floor in the main part of the bar and an upstairs area, which was more of a lounge with tables and loads of comfy seats. There was a balcony that overlooked the dance floor. Exploring, Taylor saw several patrons going through a side door near the restrooms. He followed and discovered that there was another room to the bar. This room had a stage where drag queens mimed, belting out torch songs and show tunes. Every table was packed, and there was barely room to stand, even at the back. Taylor liked drag shows but hated having to stand and was about to retrace his footsteps and head back to the dance floor when someone caught his eye.

The guy was leaning against the wall, a drink in hand and watching the show. He was tall and skinny, and it was hard to make out facial features as he was mostly in the shadows, but something about the way he drank from the plastic cup made Taylor pause. The guy was watching the drag queen currently reigning on the stage and was oblivious to Taylor's stare. Taylor, frowning, moved a little closer.

It couldn't be. Could it?

He managed to squeeze his way through the crowd and get a little closer to the guy. Sure enough, the guy was bone thin but moved with an athletic grace. When the guy was jostled by someone in the crowd and had to shift back to his studiedly nonchalant pose, Taylor was sure. The dude had perfectly combed and parted hair and was wearing dark glasses, but there was no doubt that he was Ricky Yarnell.

Jesus, Taylor thought. Ricky hadn't even bothered with a wig. He'd just combed his normally wild hair and stuck on some Ray-bans. The guitarist was asking to be recognized!

The drag queen on stage was joined by another, and the two, dressed in fishnets and mini-skirts, danced and mimed, singing "It's Raining Men." The crowd roared its approval. Some of the patrons standing at the back began to dance along, making it difficult for Taylor to make his way over to Ricky. The song was nearly over by the time Taylor managed to sidle up next to his band mate.

Taylor couldn't keep the grin off his face. The object of countless jack-off sessions was here, watching a drag show! True, it didn't mean that Ricky wasn't as straight as he professed to be. Lots of straight guys went to drag shows. Generally not by themselves, though, and Taylor hadn't seen anyone that seemed to be there with Ricky. Nope, the guitarist, who had told Carl he had a headache, was alone in a gay bar. There was hope.

The queens were basking in the thunderous applause. With the crowd cheering Taylor had to shout in Ricky's ear. "Great show, huh?"

The guitarist took a swig of his cocktail before turning his head to eye the speaker. Even if Ricky had been heavily disguised, Taylor would have recognized him. Sheer cockiness oozed out of every pore. “Not bad.” Ricky spoke in a lower register than was normal, but Taylor still got a thrill from hearing his friend’s voice.

Taylor’s grin grew as Ricky looked him over from head to tow. He chuckled, waiting for the look that would cross Ricky’s face when he realized who was standing next to him.

It didn’t come. Instead, Ricky gave him a sly nod. “It’s a good show,” he said, “but I think we can find something more fun, don’t you?”

Holy crap! Taylor thought. *He really doesn’t recognize me!*

Taylor edged a little closer, allowing his elbow to make contact with Ricky’s arm. An electric thrill ran through him. He swallowed hard and asked, “What did you have in mind?”

“What?” Taylor’s voice couldn’t be heard over the happenings on stage. A new drag queen, dressed as a young but overly tall Liza Minnelli, had been joined by a lesbian dressed as the emcee from Cabaret, and the two were doing a clumsy version of “Money, Money.” Despite the ineptitude of the performance, the crowd was eating it up.

Taylor repeated himself, louder this time. Ricky smiled and leaned in, putting his face close to Taylor’s. “I’ve got a hotel room not far from here. We can take the party there.”

“Sounds good!” Taylor’s reply was unfortunately timed. His shouted words coincided with a quiet spot in the song, and several people turned to see who was interrupting the show. The Liza wannabe on stage hissed angrily, “Take him home and fuck him already!” before continuing with the song.

Ricky flashed Taylor a grin. “You heard the woman. Can’t argue with Liza, now can we?”

Throughout the cab ride back to the hotel, Taylor kept expecting recognition to dawn on Ricky. It never did. Granted, it was even darker in the back seat of the cab than it had been in the bar, but surely Ricky recognized Taylor's voice. True, Ricky was stoned out of his mind but still ...

The cab pulled up at the hotel, and Ricky tossed some bills at the driver. They stood on the sidewalk, and Taylor felt a slight chill as a sudden breeze whipped by. The cool air seemed to sober Ricky somewhat. As he swayed unsteadily, his bleary eyes examined Taylor carefully. "Have we met before?" he asked. "You look strangely familiar."

"Funny," Taylor replied. "I was about to say the same thing to you."

Ricky's grin was wicked and uncharacteristically humble. Taylor even thought he detected a hint of blush on Ricky's cheek as he muttered, "Yeah. You might have seen me around somewhere. It's not important. What's important is that we're together now." He playfully grabbed at Taylor's ass.

The movement nearly made Taylor jump out of his skin. His brain was so conditioned to avoid any public displays that might foster the notion that he might be gay that, even disguised, he balked at being pawed while standing on the sidewalk of a busy city street. The show of affection didn't seem to bother the less camouflaged Ricky, who laughed and said, "What's the matter? You're not shy, are ya?"

Taylor quickly glanced around. No one seemed to be paying the slightest bit of attention to them. "Not shy," Taylor said, hoping he sounded more assured than he felt. "You just caught me by surprise, that's all."

Ricky suddenly reached out and took hold of Taylor's shirt front, roughly pulling him close. Before Taylor could react, Ricky kissed him hard on the lips. Their teeth clunked together briefly before Ricky's tongue fought its way into Taylor's mouth. Once the shock of enamel hitting enamel wore off, Taylor relaxed and enjoyed the kiss, forgetting that they were still standing outside the hotel in full view of passers-by. Ricky was a good kisser, firm but not overpowering, and his whiskey breath was actually quite pleasant.

Just as quickly the kiss ended, although Ricky kept his grip on Taylor's shirtfront. "Let's get upstairs, so we can fuck," he hissed.

Somehow during the elevator ride up to Ricky's room, both Taylor's shirt and undershirt had been pulled off, even though Taylor didn't think they had stopped kissing long enough for the undershirt to be removed. Had Ricky ripped the damn thing off? Taylor didn't care. The two pulled and grappled with each other all the way down the hall, their lips hardly ever parting. By the time they were standing in front of Room 712, Taylor had undone Ricky's belt and had his hand jammed down the front of the guitarist's jeans. It took four tries for Ricky to get the key card to work.

The two stumbled into the room, barely getting the door closed behind them. Giggling while still lip-locked, the two collapsed to the floor when Ricky's jeans finally gave way and tumbled down around his knees. A brief tussle ended with Ricky straddling Taylor's chest. He leered down at Taylor as he tore his shirt off. Buttons flew, and the garment was tossed aside, revealing Ricky's surprisingly hairy chest. With a flourish, Ricky removed his dark glasses and threw them across the room, then he slid down and covered Taylor's body with his own. Gazing into Taylor's eyes, he whispered, "Do you know who I am?"

Taylor had been reaching up to ensure that his wig was still in place, and the question caught him unaware. After a pause he replied, "You're that guy, the one in the group, Witchcraft."

"Yeah," Ricky said with a grin. "You're about to get fucked by Ricky Yarnell. What do you think about that?" He paused to nibble on Taylor's neck. "That's something a million girls would give their left arm for, the chance to have Ricky Yarnell's cock inside them."

Taylor raised his head and licked the tip of Ricky's nose. "Stop talking, and let's get the rest of our clothes off," he said.

Ricky may have been stoned to the gills, but he had no problem keeping his erection. The two climbed onto the king sized bed, and Ricky rapidly sheathed himself and lubed up. After a brief kiss, Ricky raised Taylor's legs onto his shoulders and positioned himself for entry. Taylor gasped when Ricky's cock was forced into his ass. Ricky grimaced. "Sorry. I'll take it slower."

"Just give my fucking ass muscles a chance to relax, dude!" Taylor smiled as the pain subsided and Ricky pushed more of his cock inside him, slower this time.

One wouldn't accuse Ricky Yarnell of being a gentle lover. Soon he was smacking his cock hard into Taylor's ass so hard that Taylor worried that he wouldn't be able to walk for days. Not that he cared. Ricky felt so right inside him, pounding away. Taylor groaned with pleasure as Ricky began to fuck him even harder. Taylor had jacked off thousands of times thinking of just this situation, and now it was actually happening!

Both guys were sweating profusely. Taylor could tell the guitarist was close to coming, so he began jacking his own cock. As the grunts increased in volume something slid slowly across Taylor's right eye. He shot his load just as he figured out that his wig had slipped down over his forehead. Not surprising with all the thrashing around they were doing, he thought. Ricky let out a yowl as he came, his hard cock pulsing inside Taylor.

This is it, Taylor. *As soon as he looks down he'll realize he was fucking his band mate.*

Ricky remained frozen for several moments, his eyes closed and his hands tightly clutching Taylor's calves. Slowly, he pulled his cock out. Tossing the condom onto the floor, he fell back onto the big bed with a satisfied chuckle.

His eyes still closed, he muttered, "That was amazing."

In minutes, he was asleep.

Ricky didn't look his best at the photo shoot the following day. He arrived on time, which was unusual for him, but he looked haggard and worn out.

Carl immediately gave him hell. "You look like the pussy got the better of you last night, boy!" He slapped the guitarist playfully on the back. "You shoulda come out with me. We coulda had us a goddamn orgy! Ended up with three bitches in my bed, myself."

Giving the drummer a weak smile, Ricky said, "I did pretty well on my own, actually. Really good fuck, too. Gone when I woke up, though. Didn't even have a chance to thank her."

Carl smacked Ricky's arm with a sly grin. "And I thought you had a headache last night. You were holding out on me, you dog!"

Overhearing, Taylor raised his eyebrows and checked to make sure he still had the brown paper bag inside his jacket pocket. He waited until later when, during a lull in the shoot, he had a chance to speak to Ricky alone. Pulling out the paper bag, he spoke to the guitarist in a low tone. "So you got lucky last night, eh?"

"Sure as fuck did. Hot little thing, too."

Taylor grinned. "I thought, maybe if you weren't too tired, that maybe you and I could work off some steam after the photo shoot. Get our rocks off and then take a nap or something."

Ricky frowned. "I don't think so, Tay. Group sex is more Carl's bag. I like my sex one on one, you know?"

With a shrug, Taylor opened the paper bag and extracted his wig. "I meant just you and me. Group sex isn't really my thing, either." He tossed the wig to a surprised Yarnell.

Taylor watched as confusion, embarrassment, and finally amusement crossed Ricky's face. Grasping the wig tightly, he looked into Taylor's eyes. "That was you?" he asked, his voice so whispered as to be almost inaudible.

Taylor nodded. "I can't believe you didn't realize."

It took several moments, but finally Ricky burst into laughter. "Fuck," he said, "all this time we could have ..."

"We can try it without the wig next time, if you want."

Ricky's eyes sparkled as he replied. "Fuck yeah!"

GETTING VISUAL
By Fox Lee

It was late afternoon when my plane landed in Tokyo. At twenty-two years old, the trip was, my mother repeatedly reminded me, long overdue. She and my father were both native Japanese. They moved to the States three years before I was born, after which, finances became too tight for a family vacation overseas.

I wouldn't say I was cocky about being able to fit in. I was, shall we say, slightly over confident. My parents raised me to understand my culture, and I spoke the language pretty well. I had no doubt I would blend in with the locals in no time.

This illusion was dashed when my cousin, Yori, picked me up at the airport. I barely got a sentence out, before she burst out laughing.

"Kenji-Chan, your accent is so thick! Speak English for now, ok?"

"Am I that bad?" I asked.

"You speak very well," Yori said, "but it is very hard to understand you."

At Yori's apartment, she chatted about my aunt and uncle while I unpacked my things. They ran a *ryukan* in Osaka and were quite busy this time of year. I wouldn't get to see them for a few days, unless I wanted to take the train alone. After Yori's reaction to my language skills, I figured it was better to go as a pair.

I asked Yori what the plans were for that night. She told me about her friend, who was in a Visual Kei band.

"They have a gig tonight," she said. "Do you want to go?"

"What's Visual Kei?" I asked.

I must have butchered the pronunciation: Yori forced back a giggle and smiled at me.

"It's hard for me to explain in English," she said. "You want to see pictures from the last show I went to?"

I said sure, and Yori went to get her laptop. Visual Kei, I learned, was like glam rock on ecstasy. The hair was the first thing that caught my eye. Some of the guys fashioned theirs to look like anime school girls, others teased it high and wild. One picture had a drummer dressed in a maid's outfit. He looked as if he had a fireworks display on top of his head: an explosion of red, gold, and purple.

"That's Hayato," Yori said. "He's in Going Touch, with my friend Mitsu."

Mitsu came up a few pictures later. The lead singer of Going Touch, he had long, curly green hair and a heart-shaped face. If Yori hadn't told me otherwise, I would have sworn he was a girl. Especially when I saw the picture of him kissing Bo, the bassist. I asked Yori if they were all gay, and she gave me an odd look.

"Lots of boys in Japanese rock bands kiss, Kenji-san. It's just for fun."

Yori didn't know I was gay, so I tried not to sound too intrigued by her friend's lip-lock. Still, the idea of a bunch of straight guys kissing "for fun" gave me a giddy thrill. I wondered if it was a regular part of the shows, or something they did when the mood struck them.

When Yori showed me a picture of Going Touch's lead guitarist, Ryoichi, my dick jumped in my pants. Tall and lean, Ryoichi glowered at the camera under a mane of jet black hair that went halfway down his back. Whereas his band mates went with either gender ambiguous or women's clothing, Ryoichi wore leather pants and an ornate military jacket. His eyes, one blue and one green, stared me down to the bone.

"Does he always wear that?" I asked my cousin.

I pointed to the mask that covered the lower part of Ryoichi's face. It was made of black leather, and accentuated his high cheekbones.

"He wears it a lot," Yori said. "He has other masks, too."

I wanted some quality time alone after seeing Ryoichi. Unfortunately, Yori had a lot more pictures to show me. I pressed my knees together to stifle the swelling between my legs. Every time a picture of Ryoichi came up, I tried to think unsexy thoughts: ground beef, the woman who taught me math in seventh grade, and the time I fell off my skateboard and broke my hand in three places.

At long last, the slide show ended. I told Yori I felt grungy after the long plane ride and excused myself to take a shower. Another round of culture shock waited for me in the bathroom. I was average height and pretty thin, yet in Yori's shower I felt like Godzilla. As I cleaned myself with the detachable shower head, my hand strayed to my cock and began to gently stroke my growing erection. I thought about Ryoichi: The way the mask made his eyes look so severe and demanding.

Once my cock was fully hard, I ran my hand up the side and rubbed circles around the slit at the top. Precum oozed under my thumb, and further lubricated my efforts. I imagined Ryoichi touching me. In my fantasy, he didn't talk at all. He pressed me against the wall of the shower and slid his finger roughly up my hole. I moaned, and gripped my shaft. Seconds later, I came with such force that my legs nearly flew out from under me. Ropes of cum struck my chest and the shower walls, as I struggled for balance.

I chided myself for getting so worked up over a guy who batted for the other team. Then again, it wasn't as if I was going to rush the stage and jump him. Tomorrow, I would have "the talk" with Yori and ask if she knew where a guy like me could hook up in Tokyo. In the meantime, Ryoichi could be my eye candy: something to tide me over, until I found a man to sink my teeth into.

After the shower, I made myself presentable, and Yori took me out to dinner. It was early evening and pleasantly warm out, so we walked to the restaurant. By the time we got there, I felt overwhelmed. Tokyo was bigger, brighter, and busier than I ever imagined. The street system didn't make any sense at all to me: Without Yori, I would have kept walking until I hit the ocean.

Dinner was at a place that specialized in hot pot. I left it up to Yori to order: I was afraid to embarrass myself again. The waiter returned with plates of seafood, meat, and vegetables. Everything was delicious, and I was too busy stuffing my face to have much to say. Luckily, Yori could keep up a conversation all by herself. Mostly she talked about the other guitarist in Going Touch, Jiro. She clearly had a crush on him. I vaguely remembered Jiro as being the guy with spiked blue hair and fishnets.

"I called Mitsu when you were in the shower," Yori said, between bites of udon noodles. "He says we should all hang out at Hayato and Ryoichi's apartment, after the show."

I almost choked on a shrimp. Half of me was excited at the prospect of seeing Ryoichi up close. The other was afraid the experience would be a let-down. Part of the fun was not knowing what he was really like and being able to fill in the blanks at my own discretion.

I didn't dare say no, of course. Yori was too excited, whereas my attraction to Ryoichi was only a few hours old. I tucked back into my food, while Yori went into another monologue about Jiro. I pictured the look on my aunt and uncle's faces, if Yori ever introduced the three. What parents didn't dream of their daughter dating a guy who looked better in a skirt than she did?

The club was packed when we arrived. I could feel the thrum of excitement in the crowd. Yori told me that, although they were a newer band, Going Touch had a loyal following. I believed it. When the lights went out, the crowd roared. A yellow spotlight hit the stage, and there was Mitsu. He was dressed in a long, tight dress, and his hair was swept up into two pigtails. Women in the crowd shrieked his name, as he introduced himself into the microphone.

A second spotlight struck the stage behind Mitsu, and illuminated Hayato. Next was Bo, who blew kisses from behind his bass, followed by Jiro. Ryoichi was last. He was wearing a similar outfit from the picture; only the color of the jacket was different.

I barely heard a single song. I was too busy watching Ryoichi play. The way his fingers glided up and down the neck of his guitar riveted me. An hour so into the gig, I could see a sheen of moisture on his neck. I envisioned it trickling down Ryoichi's spine, into the small of his back. The music from the stage covered the whimper that escaped my lips. If it were any harder, my dick would have broken off.

I walked out of the club in a daze. Yori tugged me along, like I was a little kid. I'm sure she blamed it on me having no sense of direction. All I could think about was that I was going to meet Ryoichi in person. The apartment he shared with Hayato was only a short subway ride from the club. Yori called Mitsu when we got to the building, and he said to come straight up. The band was already there.

I expected it to be a party – tons of people, lots of distraction. It turned out to be the band, Yori, myself, and two girls. The girls were with Bo and Mitsu. Yori introduced me as her American cousin, and I immediately found myself presented with a shot glass, and a bottle of unidentifiable liquor.

"For you," Mitsu said. "Welcome to Japan!"

I would later learn that the liquid in question was sweet potato *schochu*, from Hayato's home town. Japanese generally drink it with hot water, to lower the alcohol content. We drank straight shots. It took me a while to realize everyone was trying to drink me under the table. By then, I was too drunk to do much about it. Someone would shout "Kampai!" and, like one of Pavlov's dogs, I would take another drink.

Ryoichi was the only one not drinking, due to the mask. I could swear he was watching me the whole night. I told myself I was being paranoid, or perhaps optimistic, but each time I looked up, he seemed to be looking right back. I could still feel his eyes on me when my own rolled back into my head, and my body made friends with the floor.

I woke up in the dark, stretched out on someone's futon. The party was going full blast outside the room. I could hear loud music playing and people trying to talk over it. My mouth didn't taste like ass yet, so I couldn't have been out too long.

There was someone next to me. I expected it to be Yori, no doubt there to make sure I didn't choke on my own vomit. That idea was dismissed, when a hand ran up my leg to cup my balls. My pants were gone, and the unexpected contact made me gasp.

I tried to turn over, but was promptly pushed back down. A face appeared over me, framed by curtains of black hair. The face tilted slightly, to regard me with mismatched eyes. Before I could ask what he was doing, Ryoichi put a hand over my mouth and shook his head. I nodded, and he returned his attention to my balls. He stroked them with long, elegant fingers. My hips bucked. I desperately wanted Ryoichi to touch my cock. I didn't care that, with the mask on, he couldn't do much else with it.

Ryoichi took his hand away and straddled my hips. Like me, he was naked from the waist down. Our cocks rubbed together, as he leaned forward to pull my shirt over my head. I returned the favor and began to lick and suck at his exposed nipples. They hardened quickly in my mouth, while my hands ran down Ryoichi's muscular back to grip his ass. Small and round, it curved into my palms as if it belonged there.

I bit and kissed a line to Ryoichi's neck, where I sucked the skin hard enough to leave a mark. He ground himself against me, and I could feel his precum smear onto my stomach. My own cock throbbed from the friction. I stuck my right index finger into my mouth, and swirled my tongue around the digit. When it was nice and wet, I rubbed the tip against Ryoichi's puckered hole.

My finger entered Ryoichi slowly. I didn't know if he had ever done this before, and I didn't want to hurt him. When he started to play with my nipples, I figured he was good to go. I began to finger fuck him – first with the one finger, then two. Ryoichi rocked against my thrusts and moaned softly from behind his mask. I knew he didn't want me to talk, but there was something I needed to know.

"Do you have condoms?" I whispered.

He pointed to a nightstand next to the futon. I eased my fingers out of him, and searched the first drawer. There was an unopened box of condoms tucked into the corner, along with a bottle of lube. I ripped the package of condoms open, and pulled one out.

Ryoichi was lying on his back. It was my first good look at his dick, which was long and curved, and ended in a sleek mushroom cap. He was still leaking precum. It trailed down his shaft and all the way to his balls. Ryoichi caressed the back of my head, as I sucked and licked his testicles clean. When I felt them tighten, I moved upward.

I knew Ryoichi was close, even before the last of his seven inches disappeared down my throat. My nose was buried in his pubic hair when he came. It smelled like leather and musk. His orgasm seemed endless, and I struggled to keep up with the waves of cum that shot into my mouth.

I've never gotten a condom on so fast in my life. Ryoichi's legs were a blur of motion, as I swept them over my shoulders and applied a healthy coat of lube to my erection. I steadied Ryoichi's hips and aimed my cock head at his hole. When I got about halfway, I began to gently move back and forth inside him, until I was flush with his ass.

He never took his eyes off me. It made me feel exposed and reckless. I forgot about being a gentleman. All I wanted was to fuck him hard. My balls slapped against Ryoichi's smooth, perfect ass, as I angled deeper with every thrust. He pumped his own dick, already hard again, with one hand. With the other, he ran his fingernails along the back of my neck. His muscles clenched around my cock, and I lost myself. The condom inflated with my cum, as Ryoichi released himself onto my chest and chin.

We collapsed into a heap on the futon. The sounds from outside filtered into the room, and I realized how easily we could have gotten caught. I rolled off Ryoichi and tossed the used condom into his wastebasket. When I lay down again, he pulled me over, until my head rested on his chest. I could hear Ryoichi's heartbeat, strong under his slender ribcage, and feel his mask scratch against the top of my head. I decided I didn't care so much about getting caught and let myself fall asleep beside him.

STEAMY FOR THE CREW BOY
By Jay Starre

Carter was hired in Cleveland. He sucked cock in Cincinnati. He got his ass fucked in Indianapolis. And finally in Chicago, after a month long bus ride through the Midwest, he got to fuck some ass himself – some hot, tight rock star ass.

The up-and-coming rock band, Savage Sucks, played some cool venues on their late summer tour. Their savvy production manager, Tyler, had arranged it. Hot new clubs scattered on the edge of the big cities offered sold-out enthusiastic crowds.

Tyler had also hired Carter. The young blond's job was simple – do whatever he was told. Technically, he was a P.A., a production assistant, which meant he spent hours outside club back doors holding off the fans or hovering around the tour bus keeping the groupies from seductively planting themselves aboard without permission.

It was in Cincinnati when he discovered the true reason Tyler hired him. He was standing outside the band's dressing room fending off unwanted callers. Even though he worked for a rock band, Tyler required him to wear a dress shirt and slacks, although a tie wasn't necessary. With his neatly combed blond hair and peach complexion, he looked young and harmless. But his sturdy frame, with broad shoulders and powerful thighs filling out his dress clothes, sufficed to block doorways by sheer size alone.

He heard his name yelled out from the other side of the door.

He came in to find only two of the band members present. That was no surprise, as the drummer always showed up at the last minute. Ford paced the room, again no surprise. He was always nervous before they went on stage.

The lead guitar player sat on the couch strumming his instrument and grinning. Giorgio, tall, dark and handsome, was never nervous.

"My fucking pants are too fucking tight! My dick feels like it's in a vice. Fuck! I need another pair right now!"

Carter figured Ford would want him to head to the bus and fetch a replacement pair. That was his job, standing around doing nothing – or running around in a panic on last minute errands.

"All your pants are too tight, Ford baby. I think you need something else. You got a big old boner, as usual before our gigs. Get Carter to suck you off, then your dick'll fit in your pants."

Giorgio winked at Carter and laughed, still picking at chords on his guitar.

The totally startled look on the young blond's face must have been easy to read. Ford let out a snort of laughter, then set the P.A. straight. "Yep, Kid, that's why Tyler hired you. You got those big fucking blue eyes and that big wide mouth and those big fat fucking red lips ... yum! A mouth made by God himself to suck cock."

Carter gawked open-mouthed as Ford tore open his belt and fly to release his rearing hard-on. It was a big one. Bright purple, it was lined with veins and had a swollen knob that twitched and jerked in the air to match the mood of its owner.

He was momentarily speechless. Were they fucking with him? Both guitarists were laughing, but Ford was moving toward him, that bobbing cock leading the way. The guitar player looked exactly how you'd imagine a rock star might. Shaggy auburn hair fell nearly to his shoulders. He was lean, from head to toe, those tight jeans only emphasizing his slimness. Colorful tattoos splashed his bare forearms, and half a dozen earrings inhabited each ear while one also pierced his right brow. His choice of shirts was always outlandish, today's a flaming emerald with the buttons open half-way to his navel. A gorgeous smile offset somber brown eyes, while a voice that could bring the house down with its shrieking power had his fans drooling and swooning during every performance.

Carter's knees were weak. Not only did that cock look might tasty, but also he'd secretly been one of those drooling, swooning fans ever since he'd first seen the band play a year earlier. Ford strutted the stage with a hypnotically sensual bump and grind while he belted out his vocals and banged away at his guitar. He was a live wire of energy.

Now, all that energy needed a quick release, obviously. It was for real! That waving cock came at him as he found himself dropping to his knees and emitting a wordless moan of surrender.

"Fucking sweet! Open that big mouth and show me some fucking tongue, Carter!"

The kneeling blond obeyed, trembling all over and feeling his own cock spring to attention under his slacks. He stuck out his tongue and swiped at the oncoming hard-on. The vein-lined shank slapped against his face and mouth as Ford laughed out loud and toyed with the kneeling P.A.

"Fuck yeah. Tongue that cock. Lick it all over. Un-huh! Open wide now, so I can feed you the juicy head. Yeah! Hey Giorgio, get your lazy ass over here and join me. His mouth's fucking big enough for two."

Carter gurgled loudly as Ford jammed the flared crown between his slurping lips and began to pump in and out. The rock star never did anything half-way or half-heartedly. He grabbed hold of him by the back of the neck and held his head in place as he drove his cock in and out of the kneeling P.A.'s wet lips with grunting enthusiasm.

He didn't see Giorgio coming until a second cock was shoved in his face. Dark brown with a wicked curve and a slender tapered head, it rubbed all over his cheek and nose and forehead then vied with Ford's pink boner for space in his wide-open mouth.

Two cocks forced their way between his lips. He slobbered and slurped as he reached up to clutch at the two guitarists. Both their pants and underwear were down to their knees leaving their butts bare. Carter grabbed hold of a cheek of each and squeezed.

The two asses were totally different. Ford's was clenched and compact like solid marble. Giorgio's was round and full and jiggling. He held onto both and pulled himself into their crotches as he gobbled cock with all the enthusiasm he could muster.

And he was enthusiastic. The pair were like demi-gods to their thousands of fans, any number of which would gladly exchange places with him. Besides, it was something he'd never done, sucking two cocks at once. It was really hot.

Ford thrust his hips energetically, jabbing at Carter's face and mouth, while Giorgio slid his plumper meat all over the blond's cheeks and nose, even his eyes and forehead, before he'd slide it around his wet lips and then dip it between them with sensual ease. Their tactics were opposite, but exactly like their music, it meshed perfectly. They played Carter's mouth like a wet, warm instrument.

The kneeling blond added his own voice to the music, slurps and smacks and gurgles, and even some choking as Ford buried his knob deep in the P.A.'s throat. The pair of guitarists used his face for their pleasure, pumping his wet mouth, sliding their dripping cock-heads over his smooth cheeks, or rubbing the big shanks over his nostrils and chin.

Although it seemed like a battle for his juicy lips, warm mouth and tight gullet, their shared laughter indicated it was not. In fact, Giorgio draped an arm across his slim partner's shoulder and pulled him close, kissing him passionately.

After a few moments of deep-kissing, Ford pulled away with a slurping gasp. "Carter, I'm about to blow, and I want to see your cock and ass! Pull down those slacks. Come on, kid. Now!"

The slender rock star shoved his cock deep into Carter's throat and held it there, hands clasped behind his neck. The young P.A. flushed bright red as he tore at his belt and unbuttoned his slacks. Down came his pants and underwear in a frantic rush.

Giorgio clamped his mouth over Ford's again as he rubbed his wet cock over Carter's smooth cheek while the kneeling blond reached back up to grab hold of their butts again. He loved the feel of those bare rock star asses!

Ford pulled out just in time. Carter snorted for air as both cocks erupted on either side of his face, coating his peachy complexion in gobs of nut-cream.

That's when their drummer came waltzing in.

"I'm here, dudes. Just in time I hope ..." Montana's quiet voice halted as he took a moment to survey the situation. But then, he continued just as quietly. "Fuck, just in time, all right. In time to catch our buddy here on his knees getting creamed. Sweet ass, Carter. Very sweet."

"Nice cock, too," Giorgio murmured as he disengaged from his fellow band member and stood back to check out their kneeling P.A's bobbing hard-on.

"Get us some paper towel or something to wipe up, kid. And you better wipe off your fucking face, too, before you head out to the bus to fetch me another pair of fucking jeans."

Giorgio slapped Ford on the shoulder and scolded him. "Is that any fucking way to say thank you? Carter just gave us both a first class blow job. Say thanks, you fucking idiot."

Ford offered the room his glowing smile, then impetuously bent down and licked at Carter's cheek, swiping up a dribble of his own cum. Gazing into the blond's bright blue eyes, he winked and licked his lips.

"Thank you for the excellent fucking blow job, kid. Now, get us cleaned up and then get your butt out to the bus for my jeans. And I mean now!"

Carter scrambled to his feet, pulling up on his slacks at the same time. His fat cock was still hard as hell, and the trio watched him speculatively as he reined it in with fumbling hands to pack it out of sight.

Montana said nothing. He'd already spoken about as much as he cared to. Carter glanced over at him as he passed by on the way for some paper towels. The drummer looked nothing like his fellow band members. He buzzed his hair so close it nearly looked shaved, while his face had a perpetual stubble he trimmed only every few days. Intense blue eyes dominated his broad face with its regular features. He rarely smiled, but when he did, white teeth gleamed. He was quiet and moody and somewhat detached, but when he got on stage, he became one with the band. Every note the two guitarists played, he countered with his riveting beat.

He said nothing, but his thoughts were busy. He'd taken a good look at their P.A.'s creamy-white bubble butt. A good look. He intended on getting an even closer look, and soon.

Twenty minutes later, Carter watched from back-stage as the trio shook the house with their savage brand of throbbing rock. Ford offered up one of his best vocals that night, a throaty croon of gut-wrenching loss that had the audience moaning as they swayed and rocked to his tune.

Carter tore his eyes from that mesmerizing performance to contemplate the band's drummer. Montana followed Ford's every move with those intense blue eyes, measuring out a steadily pounding beat that accentuated the sensual throb of the vocal while taking nothing away from it. He was the least greedy for recognition of the three, content to remain in the background, but just as engaged and talented.

Giorgio broke the spell just at the final moment, stepping up beside the sinewy vocalist to smash out a jarring string of chords that had the audience rocking back on their heels and shouting out loud.

The blond in the wings had to grin. That had definitely been one of their best performances. Maybe they needed a good suck job before every gig. Maybe he'd be the one to give it to them!

He least expected what happened next. From Cincinnati they swung west and north to Indianapolis. Nothing was mentioned about their cock-sucking adventure. Tyler and the three band members acted as if it hadn't happened and treated him exactly the same as before. He was disappointed but also relieved. He'd been a little afraid they'd dump him now that he'd provided them what they obviously hired him for – his sweet eager mouth.

There was nothing unusual about the fact Montana was in one of his moods when they reached their next destination. He merely grunted his thanks when Carter returned to the bus with the late night meal of pizza and beer they'd requested.

"Help me haul my equipment into the club, Carter."

It was almost three in the morning, but the P.A. didn't complain. By now, he was used to the band's idiosyncrasies. The others ignored them as they left the bus and then rummaged around in the cargo bays to get out Montana's drums.

The club had been cleared out more than an hour earlier and was already cleaned up. It was as silent as a tomb. Montana made no effort to keep from banging around noisily as they clambered up to the stage and set up his drums. Neither did he speak to Carter, who didn't need any direction. He'd helped with the chore a half a dozen times already.

When they were done, Carter waited for the drummer to dismiss him but still he remained stonily silent. The blond sighed and took a seat just off the stage in the wings to await any forthcoming orders.

It wasn't likely he'd get in a snooze as Montana began to flay away with his drumsticks in a raucous rattle and bang that echoed and reverberated in the empty hall. Even though it was late and his playing was disturbingly loud, there was no denying the talented power of it.

It wasn't unusual for any of the band to practice at odd hours. What happened next was unusual. As Carter slumped in his chair and watched from the sidelines, Montana suddenly rose from his stool. Now, he was standing. His hands flew in a cascade of wild drumming that had Carter rising up and taking notice.

Those intense blue eyes swung his way. They locked with his. The drumsticks reached a crescendo of furious flaying before he abruptly ended it with a smash against his cymbal.

It was all at once deathly silent. Their eyes were still locked, and Carter's heart pounded.

"Come on over here."

Montana's voice was calm enough, although he was breathing heavily and sweat poured down his face. Carter had no idea what to expect, although his cock stiffened up under his slacks, and his asshole clenched a little.

He reached the drummer and stood uncertainly before him. Montana wore a grey T-shirt that fit snug across his broad chest. His arms were bare, thick with muscle, especially the forearms. He began to tease the drums with his sticks in what seemed like a nervous little tick.

What the fuck was going on? Carter felt his tongue stuck to the roof of his mouth, unable to ask those words out loud. His cock tented his slacks obviously, and he tried to cover it with his hands, but those intense blue eyes found the bulge before he succeeded.

"I need to fuck some ass."

Montana's simple statement had him emitting a little gasp as he shuddered all over. That was not what he expected at all! The light rap of sticks continued, as did the riveting stare. Then one of the sticks rose and pointed in an unmistakable gesture.

"Here. Now."

He felt trapped. Those eyes, that insistent drum beat. Those sexy forearms. He moved forward in a jerk-like motion, his feet like lead and his heart in his throat. The muscular drummer was a little scary!

The hands continued their rhythmic movement as he slid between the solid body of the drummer and his drums. At the same time, he unbuckled his belt and unzipped his fly. Was this for real? Was he about to get fucked onstage while Montana practiced?

His slacks fell to the floor. He felt Montana's hefty body pressing into his from behind. Was that a stiff cock bulging his jeans? Of course it was!

"Pull down your underwear."

The drum beat continued on either side of him. He leaned over the central drum while Montana's sticks rose and fell over the two others suspended from its side. His hands trembled as he shoved down his underwear, and his cock bobbed out to smack against that drum. His bare ass jiggled nervously as Montana's buckle and jeans pressed against it.

The beat increased just slightly. "Get out my cock."

Carter fumbled behind his back to find the buckle and fly. It only took a moment to undo it and release the monster trapped behind. He couldn't help himself as he seized it with both greedy hands and jammed it between his own butt-crack.

"Sweet ass. Yeah. There's some lube in my front pocket. Get it out. Lube your asshole."

The words were punched out between staccato beats. A little faster now, a little more insistent.

He bit his fat lower lip and groaned. That cock was thick! And the head was shaped like a fucking battering ram! But there was no use denying it, he wanted that thing up his ass, and he wanted it bad.

He fumbled around with one hand behind him digging in Montana's jean pocket while the other held the base of the drummer's huge cock and pushed it between his round butt-cheeks deep into the sweating crack.

That giant knob slid around in his butt valley, leaking an ooze of precum. He could only imagine how it would feel once it punched its way up his ass gullet! He succeeded in fishing out the small bottle of lube, and for the first time realized what that meant.

The drummer had brought the lube to his practice session for one reason and one reason only.

"Lube your hole. I'm going to fuck your big, hot white butt."

Yep. That was the reason! He'd planned on fucking Carter from the get-go.

He squirted a stream of the slippery stuff into his crack. Then another squirt. The more the better – that cock was enormous. Montana's hands continued their work without any break, but his hips began to hump forward, driving his slippery cock deeper into Carter's crack.

"You want my cock? Do you?"

"Yes," he answered. His voice came out like a little shriek though as the flared knob settled right on his asshole and suddenly punched inward. "Yes! I want your cock. Ohhhhh! Unnngggh! Yes!"

The dark-haired drummer thrust his hips forward viciously, impaling the young blond with half the fat shank, then pulling back and repeating the action to the steady beat of his drumsticks.

Carter arched his back, bit his lip and closed his eyes. He focused all his attention on the feel of cock probing his tender hole in that harsh, deep rhythm. He quickly succeeded in willing his anal muscles to relax, then found himself writhing backwards to swallow up the jabbing meat with grunting enthusiasm.

"Sweet. Yeah. I fucking love your jiggling white butt."

The slap of hips against his bare ass was steady, a rhythmic beat countered by the play of drumsticks now growing more creative and wild.

Montana's muscular forearms tensed as his hands flew and his playing became increasingly frenetic. The pounding reverberated in Carter's ears as that cock continued its steady plunge, in and out and balls deep.

His own cock reared up over the lip of the drum in front of him, pink, jerking and dripping precum. He could feel the vibrations of the drums rocking through his body. The flurry of bashing all around him drowned out his grunts and squeals.

It was a hard fuck. Very hard. The drummer rammed home, yanked out his cock, and thrust deep all over again, punctuating each thrust with a flurry of drumming. Carter shook all over, his cock drooling and his white ass jiggling. He felt gutted, gored, impaled to the hilt. His asshole burned and ached and felt absolutely wonderful.

It was easy to tell when the end was coming. Montana's drumming reached a crescendo. His hands flew. The steady plunge of his cock up Carter's hole increased in tempo all at once. Then the drummer pulled out. His cymbal slammed in an ear-splitting crash.

"Fuck yeah!"

The warm spray of cum spurted all over his lower back to drip down into his sweat-covered ass-crack. His legs trembled violently. His own cock throbbed and drooled as it reared over the drum in front of him. It wouldn't take much to make him blow, too!

He felt warm breath in his ear. "I'll be thinking of you, and this drumstick, the next time I perform."

That's when he felt something hard and blunt slither up his just-fucked asshole. Montana was shoving his drumstick up Carter's butt! That did it for him. The feel of that stiff thing sliding in and out of his ass and the thought of getting probed by the rock star's drumstick was a lethal combination.

"I'm shooting ... all over your drum!"

Laughter in his ear was followed by a wet lick as the drumstick rooted around in his quivering hole and he shot gobs of cum all over Montana's drum. "Don't worry about it. I'm through for the night anyway."

The drumstick slid out of his asshole. He felt Montana's body pull back and away. He was left there, cum dripping from his twitching cock and lube leaking from his battered butt-hole. He'd been fucked and fucked good!

But now he had to clean up his mess before he could get some much-needed sleep. The drummer was nowhere to be seen. With a satiated smile on his face, Carter set about his task.

Again, nothing was said about the late-night escapade afterwards. He did catch Montana's eye once during the next performance as he stood in the wings and watched. Those intense blue orbs held his briefly as the drummer flourished one drumstick in a twirling blur and winked then continued on with his drumming.

Carter flushed. That must have been the drumstick that got shoved up his butt!

They reached their final set of gigs in the busy suburbs of Chicago. Here music was king. The crowds were wild, and it was a real chore to keep them from harassing the trio before and after the show. All that frenzy only made them play better.

By the time they returned to their dressing room, they were drenched in sweat and exhausted. Carter blocked the doorway with his placid bulk as usual. It took half an hour before the most persistent were convinced to leave.

He knocked on the door and called out. "All clear, guys."

Montana exited first. His bright eyes met Carter's for a moment as he breezed past. "They want to see you." There was a ghost of a grin on his face, and even more surprisingly, a hand snaked out to quickly grope his crotch, then just as quickly pulled away.

He was gone without another word.

Of course, the young blond was sporting a hard-on as he entered the dressing room and trying to hide it with his hands in front of him. "Montana said you wanted me," he murmured, eyes sliding from one to the other.

The pair were seated on the couch. For once, Ford wasn't pacing. Obviously, he was tired from their hard work on stage.

It was Giorgio who smiled and spoke. "Don't try to hide that cock of yours. Montana speaks highly of it. Show it off for us."

Ford was even more blunt. "Get naked, kid. Get fucking naked right fucking now."

Carter was used to doing what they asked, whatever it was. Still, his hands trembled, and he flushed bright red as he shed his dress shirt, undershirt, dress shoes and socks, and finally while the pair laughed and urged him on, his slacks and underwear.

His cock, fat, pink and juicy, thrust up from his sturdy hips in full-blown stiffness.

"Fuck! You look good naked. Maybe we should make you work butt-naked all the time! You're packing a lot of fucking muscle. Why don't you come on over here and give us a closer look at that big boner."

Ford again was more blunt than his smiling partner. "I got something for you to shove that big cock in. My tight ass could use a good fucking!"

With that, the lean rock star rose and twisted around to kneel on the couch, wriggling his compact butt lewdly and smacking it once with his hand. Carter flushed even brighter pink but scurried forward in a state of semi-shock. Ford wanted his ass fucked? By Carter?

The shaggy-haired rock star craned his head around and glared, his somber brown eyes mesmerizing as he yanked down his tight jeans to his knees and bared his butt. "Eat my ass before you fuck it, Boy. Get in there and tongue my fucking ass!"

Giorgio laughed as he smacked Ford's naked butt-cheek. "You are a fucking rude bastard. But you got good ideas. Carter, baby, eat my buddy's tight little ass before you fuck it. And you can play with mine while you're at it. You got two butts to fuck tonight. Are you up for it?"

The dark-skinned guitarist flashed his winning white smile and winked as he lay back on the couch and began to strip.

It was all happening so fast the young P.A was still a bit stunned. He dropped to his knees behind Ford's wriggling white butt like a stone and reached up with shaking hands to grab hold of that compact ass in an effort to steady himself.

"Get in there and eat my fucking butt," the rock star ordered in a near-growl.

The blond spread the cheeks apart and found himself staring deep into the pale crack. Right in the center, a tight pucker stared back at him. Smooth and hairless, it beckoned to him with a little pout and clamp. Ford wriggled around and arched his back, his compact ass tensing and squeezing.

Hardly believing it could be happening, he held those tight cheeks wide open and buried his face in rock star butt-crack. His tongue swiped over the smooth flesh, tasting salty sweat as he lapped it up and searched out that snapping pucker. He found it and began to tickle and tease it with slobbering enthusiasm.

"Oh fuck yeah! Giorgio, that boy can sure lick hole damn good! Get him to taste yours!"

The other guitarist had stripped naked by then. Out of the corner of his eye, Carter could see him move around as he squirmed beneath the kneeling Ford to lie on his back and lift his legs up to hook them around his buddy's lower back.

"Take turns. Eat us both out before you fuck our butts," he heard Giorgio order from beneath Ford.

Just as he'd sucked both their cocks before, he sucked both their asses now. Pulling out of Ford's white crack, he dove down to bury his face in Giorgio's lush brown butt. His legs were split wide open as he hooked them up around Ford's back. The guitarist's hole pouted outward eagerly. A light down of brown hair swirled inward over amber flesh to disappear around the pink hole.

Carter crammed his tongue deep into it, amazed at how it bloomed outward for him and seemed to pull his tongue inward.

The pair of nasty rock stars urged him on as they gave him his orders. He was told to strip off Ford's jeans and boots so that all three were naked. He was ordered to eat one ass, then the other, and eagerly did as he was told.

When he licked on Ford's tight pucker, the rock star reached back and held his blond head in place with a fierce grip, making him rub his peachy cheeks all over the smooth crack as he tongued and sucked. The rock star had seemed exhausted at first, but now was back in his usual frenetic form.

When he dropped down to eat out Giorgio's sweet brown hole, it was a different story. The laid-back guitarist sprawled back wide open, pulling his own ass apart for the blond's busy mouth. His hole was a gaping pit for Carter to slobber over and suck inside out. He rooted deep in the warm slot with his tongue to the sounds of Giorgio's loud moans.

Ford got impatient first, naturally. "Time to shove that fucking cock up our butts, Boy. Get the lube out of that drawer and grease us up. Now, Boy!"

The lean rock star wriggled his white butt in circles and reached back to shove a finger up his own spit-wet hole. "My tight pucker needs a good stretching. Feed me that cock!"

Carter pulled his face out of Giorgio's delicious crack and crawled over to the nearby lamp table. In the top drawer he found a big bottle of Anal Glide. Briefly he wondered who had put it there, since it hadn't been he. They must have done something for themselves for once.

He crawled back to the waiting asses, his stiff cock bobbing between hefty thighs. Ford still wriggled his white can impatiently while Giorgio gripped his own ankles and pulled them back toward his face. The pair hadn't moved, Giorgio underneath and Ford kneeling above him.

"Who should I fuck first?" Carter blurted out, amazed he still had the power to speak.

"It doesn't matter. Just fucking lube us up and fucking shove it in. One hole then the other."

Giorgio laughed from underneath his buddy. "Don't mind him, Carter. He's rude, but he's got a tight ass you'll love! And he likes it when you just ram it home. In fact, he loves that. Ignore his squeals."

Carter got up on shaky feet and squirted a stream of lube over Ford's tight white butt first. There was so much it drooled down to splatter Giorgio's splayed crack. He squirted more, this time all over Giorgio's ass and then his own cock.

Gripping the base of his fat joint, he thrust forward into Ford's wriggling butt-crack. All that squirming along with all that lube, had his cock-head sliding around just off target until the shaggy-haired guitarist managed to snag it with his tight pucker. Carter lunged with his hips.

"FUCK YEAH! SHOVE THAT COCK HOME!"

The shouted order startled and frightened him, but he was already leaning forward and thrusting against the snug ass-lips. Not exactly on purpose, he rammed the blunt knob deep into Ford's vice-like butt pit.

Seething heat enveloped half his cock. He stared down at the juncture of cock and hole, amazed at how those tightly clamping lips strained around his fat shank. Both his cock and the hole were flushed bright pink, while the rest of their bodies were creamy white. The pulsing muscles of Ford's sphincter massaged his cock like a squeezing fist, and all he could do was grunt and grit his teeth. And shove deeper.

"OH GOD! YEAH!"

He'd plunged balls-deep. Ford continued to howl, while Carter managed to rear back and pull out. A loud slurp and a drool of lube followed the exit. The hole flushed red and quivered wildly. Carter did what he thought he was supposed to, crouching down enough to drive his cock into the second hole awaiting his services.

A totally different experience there. Giorgio's hole welcomed his fat meat with gaping avarice. Wide open, it took him to the balls in one squishy slide. The handsome rock star lay back and accepted all that cock with a moaning surrender.

He took turns, slamming up Ford's tight hole, then crouching to plunge into Giorgio's gaping brown slot. The shaggy-haired drummer's pucker remained vice-tight regardless of how hard and deep he drilled it. Giorgio's hole grew sloppier and sloppier, gaping open even when he wasn't ramming it with cock.

The young P.A. was drenched in sweat. His powerful hips slid over the pair of rock star's equally sweaty butts. His pink cock rammed in and out of white and brown hole with slurping regularity, one then the other, then back to the first again. A few pumps into Ford's tight pink hole, then a few squishy pumps into Giorgio's blooming slot.

Ford wiggled his white butt in nasty circles, arching his back and presenting himself like a total slut. Giorgio pulled his own ankles up and apart to display himself in an equally nasty lust for cock. Carter's big blue eyes took it all in, totally amazed at his good fortune. He gawked and drooled as he fed his cock to the white rock star butt, then the amber rock star ass. Soon enough, he was thrusting and pounding and fucking like a jack hammer gone berserk.

"That's it! I'm gonna fucking blow!"

Ford was first. As the young blond fed him his big shank, pumping it deep and hard, the shaggy-haired rock star squealed out and lunged forward, shooting a geyser of nut-cream all over Giorgio's face below.

"Yeah! Gimme that cock, Boy, and I'll shoot my wad, too!"

He yanked his cock out of Ford's snapping slot and plunged it into Giorgio's. The eager pit swallowed him whole and began to milk him rhythmically as the rock star shot his load, too. The sensation of those quivering butt-lips pulsing around and sucking on his buried cock proved too much for the blond P.A. as well.

"I'm coming, too," he panted out.

With a slurping suction, he pulled out just in time to add his steamy juice to the rain of cum the pair of rock stars already spewed.

Shaking and panting, he was taken by surprise as the two grabbed him and pulled him up on the couch. All three naked and slippery with lube, sweat and cum, they proceeded to make out in a sloppy three-way kiss. Carter had never done anything like that before!

When it was finally over, he was ordered back to work, and that was it.

Their summer tour was almost over. It lasted only another week, and during that time no one mentioned the sexual games they'd played. He continued on as before, scurrying at the spoiled band members' beck and call day and night.

Carter actually didn't mind. He certainly wasn't fooling himself into making more of it than there was. The trio of rock-stars had used him to get off. He didn't mean anything to them. He'd done a good job as P.A., and without complaining. There was nothing more to it. He'd have some hot memories from the summer tour anyway.

They casually waved goodbye when he left them in Chicago. Tyler drove him to the bus station and handed him a final paycheck. "There's something in there from the band. They appreciated all your hard work."

It was a thousand dollars in cash. He was totally shocked.

Even more shocking was the phone call he received a month later. It was Tyler.

"We're going on a European tour in a few weeks. The boys want you and no one else to P.A. for them. How about it?"

What could he say? "Fuck yeah. I'll be there."

His cock was hard, and his mouth drooled. His asshole twitched, too. No doubt all three, cock, mouth and asshole, could look forward to some hard work soon enough!

AKI'S LOVE SONG
By Sedonia Guillone

As usual, Aki was magnificent. Sweat gleamed on his flawless torso, most of which was exposed by the flimsy costume of black leather straps criss-crossing his lean muscles. Aki's ass and thighs looked poured into his tight leather pants, the black of which only emphasized the perfect roundness of each ass cheek. His Fender Jaguar moved with his undulating body as if the two were fused together. Each movement caused Aki's ass to strain in the most mouth-watering way.

Aki's silver-tipped black hair stood out in exaggerated spikes, like the mane of a lion emerging from the dark side, and the heavy black eyeliner circling each large, chocolate brown eye gave Aki the appearance of a wild, seductive demon coming to enslave those who desired him.

Tamotsu stared at him from his customary spot in the sidelines. Though his role as manager of Spider's Web was to make sure everything went smoothly, once Aki got on stage, his slim lanky musculature emphasized by the dramatic lighting stole Tamotsu's attention.

The way Aki had already stolen his heart.

True to the name of Aki's group, every one of the fifty-thousand screaming fans in the stadium was ensnared in Aki's web, trapped by his intoxicating mixture of flawless physical beauty and existentially jarring music. To listen to Aki's voice of creamy velvet, to watch his graceful body wind and bend under the lights, and to see the blend of vulnerability and angst in his eyes was to become his prisoner. Aki was a drug one couldn't live without.

Especially Tamotsu.

Aki was playing one of his greatest songs, "Wildfire," and had just reached the bridge. The fans' screams increased in volume, rising with the cascade of sounds Aki released from his guitar. Aki's own passions drove him to his knees, head thrown back, spikes of hair waving with the thrashing of his head. Eyes closed, Aki's rippling torso undulated with the riffs he played. Aki's demonic yet innocent nature poured from beneath his plucking fingers.

Tamotsu's heart sped up. Aki absorbed him, made the entire world vanish except for Aki. Truthfully, it had always been that way, from the first time Tamotsu met him in the Music Club freshman year in high school. Even then, with normal hair and no eyeliner, slim form hidden in the navy blazer and striped tie of their school uniform, Aki was, in Tamotsu's eyes, an artist whose gentle nature had been completely overlooked by his family. They'd seen only the kernel of his musical talent and had driven him into the classics, forcing him to practice the piano hours a day. By the time Aki was fourteen, he rebelled, pulling Tamotsu into his world by asking him to play drums for the underground band he was forming.

In spite of his own painful stage fright, Tamotsu immediately accepted and had the time of his life for four glorious years playing clubs late into the nights on weekends. He'd wanted that life to go on forever, until he and Aki were old men, getting onto the stage with their walkers. The only painful part had been suffering silently in his love for Aki who of course, had scores of girls – and guys – following him around like love-starved puppies. Aki had a steady supply of companionship and sex, whenever he wanted it. Tamotsu bore Aki's busy sex life as the price of his flourishing friendship with Aki. After all, he was the one Aki came to for solace, whom Aki hung out with when he wanted to relax completely and feel safe. Even when Tamotsu had been forced to leave the band and take over his ailing father's tatami mat dealership, Aki came to him. The connection between them hadn't ever been lost, and Tamotsu couldn't bear to think of life without Aki.

So when Tamotsu's father died and Tamotsu eventually sold the business, Aki had asked him to manage Spider's Web. Of course, Tamotsu had jumped on the chance even though it didn't mean his passion for his friend would be requited. Tamotsu never wanted to violate his special place in Aki's life, so he'd kept his mouth shut for more than twenty years. Even though it meant not being in Aki's bed.

Now they were both thirty-six, and things were the same.

Except for the recent dulling in Aki's eyes, some of Aki's fire had burned down, and Tamotsu didn't understand why. Aki didn't talk about it, and Tamotsu didn't push beyond the occasional offer to talk.

"Wildfire" ended on a wailing screech of Aki's deft fingers over the steel strings. The last note of the song reverberated through the stadium, drifting away as if fading into a mist. It ebbed into silence, leaving only the screaming voices of the fans. Aki remained where he was, head thrown back, eyes closed, hands frozen on the guitar. Were he anyone else, the pose would have come off as melodramatic, but Tamotsu understood his longtime friend. Aki poured his whole heart and soul into every note he composed as well as every movement he made. Everything was significant to Aki, even the way his knees touched the floor, as if he wanted to take root there and never have to leave. The stage was where Aki felt alive, in control, seen and appreciated, desperately trying to make up for the horrifying invisibility he'd suffered in his family.

You're never invisible to me, Aki-chan, Tamotsu thought, watching Aki open his eyes and slowly rise to his feet amidst the din of cheers from his fans. If Aki could just feel, just once, how much Tamotsu loved him, perhaps he'd understand.

Tamotsu sighed and continued to stare. Aki was moving to the microphone, one hand raised in acknowledgement of the appreciation showering the airwaves. He gestured to his fellow band members, causing the cheers to escalate with each man he indicated. Aki was humble that way, always appreciating how the other musicians completed their sound and image. Without each and every one of them, Spider's Web wasn't. And Aki knew it.

"Thank you! Thank you so much!" he said into the microphone.

Cheers and yells met Aki's words. Aki waited several moments, hand up, for the tumult to calm a bit before continuing. "Friends," he began again, "Tonight, I'm playing a new song, one you've never heard before. I wrote it from the deepest place in my heart." His hands went to his guitar, one on the neck, the other in placements over the strings.

Tamotsu frowned. *A new song?* As far as he knew, the band's repertoire on this tour held only songs from their previous albums, the most recent of which had been released nearly eight months earlier. Aki had never mentioned playing a new song during this concert.

"I call it, 'Because You're Here.'" Amidst the rising tumult of cheers, he strummed across the strings, a cascade of notes at once eerie and soul-searing. The lights faded to black, leaving only one halo of glowing light around Aki, now a solitary figure in the center of the stage.

Again, Tamotsu's heart sped up. Aki always shared his songs-in-progress with him and Tamotsu couldn't recall a song with that title. His breath shortened as Aki began to sing, a slow, heart-rending ballad about unrequited love and the tremors of his heart in the presence of the one who was completely unaware. Tamotsu's chest tightened with a pang. His mind reeled at Aki's secrecy. Aki's love life had been a string of passionate, flaming affairs that burned out quickly, always with someone who'd courted his attention. No one he'd ever seen Aki go with had been able to sustain a romance with the fiery artist who could go so deep inside himself he made others feel utterly ignored. No matter how gorgeous and intoxicating Aki was, the excitement of getting intimately close with him wore off his partners very quickly.

Still, the mystery burned itself into Tamotsu's heart. Who the hell could Aki possibly be in love with, that such passion would inspire this incredible song? Or had the song just come from Aki's depths simply because he was an artist with access to the widest range of human experience?

The song was spellbinding, and even after Aki had played the last note, silence reigned for several moments before the cheers rang up again.

Tamotsu finally found his breath and turned away. For the remaining songs, he spent the time backstage, making sure security was in place for when the musicians came offstage. When they did, he was ready to escort Aki and the others in a quick stream to the green room where they all huddled for several moments, arms around each other. It was a ritual they followed before and after every performance, demonstrating their unity. Afterwards, they usually hung out in the green room for a while to cool down before leaving the concert hall to return to the hotel.

As usual, Tamotsu sat next to Aki in the limousine. Aki sagged back against the velvety dark seat, his beautiful eyes distant. Wanting only to return to the hotel room, he'd already refused to attend the after-party, which some of the traveling groupies flocked to amidst fizzing champagne bottles and huge platters of catered food. "Do you mind, Tamo-chan?" he said to Tamotsu as the limousine turned the corner to the hotel. He sounded worried that Tamotsu would be annoyed with him.

"Of course not." He studied Aki's downturned profile, not sure how to proceed. "Do you need to be by yourself?" It wasn't difficult to give Aki solitude. Their hotel room was a double suite with separate bedrooms. One could easily hang out in the main room or one of the bedrooms without disturbing the other.

Aki looked up, causing Tamotsu's breath to catch. Aki's heart-shaped face with its frame of shaggy hair, huge eyes and delicately arched lips made his friend look like one of those devastatingly beautiful anime characters. Aki shook his head. "No, I don't."

Tamotsu released a breath, both from relief and from having forgotten to breathe the moment before. "Okay," he said, trying to act casual. "Because I wasn't really up to going either."

A smile touched Aki's lips. "Cool," he said, "We can hang out. Like old times."

Back at the hotel, the bodyguards accompanied them into the back entrance of the hotel and up the elevator to their suite where they'd remain stationed outside in the hall. Inside the suite, Tamotsu closed the door behind them and heaved a breath. He and Aki were finally alone.

In the main area of the suite, a gift basket overflowing with fresh fruits, caviar and a bottle of champagne sat on the center coffee table. Aki glanced at it. "I'm going to shower before we open this," he said.

"Okay." As always, Tamotsu would have loved nothing but to follow Aki into the bathroom and watch him shower. How incredible it would be to see the water stream over Aki's perfect skin and bead off his dark nipples the color of bittersweet chocolate! Instead, he, too, took a quick shower and dressed again. He was on the sofa, pulling the foil off the top of the champagne bottle when Aki came in and flopped down next to him. Aki's nearness gave off the fresh aroma of soap, and Aki's damp hair glistened in the soft lighting. When Aki sat back, his thin white T-shirt rode up, exposing his navel in the center of a strip of skin above the tattered low-slung jeans he'd put on.

Ignoring the tightening in his cock, Tamotsu opened the champagne and poured the fizzy golden liquid into two of the flutes on the silver tray. He picked one up, handed it to Aki then picked up the other one. "What should we toast to?"

Aki held up his glass. "To friendship."

Tamotsu's heart did a strange dance. "To friendship," he said softly and clinked his glass against Aki's. He sipped from his glass and watched Aki take a large gulp of champagne. His eye fell on Aki's Adam's apple as it slid up and down. Aki had a finely arched neck of smooth golden skin that made Tamotsu want to lick it each time.

Aki set his glass on the table and wiped his hands on his jeans. "Hey, Tamo-chan," he began, "What did you think of the new song?"

Tamotsu's insides jumped, and he nearly choked on his sip of champagne. Quickly, he swallowed. "It was beautiful.

Amazing." He shook his head. "I had no idea." His stomach tightened, and he set his glass down, so he wouldn't drop it.

"Tamotsu, there's something I have to tell you." Aki exhaled and glanced away. "It's frightening and may change everything."

Shimatta. Tamotsu stared at him. Was Aki about to fire him? His stomach lurched. What could Aki have to say that would be so earth-shattering? "What is it?"

"I–I wrote that song for you, Tamo-chan. Because … I didn't know how else to tell you how I feel … about you."

Tamotsu's vision blurred. His heart raced. Was this possible? Was he hearing things? Couldn't be.

Aki frowned. "Oh, shit. I shouldn't have said that." He vaulted from the sofa and went to the window, pacing back and forth against the backdrop of the night sky and twinkling city lights of Kyoto. "I should have kept my mouth shut. Please tell me I didn't just ruin our friendship."

That jolted Tamotsu out of his shock. The thing he'd wanted most in the world was being handed to him, and he was messing it up. He got up and went over to Aki, staying him with a hand on his shoulder. The contact with sinewy muscle made Tamotsu's insides jump again. Aki's skin was warm through his thin shirt. Aki's large distressed eyes, still ringed with a shadow of dark eyeliner stared widely into his. "You could never ruin our friendship, Aki," he said gently.

Aki looked down. There were moments when his vulnerability was so poignant, it made a pang in Tamotsu's chest. This was one of those moments. "But you don't feel the same way, right?" Before Tamotsu could answer, his gaze whipped up. "You don't have to, Tamo-chan. It's all right. Just forget all of this." He looked down again.

Just then, Tamotsu felt his own largeness. He was several inches taller and wider than Aki. Years of working in his father's business, moving furniture around and unloading trucks had given him a broad, solid physique. Standing this close to Aki, a mere few inches, he felt his body suddenly, naturally, envelop Aki's. As poignantly as he felt Aki's vulnerability, he now felt the way Aki had looked to him for protection all these years, a role Tamotsu had fallen into more naturally than anything else he'd ever done.

Aki's bottom lip trembled. The traces of dark eyeliner made his already luminous eyes appear even larger. "I have everything," he said in a near whisper. "But it doesn't matter anymore without you."

Aki's words infused him with courage. Reaching up, he slid one hand along the other man's cheek and rested it there. Here it was. Aki was offering himself, offering his heart, the wild dream Tamotsu had held onto all these years. "It's all right, Aki-chan. I've felt the same way about you for a long time."

The slimmer man's lips parted. "Oh," he breathed, and his eyelids fluttered.

Heart hammering, Tamotsu descended and kissed him. The tiny sound of their lips meeting almost made him melt. A sigh escaped Aki's throat, a tiny sound in which Tamotsu swore he could hear relief and passion all mixed together. He slipped his tongue between Aki's lips and tasted him more deeply. Aki's flavor was as beautiful and intoxicating as his beauty and his voice.

One of Aki's hands came up and rested on his chest. The sweet feeling made energy skitter through Tamotsu's body. He pulled Aki against him so that their chests rubbed together. Sparks zinged through his nipples at the sweet contact. Aki's wiry body was at once pliant and hard in his arms. Aki was kittenish yet strong. And he loved Tamotsu. Was giving himself to him. The heart-rending melody of Aki's love song spiraled through Tamotsu's memory, fueling their kiss.

He danced his tongue against Aki's. The sound of their lips and tongues chafing together filled Tamotsu's ears. Aki's scent, soap and musk, wafted into him. He loves me. The emotions came through in Aki's kiss. Aki, who'd had so many lovers, loved him. Aki had to know he'd love him no matter what because he'd proven himself already.

Now he was free. Free to show Aki everything he was feeling. Everything he'd felt for him all these years.

He grasped the hem of Aki's shirt and pulled it up. Aki broke from their kiss, large eyes simmering and lifted his arms. Tamotsu slid the shirt up, over Aki's sleekly muscled arms and dropped it to the floor. He barely had a moment to savor the vision of Aki's equally sleek torso when Aki took hold of his shirt and yanked it up. Tamotsu pulled his shirt the rest of the way off and tossed it away. The slimmer man's eyes darkened yet more. His lids came down halfway. "You're so amazing," he breathed.

If Tamotsu hadn't been so aroused and overwhelmed, he would have laughed. Here was one of the hottest, most popular J-rock stars in all of Japan and Southeast Asia, telling him he was amazing. Tamotsu thought of his face as indistinct, not ugly, not handsome, just ... strong and earthy, not a face to attract Aki who could have anyone he wanted.

But Aki seemed to feel differently. Reaching up, he cupped Tamotsu's cheeks and kissed him again, a series of tiny nips and licks that seemed to beg Tamotsu to love him, to appreciate him forever.

As if he didn't already.

When Aki broke the kiss again, he picked up Tamotsu's hand and tugged. "Come to my room," he whispered, his voice thick now from desire. His already voluptuous lips were swollen from kissing, and his smooth golden cheeks were flushed.

Wordlessly, Tamotsu followed him. Part of his protectiveness had always been to let Aki lead, which he was doing now, into the bedroom. Aki sat on the edge of the bed and tugged him over, thighs spread so that Tamotsu stood between them. Without another word, Aki's hands went to Tamotsu's belt and yanked it open.

Tamotsu pulled in a breath. Just the sensation of Aki's nimble fingers tugging his pants, brushing the skin of his stomach made him wild with need. His cock bulged out mercilessly, and Aki freed it from the confines of elastic and cotton. The thick rod popped into his face, and without hesitation, Aki covered the head with his lips and tugged more than half the lard length in.

The entire world blurred. Tamotsu groaned, prisoner of Aki's sweet mouth. All he could do was stand there, hands on Aki's shoulders, staring down at Aki's silver-tipped head bobbing up and down, pulling him into sweet oblivion. Aki's hands smoothed over his ass cheeks, up the sides of his waist and back down again. The rhythmic slide of Aki's full lips and hot wet tongue made his eyes squeeze shut while everything else in existence vanished. He groaned, forcing himself not to pump his hips so that his cock would go deeper into Aki's mouth.

When Aki finally released him to come up for breath, his eyes were wild. His swollen lips gleamed and his lightly carved chest heaved. Like when he was on stage, his shaggy hair streaked out at all wild angles, making him appear devilish and otherworldly. Yet to Tamotsu, he was beauty incarnate.

Staring up at him, Aki undid his jeans. Lifting quickly off the bed, he slid them down and kicked them off. Without pulling the covers down, he scooted back and lay down. “Everything we need is in the drawer, Tamo-chan,” he breathed.

Tamotsu pulled in a breath. When the day had begun like every other day, he’d never imagined it would finish like this, his most coveted dream fulfilled. His hand trembled slightly as he pulled the drawer open and got out a foil packet. He pushed his pants down and worked his feet out of them, aware of Aki’s large gaze on his naked body. Aki levered up on his elbows, watching, his expression almost greedy. “I want to watch you put it on,” he said softly. “I’ve thought about it so many times.”

Tamotsu paused. “You have?” Hard to believe. Tamotsu had seen Aki’s lovers. Male and female, they were like models out of magazines or on film, not a broad meaty workman such as he was. What did Aki see in him?

Aki nodded. “Yes.”

Tamotsu didn’t get it, but he sure as hell was grateful. He ripped open the packet and tossed aside the paper. Under Aki’s hungry gaze, he rolled the rubber on, glad for once that his cock was big and thick. That at least, was something he had to impress beautiful Aki with.

Reaching back into the drawer, he found one of those small, one-dose tubes of grease. He ripped off the tab and squeezed the slippery cream onto his fingers. Then he knelt between Aki’s sloping thighs and spread the lube over the man’s hole.

“Ohhh.” Aki’s head tilted back, his eyes closed, the way he did on stage, only now, the smile on his lips seemed to say, ‘I’m in Heaven.’ He fell onto his back, legs open.

Encouraged, Tamotsu played around the tiny puckered bud of flesh. Each tiny moan Aki gave shimmered through Tamotsu's very being. He wanted Aki to feel nothing but pleasure. Nothing but bliss. He pushed his index finger in and wiggled it back and forth.

Aki let out a pleasure cry and arched his hips. Tamotsu pushed in deeper, moving in circles that stretched Aki's entrance open wider, preparing him. Leaning down, he licked his tongue up the length of Aki's cock and pushed the tip into the tiny opening. In a rhythm, he licked and pumped his finger in.

"Oh, oh, oh!" Aki's hands fisted the bed covers and his head thrashed back and forth.

He was ready.

Tamotsu straightened and looked down at the other man. The vision captured him again. No matter how many times he looked at Aki, the man took his breath away. Every inch of Aki was smooth, perfectly carved, artful, down to the tiny trail of dark hair under his bellybutton. Tamotsu took a moment to trace it with several fingertips.

Aki's slim cock tapped his hand, as if begging for his attention. Aki's chest heaved, and he lay quietly, seeming to relish the appreciative way Tamotsu touched him. Tamotsu liked to think no one else had taken such time with him. They'd probably just were thrilled to get so close to Aki, not seeing his true beauty, the sweet vulnerable creature he was inside.

As soon as their bodies touched, Aki lifted his legs, locking them around Tamotsu's hips. The movement of submission sent an electrifying thrill through Tamotsu's entire body. The head of his cock bumped Aki's slippery opening, yet Tamotsu waited, took a few moments to nuzzle the other man's chest, to taste his dark nipples, savoring each one with sensuous licks back and forth. Aki's hands curled into his short hair, grasping, while his hips undulated against Tamotsu's, silently begging for penetration.

Tamotsu obeyed. He couldn't deny Aki anything and never had. Only when he thought something Aki wanted to do was bad for his career, he fought with him. Otherwise, Tamotsu was his, to do with as he pleased. Forever, if Aki wanted it that way.

He pushed the head of his cock in. Aki gasped, and his hands tightened on Tamotsu's upper arms.

Aki's large eyes took on a glazed look, and a smile spread on his lips. His inner thighs pressed harder to Tamotsu's hips. "I've wanted this for so long," he whispered. "I was afraid to tell you."

Speech was difficult for the erotic thrills cascading through Tamotsu's body, especially his ass and thighs, but he smoothed back Aki's hair. "Don't ever be afraid," he said softly. "Not with me." He followed his words with a deep, wild kiss. Aki tasted so good, and the sounds of their lips and tongues chafing together was as erotic as the sensation of his cock sliding inch by inch into Aki's tight passage.

Aki squeezed, drawing him in. Tamotsu could do nothing else but go, drive in deep until their bodies bumped. He panted, fighting back the urge to drive wildly in and out of Aki's channel. At first, it worked. He slid back and then in again slowly, alternately kissing Aki and lifting up to stare down at him in disbelief at his good fortune. But then Aki squeezed his ass tight, a devilish smile on his lips. His hands squeezed Tamotsu's ass cheeks, kneading and rubbing them with barely disguised greed.

Tamotsu gasped and drove in harder. He couldn't refuse. Even this, he couldn't refuse Aki. Sheer driving need took over, and he rode Aki, taking him as if each thrust could make their souls blend along with their bodies. Why had they waited so long for this? It seemed they'd wasted so much time.

The thought drove Tamotsu harder. Aki's tight passage massaged his cock so perfectly, the pressure built hard and fast. Aki groaned and let out several harsh panting breaths. His hands slid up Tamotsu's back and landed on his upper arms. His fingers dug into Tamotsu's triceps, and Tamotsu felt the hot splash of Aki's climax on his chest. Droplets hit his cheeks and lips, too.

Instead of wilting beneath him, Aki grinned. The devilish gleam in Aki's eyes remained, and he squeezed his ass harder, pumping his hips against Tamotsu's thrusts. Even though he was underneath Tamotsu, taking Tamotsu into his body, he was in complete control. Aki needed the control, Tamotsu knew because he understood Aki so well for so long. It only made Tamotsu love him more.

Tamotsu heaved another breath, and the pressure released. Mindless with the ecstasy of release, he thrust in short jerks until he was empty and collapsed on top of Aki, one hand laced into Aki's thick hair. Their heavy breathing intermingled, filling the air.

Wow. Mind-blowing sex. Tamotsu closed his eyes and breathed in Aki's musky scent. The man's hair was like ebony silk against his fingertips. He pressed a soft kiss to Aki's shoulder, damp with sweat. One of Aki's hands stroked his back while the other rested on a hip.

This was Heaven, pure and simple.

"I'm glad I wrote you that song," Aki said softly. "I'm just sorry I waited so long." Underneath the breathlessness, his voice held deep regret.

Tamotsu lifted up and gazed at him. Aki's bewitching eyes regarded him with a blend of desire and sorrow. Aki was right to be sad. Life was a fleeting thing, a breath that was extinguished all too soon. They weren't old yet, but they weren't kids, either. Neither of them would last forever. "I also waited too long," he said finally, "but at least you did something about it." That song was as hauntingly beautiful as the man who'd written it.

Aki lifted his head and kissed Tamotsu, a soft brush of their lips together.

Tamotsu's heart surged. When he pulled back, Aki's eyes were simmering yet also tender.

Aki smiled and arched his back slightly, pressing into Tamotsu's chest. "I know you'll make it up to me, Tamo-chan. No one else has ever been better to me. I mean it."

Tamotsu caressed Aki's hair again. "It's because you're so beautiful and wonderful."

But Aki shook his head. His smile faded. "No. You've made me that way. I've become those things because of you. Because you've believed in me. Because you're here."

ALWAYS CRASHING IN THE SAME CAR

By Martha J Allard

1983, Los Angeles

Ziggy stands in the wings backstage at the Refugee Club, a narrow shadow. He lights a cigarette, shielding the flame with his hand to protect the darkness. In the full house beyond the curtain, Ziggy counts dozens of reflections of himself. Boys or girls, hair cut spiky with spaghetti-o colored dye-jobs, all waiting for him. He exhales a lungful of smoke. Every night there's more of them, but it's not enough, not yet.

"Ziggy." Asia Heyes, Black Light's bass player calls him from the doorway to the basement dressing room the band shares. "Weird's real sick."

"No he's not." Ziggy says, turning.

"Yeah, Zig, he is. He's not gonna be able to play the show tonight. He should be ..."

"He should be shootin' the hell up, Asia. He's the guitar player, and this isn't fuckin' Charity's Place back in Ann Arbor anymore. It's the Refugee Club where somebody important could be listening." Ziggy moves farther backstage, past Asia, down the rickety stairs. He smells it, bitter on the air before he hits the bottom step. Then he hears Weird choking.

Asia is right behind Ziggy, protesting. "He's almost clean. Don't fuck it up for him."

Ziggy doesn't answer. Instead of going down the short hallway to the bathroom, he heads into the dressing room. Weird's guitar case is propped against the broken-down leather couch that sags in one corner. Tucked inside, along with the instrument are Weird's works, just like Ziggy knew they would be. He grabs the pouch and steps around Asia to cross the hall. Without knocking, Ziggy opens the bathroom door.

It's a remodeled storage closet, too small for three people. Ronnie, their drummer, hovers, worry lining his pretty face.

Weird's on the floor, back against the wall, arm draped around the toilet seat, like it's his best friend. In the buzzing fluorescent light, his skin is the color of spoiled milk. His face is covered in a thin sheen of sweat, long red-blond hair stuck down with it. He wipes a hand over his beard, looks up at Ziggy through silted eyes and grins. "Hey you gonna hold my hair while I puke some more?"

"Are you're gonna? I mean, you are gonna be okay, aren't you?" Ronnie's face turns even paler as he squeezes himself against the sink to let Ziggy all the way in.

"Oh sure." Weird groans, sucks in some of the sour air. "Yeah, I'm great." Then he looks up at Ziggy again. "Gimme my damn smack."

"No." Ronnie gasps. "No, Weird."

Weird stares hard at Ziggy. "Gimme m' works, cuz neither one of them will."

Ziggy nods. He hands the pouch over and turns away.

Asia is leaning against the hand railing of the stairs, shaking his head as Ziggy exits the bathroom. "So let him go back to killin' himself, and you don't even care, do you?"

"You think he can play clean, Asia?" Ziggy says. "You wanna take that away from him?"

"That's bullshit. You don't really think that." Asia laughs. "You get what you want, and that's all that matters."

Ziggy looks into Asia's eyes, rust/green, and takes a breath. All he ever gets from Asia anymore is anger and disappointment. Ziggy reaches up to brush a stray lock of wavy ginger hair back from his face, but Asia flinches.

"Whatever you wanna think." Ziggy says softly. "It's done. Get ready for the show."

He goes back upstairs without waiting for Asia's answer.

Asia shakes it off. He moves to stand in the doorway. "Wait, Weird. I can play your shit tonight and Zig can play bass."

Weird is up, unsteadily leaning against the sink, already cooking his shit, Ronnie looking on, stricken. Weird snickers. "How you think he's gonna do that? Faggot can't even walk and chew gum."

"I don't care." Asia knows he's pleading. This had all depended on the heroin staying out of Weird's reach. Until he got strong enough to turn it down. "We can do it."

"See, Ziggy's a bastard, but he's right." Weird says. His hands don't shake at all when he pulls the plunger back on his syringe to suck the liquefied drug up. "You think that bein' a junkie's ruinin' my life, right? That it's what's gonna kill me? See, no, because it's all I am, Asia. Junk's what makes the rest of my life livable."

Weird is tying a piece of tubing around his upper arm. He looks from Asia to Ronnie. "You guys got shit to do before we go on, right?"

Not really, Asia thinks, but feels himself give in. He turns away, and Ronnie follows him.

They stand outside the back door, in the alley that runs behind the Refugee Club, leaning against the scarred brick wall.

"Ziggy was right." Ronnie says finally, combing his long pale bangs back from his face.

"He's an asshole," Asia corrects.

"Weird's never gonna get clean. He doesn't want to." Ronnie laughs bitterly. "Cos where'd his works come from, huh?"

"His ... Ziggy got 'em outta his guitar case." Asia frowns. "But, so?"

"And there was what? Like a half a gram of smack? When d'ya think Weird bought it?" Ronnie looks at Asia.

"I don't know." Asia shrugs, but gets the sinking realization. He lets out a long sigh. "I wish ..."

He doesn't get to finish before the door opens, and Ziggy appears, now ready for the show. As he steps into the halo cast by a street light, his tight T-shirt sparkles. A cigarette trails from his fingers. His eyes are lined in heavy blue, making them electric; the blush against his cheekbones makes them sharper. None of it can make him more beautiful, Asia thinks, it only accents the fact.

"Are you ready?" Ziggy asks, eyes on Asia.

"Yeah, I guess." Asia looks down at his faded jeans and crackled Harpo's T-shirt. "How's Weird?"

"He's okay. He's cleaning up." Ziggy shrugs.

"I'm gonna do my hair," Ronnie says, ducking back inside.

Ziggy gives Asia a half-smile. "I know you're pissed. If you wanna hit me, now's the time."

"I don't wanna." Asia steps back, as though to get out of range anyway. "I'm not … I just wish things were different, that's all."

Ziggy takes a drag from his cigarette and drops it on the pavement. He laughs. "Asia, it is gonna happen. Soon. It has to, I can feel it."

Not tonight, Asia thinks, looking away again. Please, not tonight.

# # # # #

The sidewalk outside the Refugee Club is crowded with the tragically hip. They wait, in spiked heels and purple eye shadow. Albrecht Christian stands in this sea of restless youth unmoving. It is all familiar to him, but there are differences. Shorter hair, tighter clothes. This new decade has a harder edge. Albrecht catches the eye of a girl packed into a black tube top and red plastic mini. She stares past him, and Albrecht smiles like a shark in the neon night, like it means nothing. But the truth is he craves youth. He hungers for it.

Not his own-not the way other men do. Quite the opposite. Albrecht craves youth that will wash away his past.

Now, standing under the Refugee Club's marquee, he feels the ghost of Sean Wilder touch his sleeve. Albrecht's smile softens, and he imagines he can catch the faint scent of ginger and cinnamon on the exhaust-laden air.

Sean, Albrecht thinks, savoring the pain of it. And, just like that, he is slipping the snare of time. He closes his eyes, lets the current take him back.

1976

Albrecht guided the pearl colored Jaguar away from the well-lit boulevard to a deserted street. The place between Albrecht's shoulder blades itched. Two blocks back, they had been cruising a fashionably seedy area of West Hollywood. Wherever Sean was taking him now was in a feral pocket of the city.

"Turn down here," Sean directed, pointing across Albrecht's arms as he held the wheel.

"Why?"

"Y'scared, baby?" Sean grinned in the shadows, hand wandering to Albrecht's leg.

Albrecht tasted the boy's excitement, felt a warm jolt at the contact. Good, clean, not fueled by cocaine for a change. Albrecht smiled indulgently. "I've got you to protect me, yes?"

"We're almost there, anyway." Sean laughed. "Turn left at the corner. It's half way up the block, on your side."

Ever patient, Albrecht followed orders. He let the Jag slow to a creep around the corner onto an even more desolate street. There was debris strewn across the pavement now, and Albrecht didn't assume that Sean would change the tire if things went badly. Nor did he think they'd get very far on foot.

"See it?" Sean gestured again. "This is what I wanted you to see."

Albrecht pulled the car to the curb to regard Sean's find through the windshield. An enormous old theater hulked in the darkness. The surrounding street lights were out, its marquee dead. Above it were the remnants of the name, 'A-onis.' Not very god-like now, Albrecht thought. Broken glass littered the pavement beneath as though it had just shattered.

Still, in the white of the car's headlights, Albrecht saw what Sean saw in the place. It had the air of something fine about it.

"It's perfect." Sean touched his hand, and Albrecht felt the spark of the boy's energy jump between them again.

"I'll have my office find out who owns the property." Albrecht told him. "We'll make an offer."

# # # # #

Albrecht knows that standing on queue at the door is unnecessary, but he enjoys the anonymity. The bouncer sizes him up through wraparound sunglasses. Albrecht lifts his chin and sharpens his smile again. A muscle twitches in the big man's neck, and he passes Albrecht through.

The Refugee Club folds itself around him as he enters. Now it is the '80s, and Sean is a legend. Inside everything has changed, yet nothing has changed. The concession stand in the lobby is still all brass and glass counter-tops. The main room still echoes the movie theater it once was. Though the seats are all gone, the dance floor still slopes gently down to the stage. The bar runs along the far wall, carved cherubs and devils above it. Albrecht takes his place there.

He lights a cigarette and waits for one of half dozen bartenders to bring him an ashtray. It is a girl in endearingly clumsy drag makeup, the mascara mostly in dark shadows under her eyes, blush streaking up her cheeks in two red bars. Horrifying, thinks Albrecht, amused. The girl's eyes travel from the slim gold lighter Albrecht places on the bar top to the platinum Rolex on his wrist, to the suit he wears. The custom cut of the grey silk is lost on the girl, but Albrecht knows the impression he makes. Wealthy. A little desperate.

It is a lie, Albrecht tells himself.

"May I have a gin and tonic?" He knows there is enough Austria left in his voice to set him even further apart.

The girl nods, complying quickly. Albrecht takes a drink and smiles his thanks, but the girl has disappeared.

Albrecht shifts on his stool. There are more people on the dance floor than at tables, all moving savagely to the music that pulses from the sound system.

Sean, Albrecht thinks again, losing the thread of the lyric. He scans over the surface of the dancers, hair sprayed and glittered, lip gloss flashing in the lights. Beautiful, he thinks, but can't feel anything beyond that. They could be mannequins for all they hold his attention.

The music plays out, and in the relative silence lights on the stage go up. Albrecht spots his little bartender, now turned ringmaster. She steps into the white of the tight spot light, framed by a heavy red curtain. "You know who I got back here, doncha?" She teases, winking.

The crowd surges forward to pool around the edge of the stage, chanting a name. "Ziggy. Ziggy." Albrecht feels himself lean in, muscles tensing.

The bartender grins. "Yeah, that's right." She has to shout over noise, even into the microphone. "Ziggy. Ya think you're ready? I can't hear you."

More screams, and she has to take a step back from the dozens of hands that reach up to her. The curtain lurches aside, and the band is there, waiting. Guitar, bass, drums. So far Albrecht isn't impressed.

The bartender steps away. The lead singer moves into the spot light, and the room explodes. The chant turns to a prayer.

"Everybody comes to the Refugee looking for just one thing, don't they?" The singer grins as the crowd screams. "Well, it's okay. I'm here now."

All lines and angles, his spiky hair is the color of flame. His black T-shirt has the word "Bitch" spelled out tight against his chest in rhinestones. Albrecht feels the collective intake of breath as the band grinds out the first chords of the song. The energy in the room turns sharp, rakes past Albrecht, hones in on the stage.

Yes, something speaks inside Albrecht. Yes.

Ziggy wraps one thin hand around the microphone, body coiled tight, like a bull whip. His voice opens a raw, hungry place in Albrecht. Everyone else in the world recedes until it is just him and just Ziggy.

At the end of the set, Albrecht is breathless. The hunger increases in him as Ziggy disappears behind the curtain

"I fucking love him."The bartender sighs, returned to her post.

Albrecht is surprised at how true the sentiment echoes within him. He extracts a card from the holder in his breast pocket. Black with grey gothic lettering, it reads; Albrecht Christian, Parabellum Records. He offers it to the girl along with a fifty dollar bill. "See that Ziggy gets the card, please. Tell him I wish to speak with him tonight without his band."

# # # # #

Ziggy is quiet in the back of the car as they ride from the Refugee Club to Albrecht's penthouse. Albrecht watches the street lights play across Ziggy's skin shadowing the bone structure of his face, the hollow at the base of his throat. The power that had crackled off him from the stage is barely contained now by that translucent skin. Ziggy catches him looking and gives him a slow smile, Albrecht feels those ice colored eyes lingering. He is charmed by the honest appraisal.

The Algonquin is not the largest building on the block. Sleeker, taller glass and steel monstrosities have grown up around it in the time Albrecht has kept rooms here. This building is like him. It echoes the past with its art deco stone work and lead glass windows. When they arrive, he leads Ziggy through its hushed lobby to the elevator, where he slides his key into the panel.

"Shit." Ziggy says as they begin their assent. "You're either really rich, or you're a serial killer."

"Oh dear," Albrecht laughs softly. "What if I'm both?"

Ziggy shrugs. "It's a chance I'll have to take."

They come to a stop, and the door slides aside. Albrecht steps off. "Here we are."

The main room of the penthouse is entirely black and white from the tiles on the floor to the walls and furniture. The only color in the place is the Warhols. Blue, red, and green backgrounds, they stand out like graffiti on fresh paint. Ziggy's jaw drops slightly when his eyes catch on them.

On the canvases, Albrecht is larger than life, blond hair tinted gold and slicked against his skull. His face is lean, sharp, the skin pale and smooth, ageless except for his ancient eyes. His lips are thin, a smile just tilting the corners. The Albrecht Christian frozen in time. "Do you enjoy Warhol?" His smile mirrors the silk-screens.

"Damn," is all Ziggy says.

"Please. Make yourself at home."

Ziggy chooses one of the white couches at the center of the room. Albrecht interprets that as an invitation, and sits next to him. He reaches for the onyx box on the table in front of them for a cigarette. "Would you like one?"

"Thanks."

Albrecht extracts two, lights Ziggy's first. As he offers it, he asks, "How do you like playing the Refugee?"

Ziggy smiles faintly, pauses to take a drag then laughs. "It's the biggest stage we've ever been on. It's beautiful. My guitarist is all hot to play at the Whiskey, but this is better ... everybody comes to the Refugee."

"It's always been that way." Albrecht tells him, lighting his own cigarette. "It's mine, you know ... the Refugee. Though I haven't visited it in years, until tonight."

"No shit? But your card said you work for the record label."

“No, I own Parabellum as well.” Albrecht explains. “When I bought the club it was because ... there was a man I loved very much. It was for him.” He watches Ziggy for reaction. If anything, the news of another man relaxes him more. “When Sean found the place, it was deserted, except by the junkies and homeless. He had this vision, though, of what it could be, and I ...” Albrecht smiles, looking away from Ziggy. “I had the vision of what it had been.”

“What do you mean?”

“Oh, I had memories, from pictures I’d seen as a boy, in Austria.” Albrecht lets regret tinge his expression, the story. “It was the Adonis back then, famous, like your Mann’s Chinese now. I remember seeing Errol Flynn going in to some premier. It was very fine and beautiful.”

Amused, Albrecht knows that Ziggy is refiguring his age from older to really old in his mind. Albrecht continues anyway. “It was how I thought of America, I suppose, before I came here, all glittering and crisp and new. So you see I had to help Sean save it.”

“Wow. I never even heard of it before.”

“Of course not.” Albrecht says. “In America, forgetting the past is as easy as knocking a building down or putting up a new one. You aren’t drowning in your history here. Sean wanted to make it into something new, and I never told him about my memories.”

“Why did you let him change the name?”

“That was my choice. The Adonis had gone, no matter what I wanted.”

“Because this is America.” Ziggy guesses.

Albrecht is surprised that Ziggy understands. He changes the subject. “What do you see as your next move from here?”

Ziggy’s laugh has a hard edge to it now. “Why? Is this where you tell me that I could be rich and famous?”

“Do you need me to tell you that? Because I think you know exactly what will happen, and what you’ll do to make it so.”

“Really? You think I got it all figured out.”

“After seeing you perform, I’m sure of it.” Albrecht tells him.

Ziggy takes a drag on his cigarette and taps ashes into the crystal tray in front of them. Albrecht sees a crack in the thick armor of cool he wears. His grin is wide and unguarded.

Albrecht moves closer, reaches to trail his fingertips across the sharpness of Ziggy’s cheekbone, along the curve of his jaw. “I didn’t know what I was looking for tonight. Not until I saw you.” He leans in, and as their lips meet, Ziggy’s eyes close. He opens his mouth to Albrecht’s. His mouth tastes of beer and smoke and something deeper. Albrecht tastes the promise of power burn against his own tongue, and he swallows it down, lets it bleed into him, feed him. He steals Ziggy’s breath; he could easily use him up but stops himself.

Too beautiful a thing to be squandered in one night. “I’d like you to stay.”

Ziggy sits back a little and touches his lips with his fingers. “Yeah. Good.”

# # # # #

When Ziggy twists away from Albrecht, in sleep another form, more compact, softer, takes his place.

Why most especially you? Albrecht wonders, smelling cinnamon and ginger rise from the sheets. Why not some other empty ghost? He does not want this now, not while he has someone warm and alive in reach, but he can't maintain his hold on the present.

Sean curled away from him, small body stark against the dark sheets. "I know you're doing it to me."

"Cocaine is doing this to you,"Albrecht reasoned, gathering Sean against him.

"You know that's not true." Sean took in a breath and Albrecht felt the expansion of his ribs, sharp against his skin. "The coke, it's the only way I can hang on. I want you, but when you touch me, I ..."

This time it was a sob. "Shh." Albrecht whispered it into the inky silk of Sean's hair. "I don't want to hurt you. Not ever. I love you."

So he did, but even as he spoke, he felt the robber cells of his body stealing Sean's life to feed him. Once it came in torrents off Sean so strong it dazed Albrecht, now it was like a trickle of sand, the grains barely brushing his surface. The emptiness was growing in Albrecht, deep and gnawing. He held Sean tighter. "Think about tomorrow. Your opening at the club."

Albrecht shakes the memory off and gets out of bed. He slips through the French doors to the balcony. He stands naked at the railing, breathing deep lungfuls of heavy, dirty Los Angles air. This city suits him, more than any other. It is his mirror, in many ways. It is something hard and old, covered in a new skin.

Albrecht smiles. He smells fresh cigarette smoke from the doorway and turns. Ziggy is lounging on the threshold, skin turned blue by the moon.

"I've never seen L.A. from this high up. It looks just like the movies. Beautiful."

Albrecht laughs softly. "Everything is beautiful from far enough away."

"The lights go right up to the stars." Ziggy joins him at the railing.

"It'll be dawn soon." Albrecht warns. "Do you have to leave?"

"I don't want to." Ziggy leans down to kiss him. This time Albrecht tastes himself.

"Good." Albrecht leads him back inside and shuts the doors behind them. They settle back in bed, and Albrecht says, "I want to sign you to my label. We have a studio here in Los Angles. I want to get a producer in to record with you."

Ziggy stretches like a cat and turns away from Albrecht. "You heard me sing two sets tonight, and then we fucked. Which performance is this offer based on?"

"Do you truly care? Do you think I value your talent less because I may be falling in love with you?" Albrecht fits himself against the sharpness of Ziggy's back. The press of the full length of his body is like an electric shock, makes Albrecht's heart hammer, his blood pound. Some part of him wants to take this slower, but he can't. He knows that once they leave this room the world will tangle them up. Other people will intrude. It will never be pure like this again.

Ziggy turns to move down, and Albrecht feels his tongue, quick and wet. He groans and tries to push further in, but Ziggy moves back. "I love you." Albrecht whispers it. "I don't want to let go of you."

# # # # #

When Ziggy wakes, he's entangled. Christian is coiled around him. Ziggy moves slowly, works his way out of the puzzle of skin and bone.

He stands at the side of the bed, studying Christian in the unforgiving morning light. His white-blond hair is thick, lank against the pillow. He is so thin, and so still, Ziggy thinks of a corpse. He loves me, Ziggy thinks, stepping away. He goes to piss in a bathroom as large as his first apartment. He stares at himself in the mirror as he empties his bladder. People have been in love with him before. Asia has been, since they were kids. And there is no shortage of girls or boys ready to fall at his feet when he gets off stage.

This, he thinks, flushing, is different. He steps into a shower tiled in black and dials the water hot enough to bring color to his skin. Standing under it is like a hail storm, but he takes it.

I love you. Christian had said it. True, they had met less than ten hours ago and true, he'd said it while they were fucking, but there was such a focus to it that Ziggy finds himself wishing it was sincere. Hoping it was. He thinks of getting back into bed with Christian now, but resists. Ziggy has always tried to be careful about whom he fucked. But, this happened before he could think, it was still happening too fast.

He leaves the bathroom to collect his clothes from where they'd been scattered last night. He picks up Christian's heavy platinum watch from the night stand to squint at the time. Not quite 10:00 am, still early to Ziggy, but he is amazed at Christian. Is he so rich he doesn't care if Ziggy tosses his place? Maybe, but maybe it's something else. He loves Ziggy.

"Don't trust me, though," he murmurs, turning the watch over in his hands. On the back, he reads the word, "Libeling." He has no clue what a Rolex is worth. More than a recording contract? He puts it back. Whores go through their johns' pockets. Ziggy's not a whore. Not exactly.

"Hey." He sits on the edge of the bed and touches Christian's shoulder. "It's getting late."

Christian turns toward him, completely awake, his thin lips curving upward. "Is it? You look well rested."

Ziggy catches his glance toward the night stand and wonders if it is a test. "I had a shower. I hope that's okay."

"I'd like you to feel welcome here."

Ziggy grins and leans over Christian to kiss him. "I do."

Christian shifts; fingers trailing down Ziggy's back to the top of his jeans, but stop there. "Perhaps we should have breakfast, yes?" He is pulling away, getting out of bed. "My arrival here was a bit spur-of-the-moment, so I fear the kitchen is not stocked. I could have something ordered in."

Ziggy hesitates, but shakes his head. "I gotta meet the rest of the band at the Refugee at one for practice."

If Christian is disappointed, he doesn't let it show. "Plenty of time to eat. Shall we have coffee at the club? I'll call my assistant to let them know we're coming. And perhaps we could work out the particulars of the contract as well."

# # # # #

"Herr Christian." Albrecht's little bartender looks apprehensive as they approach. "I'm sorry that I didn't realize last night. Who you were, I mean, I ..."

She blushes prettily, and Albrecht laughs. "Oh, come now. How were you to know when I didn't wish you to? Still your service was excellent."

The girl brightens at the compliment, then blushes harder when she sees Ziggy. Another layer is added to her smile, turns it more intimate. "Hi."

Ziggy seems amused. "Hi, Sammy."

"Good show last night."

He gives her a toothy grin. "Thanks."

"Uh. Any time." Then Sammy turns back to Albrecht. "Your assistant had breakfast sent over. And I have coffee made if you like."

She indicates a table nearby set up with fruit and cheese and bread. Albrecht's stomach grumbles, and he realizes he's hungry. It's the first time since Sean died that Albrecht has craved more than a cigarette.

They relocate, and he watches Sammy nearing with the coffee pot. Her eyes are on Ziggy as she pours. When he leaves Albrecht guesses, "There's something between the two of you."

"She blew me last night before I went on stage. We aren't exactly going steady." Ziggy laughs. "And even if we were ... Why? Jealous?"

Albrecht takes a drink, grateful for the kick of caffeine. “Should I be?”

“It was one blow job.” Ziggy shrugs. “And, it was before I met you.”

Albrecht doesn’t answer, surprised when he realizes he wants more from Ziggy on the subject. He is jealous.

“So. Where is your lover?” Ziggy asks. “His name was Sean, right?”

“What?” Albrecht looks up from his coffee cup, afraid that the ghost is somehow visible.

“You buy this whole place for him,” Ziggy says. “That sounds pretty intense. What happened?”

Albrecht wonders if Ziggy already knows the story. After all, it is the stuff myths are made of. “You know about the suicide, I’m sure.”

Ziggy frowns slightly. “I heard somebody shot himself in the john here a long time ago.”

“Sean was brilliant, and he was beautiful. But toward the end, I remember thinking that he ... he used his life up so quickly. When I met him, he was turning tricks on the street, and I brought him out of that.” Albrecht shakes his head. “The cocaine didn’t help, but I could never get him to give that up. I think he saw everything he ever wanted coming true here and was afraid it wouldn’t be enough.”

“So he killed himself.”

Albrecht nods. “He put one of my handguns into his mouth and pulled the trigger.”

"Fuck, that's horrible," Ziggy breathes.

"It was." Albrecht does not tell him that the gun is still in his possession. He intends the story to make him seem tragic and romantic, not frightening. "I miss him."

There is a space in the conversation. Ziggy brushes his fingers across Albrecht's hand. "I want you to give me the contract."

Albrecht nods. To someone else this may seem like an abrupt subject change, even harsh. But, Albrecht is grateful to be done with Sean for the moment. He smiles. "Of course, and I want to give it to you. I shall have my assistant draw it up, but it will be standard, to start with. An album and promotion."

"We'll need up-front money." Ziggy says. "We're pretty strapped right now, and the guys are living in a hell hole in Encino."

Albrecht nods. "William will have exact numbers, but that shouldn't be a problem. I have a producer in mind. I'd like to get him here to listen to you. You're here for the week, yes?"

Ziggy nods.

"Good." Albrecht wonders what the other members of the band will think of these arrangements. If that mattered at all. "Good. I'll call William, then, and we'll begin."

Albrecht is in a new position. Instead of the need to consume Ziggy, Albrecht feels a shift within himself like the clear toll of a bell, from taker to taken.

"Hey." Ziggy's expression falters; he tries to catch Albrecht's eyes. "Are you okay?"

Albrecht nods. He decides to make it about something Ziggy can understand. 'I was just wishing things were simpler."

Ziggy takes a piece of toast from Albrecht's plate, tears off a corner. "What do you mean?"

"I admit, having money isn't exactly unpleasant," Albrecht shrugs. "But there are drawbacks."

"You wouldn't say that if you'd ever been short on the rent."

"Perhaps not," Albrecht admits. "But when you're poor, it's easy to guess people's motives."

Ziggy laughs. "Yeah right, you think?"

"If you told me you loved me, for instance," Albrecht watches Ziggy's face, but there's no reaction on the surface. "How could I ever be sure you were being truthful?"

Instead of answering, Ziggy reaches for Albrecht, slides a hand to the back of his neck. Albrecht leans in, aware of how exposed this makes him. There is a steady stream of people milling around them in the club, cleaning, stocking. Ziggy's lips brush Albrecht's, and he is being kissed in public, by a man. This has never happened to him before, and he doesn't care. He closes his eyes, opens his mouth, lets Ziggy take his breath. He feels Ziggy's hand on his leg, drifting higher. A soft moan escapes Albrecht, and Ziggy stops. He licks his lips and grins again. "If I'm a good actor, does it matter?"

Albrecht takes another breath, lets it out slow. "I'll use the phone at the bar."

If William is surprised to hear from Albrecht, he doesn't let it show in his voice. He has worked for Albrecht more than a decade and has never so much as raised an eyebrow no matter what is asked of him.

"I want you to deal with the legalities. This afternoon." Albrecht tells him. "Can you do it?"

"Of course, Herr Christian."

As the call ends, Albrecht feels Ziggy coming closer again. Albrecht feels closed in, suddenly, and lies. "I'm afraid I have to put in an appearance at the office, but I'll be back later."

As Christian leaves, Ziggy is surprised at the wave of exhaustion he feels. The intensity of Christian's attention will take getting used to.

Ziggy ignores the hopeful looks that Sammy flashes. Not now, he thinks, and maybe not ever again, though he liked the flare of jealousy from Christian.

But, he decides not to push it. He goes under the stage to the cool dark little dressing room. He clicks a Ramones tape into the player and collapses onto the saggy old leather couch in the corner.

He doesn't need to look at the clammy wall behind him to know the graffiti signatures of all the bands that came before him in this place. He knows them by heart. Blondie, the Idiots, the Attractions. Ziggy has yet to make his mark. Soon, he thinks, shifting to peel off his T-shirt. Soon he'll be up there and past this place. Soon.

# # # # #

Albrecht escapes to the waiting car, tells the driver to drive.

"Where to, sir?"

Albrecht sinks into the leather seat and closes his eyes. "I don't care. Just keep me moving."

He has already lost a part of himself with Ziggy, feels the connection stretching thin, pulling taut as the distance spins out between them. Albrecht puts a hand to his temples, lack of sleep weighing down on him.

He opens his eyes to Sean, on the floor of the car, his cheek against Albrecht's knee. Albrecht feels the chill. He reaches down to touch Sean's hair.

"Why?" he asks. "I tried to give you what you wanted."

"It wasn't as much as you took, though."

Albrecht feels the pull of Sean's sable eyes just as if this was really happening. The old grief takes hold of him. Like the rock beneath a wave, he is never broken by it so much as made smooth.

"I knew that if I were dead, you could never leave me."

Albrecht smiles, surprised in spite of everything. Here was a strength he had never touched while Sean was alive. He wonders if it will come to this between Ziggy and him. He wonders if he even cares. It is not loss of life that Albrecht fears.

HIPPIE-LUST
By R. W. Clinger

"Free love, dude, that's what I'm talking about," Cody Wall sings down his sloped, hairy chest, sharing the lyrics to his Billboard topper "Face to Crotch." The shaggy-blond rock star pushes my head down over his seven inches of hearty prick and continues to sing, stoned and drunk, exactly the way I have worshipped him in the past four years while following his band.

The last few days are a blur for me: the life of being a groupie. I don't know how I end up in Cody's hippie van, but do. All I can seem to remember are a few of the cities we've traveled to and the concerts held in each one: Cleveland, Cincinnati, Erie, Pittsburgh. And now the van heads to Philadelphia.

Joints and gigs later, I now have my lips on the lead singer's two-inch wide cock, ramming the hippie's rod down the back of my throat and tugging on his balls with exceptional skill.

"Peace ... Love ... No war ... Mediocrity for the poor ... Doing the face to crotch in life," Cody grooves, totally into his lyrics, building a rhythm between my bobbing head and his song.

I lift my face from my work and study his skinny-hairy chest with strawberry-colored nipples, straggly beard, and a tie-dyed bandana snug around his head. My knowledge of his band, Sixties Brigade, is top-notch shit. But my special interest is in Cody himself, not the band. Wall was born and raised in Topeka, Kansas, has a five-ten frame, is twenty-four-years-old, and sounds like a mix between The Who and The Doors. Ask me thirty questions about Cody, and I will have all the right answers.

Cody studies me back: religious tattoos ink my chest, charcoal-black hair and L-shaped sideburns, bottom-of-the-ocean-colored eyes, six-foot frame, pale complexion, treasure trail and puckered navel.

He kicks off his hemp sandals, rides his shaft in my tight mouth, rolls fingers through my thick hair, and hums my name, "Danny Love ... You're so good at sucking me off."

Who is driving the van? Who the fuck cares? My mind is elsewhere, consumed by the act of van sex with the hottest singer. The sex is amazing shit, just like a drug. Every bump and brake the van makes, every jolt and jump, is unnoticed because of our connection. Mouth-to-cock is all we seem to care about.

Cody hangs onto his battered, two-person sofa in the back of the van. No longer does he have his palms on the back of my skull, keeping his cock from flying out of my mouth. Instead, his face-fuck is like a concert on speed between us, and every hump and suck is like a group of mismatched songs, a sloppy but fun cadence.

The van's interior becomes hypnotic to me: multicolored fake fur begins to blur my vision, a miniature disco ball hangs down from the roof and madly twirls, causing me to become dizzy. And Sixties Brigade sings a chart-topper on the van's radio about love, lust, and deep sex.

I'm hard inside my khaki shorts, ready to burst. I pull my mouth off the singer's beef, lick my lips, sing a line to one of his songs, and go back to my suck-gig on his plump dick, willing it to burst.

Cody thrusts his hips into my face: chaotically, repetitiously, without being gentle. A moan surfaces from his beautiful lips, blocking out my slurps and groans. He gasps with satisfaction as my mouth careens into overplay on his tool, ready for him to blow.

Accidentally, one finger falls away from his balls and grazes his furry hole. I take advantage of the situation and press its fingertip into his taut bottom, up to its first knuckle, and listen to him go crazy, finding bliss, beginning to whimper.

"Fuck me and suck me," he sings, creating a new song for me. "Let me shoot in your mouth ... Let me go wow."

I poke his bottom, pull the half-digit out, and poke him again. In doing so, my mouth is busy on his meat, and my other hand rocks his world by massaging his stick's extra skin, up and down, continuously. I slurp and groan, lodge his seven inches into the back of my throat, gagging.

Rock star squirt is nothing like other squirts; I've learned this in the past few days. Cody's spew is tainted with uppers and downers and alcohol and weed and ...

"Shooting," he murmurs, craning his neck and gritting teeth.

Quickly, I pull off and away from his drum stick, begin to stroke it with speedy fingers and a palm, and let him rock it out, splashing sap down and over my appendages in gooey lines.

A final rise of his hips and a loud harmonic B-chord escapes his lungs as he completes his shoot. White and creamy spew erupts from his pole, flowing over his cock's cut cap, oozing down and along his tight skin like a slow fountain.

Once his elation is found, growing spent and goo-free, he informs, "Get your cock up here, so I can finish you off, pal."

I unbutton my khakis, drop them to my ankles, and sit next to him on the sofa in the back of the van. In a matter of seconds, Cody finds the circumcised flag between my legs, grips it with his right palm, and begins to jack it up and down. His fingers move steadily on my shaft, building friction, which prompts my breathing to intensify and perspiration to form on my chest, arms and forehead.

Beside me, Cody sings, "Tainted lust ... In the dust ... We just want to fuck." His hand becomes crazy-busy on my rod as it pulls and pushes on my dong's excessive skin. He drives me into a heated shoot-fest, and coaches, "Fuck my fist, Danny. I want to watch you eat your own spunk after you blow."

The hippie's hand job is pure magic. Stroke after stroke causes a steady vibration of ecstasy to skirt throughout my seated body. I buck hips upwards and hang onto one of his naked thighs and ... a buzz of excitement careens throughout my sweat-slicked torso.

Cody continues to coach me, picking lyrics from one of his songs, "Let it fly ... Come in time ... Do it the right way."

His voice and hand job are euphoric for me as an unstoppable orgasm surfaces between my legs. My grip on his thigh tightens, and my chest constricts in a state of occupied bliss. Expectedly, globs of sticky sap gush out of the top of my hose and decorate his fingers and wrist.

Following my cream-fest, I devour my own juice from his fist, licking and lapping it away from his skin, hungry for my seed. I moan and groan, finding satisfaction, and become sated. Deeply intoxicated by the ooze, I whisper to the rock star, "You're my drug."

And he sings, "Hot and sweet stuff ... Just what you like ... All from Danny's spike."

We kiss, take a few pills called LostSoul with a beer, and I black out.

I accidentally miss the Philly concert, sleeping through it. Truth is I can't remember anything in the past twenty-plus hours. The only images that float through my mind are of Cody's hand job and taking LostSoul. The time between then and now is a blur, a blackout, lost time, and nothing I can puzzle together.

I wake in the van, which is parked in an underground parking lot in a Philly suburb. Cody leaves a note for me that reads: POST-CONCERT PARTY. 217 BAYBERRY STREET. BRING TEQUILA AND YOUR CHOICE OF PILLS.

I gather up a few turquoise pills of Flydom, a bottle of tequila, and go in search of the address. Twenty minutes later, I'm standing within a run-down pothouse where a post-concert party rocks inside. Clouds of marijuana smoke linger above fifteen heads: groupies, band members, and other partiers. Drunk, high, and sexual male and female bodies are crammed inside the living room-like area. Two fags make-out on a leather sofa while others share blowjobs against one of the walls. Females dance to a Sixties Brigade song that erupts from a nearby speaker. The house is on fire with action, buzzing with a bash of fun.

Some really hot guy with jade-colored eyes, Jesus-like hair, and a bare-chested bod finds me among the guests. We drink some tequila, dance to a few songs in the middle of the crowded floor, and take two pills of Flydom. Jesus decides to pull my khaki shorts down to my ankles and provide some mouth-watering pleasure to my middle. I find him interesting and attractive, but decide to pass on his sex-exploration. Instead, I find the first floor bathroom, prepared to release a healthy piss.

Like Alice in Wonderland, I discover a second door inside the bathroom area, turn its knob, push it open, and see …

A one-star bedroom opens before me: queen-sized bed, stained carpet, dilapidated furniture, smashed mirror on one wall, and a broken recliner. The room is a hole, uninhabitable in every way.

The lead singer of Sixties Brigade is alone on the bed, naked and smoking a bong. A limp shaft hangs between his spread legs. After he observes my entrance, he takes a hit on the bong, holds in the smoky substance for a few seconds, exhales, and grins at me. Cody says, "Danny, I knew you'd find me. Where the hell have you been?"

"I've been passed out for hours, dude," I confess, stepping up to the left side of the bed.

Cody passes me the bong, and I take a hit. The shit immediately kicks me in the ass, blowing my mind apart. It's not pot, I realize, obviously something stronger. When a buzz takes over my system, I start to giggle, beginning our twosome party.

From the bed, Cody coaches, "Get out of your clothes and use my dick, man."

I laugh at his request, ready to give into his needs.

He grabs the bong from me, takes a hit, places the device on a shoddy nightstand, and says, "Show me how I can be the center of attention."

Cody's request ends up being the understatement of the year. Approximately thirty seconds later I'm completely undressed, on the bed, and gaze down at his head between my open legs. I become the center of attention as he begins to rock my world with his mouth, lapping at my hole, sucking my opening and applying tongue-kisses to its tight pinkness. Hungrily, he dives diligently into my bottom, steadily at work, ready to please me.

Zen is found. I become dizzy under his touch. The rock star's tongue and lips push me into a state of queer-bliss, and I start to hear a few of Sixties Brigade's number one hits inside my head: "Lust-Rush," "Veined Love," "Freedom Eater," "Potted & Plowed," "Environmentally Sound," and "Marshmallow Land." The room begins to spin around and around as his slurping becomes heated, heavy, and sensually perfect. He falls away from my hole, discovers it again, and ... I lose my mind, reaching frenzied enjoyment.

To my surprise, I notice a digital camera on the dilapidated dresser on the right side of the room. A red light flashes, filming our performance. I listen to the device hum while Cody slurps and laps at my hole.

On his knees, hunched over, driving my bottom wild, he threatens that he's going to slip his timber inside the fold of my ass and fuck a few chords out of me. Between licks and stabs with his tongue, he murmurs, "You're the hottest groupie ever, guy."

I'm going crazy by his face-gig. He seems to build up an adequate tempo between my legs, rolling his tongue down and along my opening, pulling it away, and applying it to my hole again. Repeatedly, he caresses my insides with his longing – I swear, trying to send me into a state of orgasmic no return. Cody tongue-laps my tight bottom like a pro, driving me into a point of cock-hardening ecstasy. His licking is tender and deep and smooth. Consecutive tongue-dabs throttle me into semi-explosion, but I hold my load in, unwilling to shoot the sticky sap onto my chest.

Of course, my palms are all over my rod, pivoting me to blow cream into spirals. I massage my cock's cap and stem with fiery passion, ready to get myself off while the singer is busy at my core. Hands move continuously up and down on my rod in a silky manner, working its sliding meat with dexterous pleasure. And fingers from my left hand eventually work up and along my chest and find one of my nipples, providing it with a little pinch, twist, and release, which continues for the next few minutes. Both of us grunt and groan with satisfaction, obtaining our fixes – the rocker and groupie connecting.

With the digital camera still running, and the smell of a thick hallucinogen hanging inside the room, we perform our own two-person band. Cody uses my skin with a lyrical passion: gagging himself on my ass, slippery at work, and plugging my middle with an extension of his warm tongue. And I continue to toil with him, rolling fingers up and down on my beef, prepared to cream at any given moment, wanting to splash my tattoo-covered torso with fresh ooze. Together we master the art of sex between young men.

"I'm not coming yet," I confess, windblown and sweaty.

"Not until I fuck you."

"Don't tease me, Cody."

"Trust me ... it's not a tease."

A condom is found in his jeans and applied to his throbber. Within seconds, my legs are pulled apart for a steady and rhythmic entry by Cody's plastic-covered cock. His tool separates me while entering my insides. One quick thump turns into many thumps as its full length begins to throttle my ass. Before I know it, the rock star is fucking me, lodging his meat inside my opening, pulling out, lodging it inside again, and …

I become a guitar against him: handled and played. Cody thrusts his body against mine, dramatically thrashes in and out of my hole, and mutters, "Blasting you, Danny … Enjoy the ride."

Steady pulses of elation ripple through my body as he pounds me. Every breath I can muster is short and quick, and I lose oxygen by the seconds. Dizzy and compelled to pass out by his motion, I gasp with pleasure, consumed by the rock star's spell.

Following a concert of baritone moans between us – the language between young men of the sexually active – I cannot hold my load in any longer. My palms feel like a mouth as I continue to hump my rod. And after a continuous manipulation of my pole, finally reaching an orgasm, succumbing to its delight, sticky seed juts out of my rod and spirals a fiery-hot load against my stomach, inked pecs and firm nipples.

Cody is all wide-eyed and breathless between my legs, evidently loving every minute of his ride. His stick lodges itself inside my bulk, continuing its gig, almost ready to blow. While holding my ankles in midair, he rocks his body against mine, plunging his slick shaft inside my interior. Quickly, he removes the slab from my tight tunnel in a coarse manner, rips off the condom and tosses it over his shoulder to the floor. The rocker begins to rotate his erect stem with a greedy grip, sharing a grin of happiness across his handsome face. Hyper, almost frantic movements occur between his hips and hands. Cody definitely wants to get off. His spike is aimed at the ceiling, ready to explode and …

An arc of combustible, sticky-white jizm flies out of his prick and rises between us. The juice plummets to my face, nailing me on both cheeks. To my surprise, two more arcs twirl out of his hose, splat against my tattooed torso and sizzles against my heated and sweaty skin.

"You fucking rock, Danny Love."

"Only with you," I add, breathless and fatigued. "Now, tell me what you're going to do with this scene on your camera?"

"Keep it for myself ... and jerk off to it when you're not around."

I laugh at this and reply, "You're so ballsy and bad."

"Sounds like a good tune. I may just have to use it."

Now spent, exhausted, Cody cuddles me against his body. He finds the bong again, lights it, inhales its nameless but potent smoke, and eventually passes it to me. The digital camera still rolls. And while the party ensues in the other room, beyond the bedroom and bathroom, we share the bong, take some blue pills, and kiss like boyfriends.

The next day, somewhere between Philadelphia and New York City, Cody's van takes a left and heads west. He asks if I've ever been to Yardland.

"What's that?" I inquire, blitzed on a purple pill called Mairgold's Dream.

"It's like Woodstock. A bunch of bands get together in a field and rock the day and night away for a week."

"You playing there?"

"Fuck yeah," he replies, locking my head to his crotch, ready for the blowjob of his music career.

Approximately one-hundred-twenty miles later with a purple-blue dusk present, I'm dancing front and center in a New York field with three thousand groupies, listening to a band called The Renters. The evening at Yardland is unbelievable: twelve bands, drugs and alcohol galore, free love, peace and no war, and irresponsible sex. The field is three football fields wide and one football field long. The place is partying with bands I love and follow: Planted Pot, The Seducers, Go-Boys, Rawhide Bone, and Trilogy Buzz. In truth, I'm having the time of my life, bare-chested and drunk, barefoot and potted, totally blitzed on a fresh powder called Mustard Merman.

Following Cody's hour-performance on the stage, he whisks me away into the nearby cornfield for heated sex. Burning marijuana blows through the air, filling my lungs, adding to my musicland buzz. The night's sky opens with stars, a full moon, and a light wind. Cody tells me he's horny and doesn't want to wait another minute to get me out of my shorts.

As a band by the name of Rockerboy echoes around me, Cody unbuttons my shorts and lowers them to the dry farmland. He finds my now-firm rod, gives it a hearty sniff, and begins to lick it from its base to its tender cap. One of his hands plants itself around my meat-tube, holding it like a shovel. Slurps are added to the cock by his spirited tongue, and my joint is pressed down the back of his throat with an unbelievable skill. He holds the base of my sphincter with two fingers and a thumb, dives on my dick, pulls away, and dives on it again, which continues for the next six minutes.

Thrashing ensues to his mouth in a wicked and rock-hard manner. Dick head and stem penetrate his tonsils, down the length of his narrow and tight throat. Beneath me, he whimpers with attentiveness, hungry for my stick. He grabs onto my ass with both palms, pulls me toward his face, and crushes my swinging balls to his furry chin and neck.

I become disoriented by his sex-spell and the pot-smell lingering through the field. My body wavers above him, and I have to reach out and grip his shoulders, so I don't fall. His mouth and constant sucking blows me away. Dizziness takes over my world, and I mumble, "Cody, I'm going to spray."

Quickly, he pulls off and away from my beef, shaking his head. He instructs, "Not yet. I want you to jam your rod in my ass first."

For once, he is not singing, which surprises me. Not that it matters, though, since I'm excited to hear his request, indulging it to the fullest.

Seconds later, Cody spins around, bends over, grabs his ankles, and orders, "Lube me up with your tongue, buddy ... I can't take it dry."

And so it is done. I hunch down and become hungry behind his bottom, rimming his core with a heated and wet tongue while holding onto his hips. Darting the slippery tool into his compact opening only causes the boner between my solid legs to grow harder. I slurp and lap his cave while he burbles in front of me.

A few clear and concise words escape his front hole: "Put it in as far as it will go."

Again, I listen. Why not? What do I have to lose? I'm just a groupie, banging the lead singer of his band from one city to the next, and having the time of my life doing it. Why can't I push my sliver of heated and slippery tongue into his center? So I do, one inch after the next. Helplessly, I attempt to please him with every lick and lap, lost in both of our hungers.

Cody rides my face. He pushes his weight back and my nose slips into his tight notch. A sound of pure delight explodes from his mouth, and a possible spasm of enjoyment ripples through his body from head to toe. During his eddying, he sings, "Deeee … per, Dannnny," lost by my sensual touch.

What transpires next is why he leads me to the cornfield in the first place. He insists I remove my face from his ass and begin to the bang it with my firm stalk. He begs me for the action, unwilling to leave the field until he is fully spent from a fresh pounding.

Of course hippie-lust has its demands. I concede to his new desire, ready and willing to propel his world into a state of groupie-inside-rocker ecstasy. Before he knows it, I have one condom-covered inch at the doorway of his need, grasp his hips, and give him a murmured warning, "Take all eight inches, Cody … I know you can handle them."

Truth is I believe I have control of the moment, pushing half of my stalk into the singer's bottom. This is a total misunderstanding on my part, though. Cody roughly backs into my meat, taking all of my tool into his core with one push, and lets out a loud and obnoxious humph sound, discovering pleasure.

The rock star does all the work, riding my beam. One spirited push on my rod turns into a dozen or more. He plows his weight radically into my body, almost knocks me over, and lets out a generous moan of deep satisfaction.

I cannot have him be the star of the hour, though, and provide a naughty and commanding shove to his tight hub. The feeling provides a beat of elation that twists through my body, which I carry out again and again. Fingers cling to his hips and sweat starts to fly off my chest, sputtering on his thin back. Together we beef-up our connection and share a mind-boggling ride.

In front of me, the band leader rattles off, "Fuck me hard, dude. Punch it into my system."

I affectionately process his request, shoving all I have into him, haul out of his rigid core, and jostle inside him again. More sweat flies off the plane of my chest and stings his back.

The rocker becomes lost by my touch. Wooziness is found, and he begins to murmur incomprehensible sounds. Cody jars his body onto my shaft, putting forth his best heated effort. Madness overtakes him, and he finally rambles something I can understand, "Shoot with me, Danny. Now … Let's not wait any longer."

Following a couple more hits to his hub, I pull out and lose the condom. Ready to blow, I watch Cody stand and position himself next to me. He wraps his left arm around my back and holds me close to his skin, and together we jack our loads into the field, using our hands as instrumental tools.

Fists cultivate beef in matched accomplishment. Chests heave with delight, and our breathing intensifies. Together, we establish a band of our own, rocking it out.

Cody is the first to blow and mutters, "I'm hosing." He lets out an obnoxious roar and fertilizes the field with his sap. The white liquid decorates the tilled earth, two stalks of corn, and almost hits my right foot.

Watching him come is perfectly euphoric for me. I can't keep my load in any longer, stroking my pounder with all my might. Heaving for oxygen, following his blast, I arc three wads of my churn into the cornfield, releasing every drop of my load against the shadowy ground.

Face to face, post-sexed and spent, we pull our clothes on. A song about hippies and gay sex explodes through the cornfield. Enamored with Cody, I ask, "You going to New York next?"

"Only if you come along, pal. It won't be the same show without you there."

We kiss with intense fire: dramatically, roughly, unable to hold back.

When he finally pulls away from me, he admits, "I've got a thing for you, Danny. This song about you keeps running through my head, and it's not going to go away until I write it down."

I joke, "What it's called, 'Hippie-Lust'?"

He responds with another kiss, grinds his groin against my middle, and replies, "Stick around ... continue to be a groupie, and you'll find out."

THE RAMS
By Lew Bull

Being a reporter for a small local newspaper often has its perks, but then I suppose if I considered myself in terms of those reporters on major newspapers, I was a small fry, a nothing, an insignificant entity. You may wonder what sort of perks I'm talking about. Well, I'm talking about occasionally meeting important people. 'So what!' I hear you say, but then when you live in a small town in the back of beyond, meeting important people is something significant in one's otherwise mundane life.

My editor had phoned me in my office and told me that a rock group was coming to town in a few days' time, and she had arranged for me to interview them. I laughed at her suggestion, knowing that not many rock groups ventured out into the country towns, let alone me knowing too much about rock music. Sure, I listened to music and had a fairly Catholic taste in music, but that didn't qualify me to be an authority on the latest forms of heavy metal, hip hop or rock, but, a job is a job.

"What's the brief, Cathy?" I asked my editor.

"They're playing at the sports stadium on Friday and Saturday night, but we want to do an article for the Thursday newspaper release, and I thought it might be a good idea for you to interview the band. Do you have any reservations?"

I didn't want to tell her that I thought I was the wrong person to interview them and that she should have asked one of the female reporters to do it – you know groupies and all that. In any case, the women were probably the ones who would have drooled to have interviewed a bunch of horny young men who were on the road wanting one-night stands and slutty sex.

"Is there no one else who might want to do this," I enquired.

"Well, if you don't want to do it, just say so," remarked Cathy, rather caustically.

"No, no! I'm more than willing," I replied, knowing that jobs were hard to come by in small towns and I might be fired for not wanting to do my work. "Where am I to meet them?" I asked.

"They are booked into the Travel Inn Hotel and will be arriving on Wednesday, so I've set up a date for you at 18:00. Just go to the hotel and tell reception who you are, and they'll direct you to a room that they are going to set up for the interview."

"Is there anything I ought to know about the band, such as the band name and the names of the group members, and things like that?"

I heard a long, deep sigh on the other end of the telephone line and imagined the look on my editor's face.

"They're called the Teddy Bears ..."

"The what?"

"I'm only joking," replied my sarcastic editor. "The band's name is The Rams ..."

"Now you are joking," I sniggered.

"I'm not," was the hasty reply. "That's their name, and the individual members names are, Harry Smithers, Dave Kankovsky, Barry Merchant and Greg Merchant."

"I take it the last two are brothers."

Again there was a desperate sigh on the other end of the line.

"Who does what?" I enquired.

"I take it you mean who plays what?" asked my exasperated editor.

"You know what I mean, yes."

"Harry plays rhythm guitar, Dave is on vocals and Barry and Greg are on drums and lead guitar respectively. OK?"

"Thanks boss. I'll do my best."

Another deep sigh was heard. I don't think my editor had much faith in me somehow. As soon as I had put down the phone, I Googled The Rams. To my surprise, they actually existed. I really thought she was having me on, but there it was on the screen and what a bunch they looked from the pictures that were displayed. I thought they would all be teeny-boppers, but they weren't. They looked like guys in their late twenties or early thirties, and they certainly didn't look like the type our town was used to seeing walking around the streets – they were dressed in leathers and were full of tattoos. Naturally, I knew that the photo didn't necessarily depict what they would be wearing for their concerts, but I must admit it was a bit of a turn-on for me. I read up as must as the site gave me about the four guys and then set to work formulating possible questions for them.

Wednesday arrived and with it a sense of foreboding. I liked music, but I wasn't a rocker; I was probably more of a nerd, so I had a certain amount of trepidation at the thought of interviewing these guys.

At 5:45 p.m. I set off for the hotel and made my way to the reception area. There were quite a few young girls hovering around the reception area, probably waiting to catch a glimpse of the band.

"Hi there, I'm Chad Humphreys, and I have an appointment with the rock group for an interview," I said to the charming young receptionist.

She gushed at me when I said I had an interview with the band.

"They'll be in the Waikiki Room, sir. It's down the passage and last door on the right. Their manager will be waiting for you there."

I thanked her and headed in the direction she had told me. When I reached the door with a large sign telling me WAIKIKI ROOM, I felt nervous and gingerly opened the door. As I peered in, I saw a middle-aged man sitting reading a newspaper.

"Hi," I said, closing the door behind me.

He looked up and smiled. "Are you Chad from *The Daily Chronicle*?"

"That is I, sir."

He stretched a hand in my direction. "Ron Massey, the band's manager."

We shook hands, and I sat in the seat next to him. Although I could see he was middle-aged, he still had the remnants of a youthful look about him, and it was clear to me that he worked out as his body had no evident fat on it, from what I could see.

"The boys will be here soon," he said smiling broadly at me. "I was just reading your local paper here. Seems you cover quite a selection of topics."

I grinned and nodded.

"Is there anything extra you need to know about the band before you get started?"

I wasn't sure just what extra material he might be referring to, but I thought I had better not show too much ignorance, so I smiled sweetly and said we would play it by ear as the interview went along.

Ron and I made small talk as we waited for the band to arrive, and I soon found myself relaxing more and more. Just then, the door opened, and the four men entered. They were dressed very casually and didn't seem to appear like the pictures on the Website. To me they looked like everyday guys who could be working in a bank or a store, and not heavy rockers.

Ron introduced me to the four men, and we made ourselves comfortable. I took out my pen and had my pad ready to make notes. I cleared my throat.

"Hi guys." That was a stupid start considering that I had already been introduced to them.

They all mumbled a rather stuttering, "Hi."

"Um… let's start with who is the leader of the band?"

"Greg is," said Ron.

"Ok. Greg, can you tell me something about the formation of the group?"

Greg looked as though he might be the eldest in the group. He had a mop of dark brown hair that framed his face and reached his shoulders. His eyes were a soft blue that sort of melted into you when you looked into them. As he spoke, my eyes trailed over the length of his body, taking in his muscular legs encased in a pair of tight blue jeans, his slim waist and broad shoulders. Naturally, as I was so preoccupied with looking over his body, I had not listened to anything he was saying nor taken down any notes.

"How do the rest of you feel about being in the band?" I asked when there was a moment of silence.

Again, that was a stupid question, but it was my own fault for not picking up on something that Greg might have said, as I would do in any other interview.

My eyes roamed from one to another, taking in each man's physical attributes. As I glanced over them, I made up in my mind, that although Dave and Barry were the better looking of the four, it was Greg who oozed the most sex appeal. Unfortunately, Harry seemed to have nothing much going for him in my estimation; physically, I mean.

"Tell me, why the name The Rams?"

Greg chuckled. "Some of us like ramming."

"I beg your pardon?"

"You know, when we have sex we like to ram it in," replied Barry, joining in with the chuckling.

I wasn't sure how seriously to take that answer, so I didn't write down anything.

The interview continued for about half an hour, thanks to prompts from Ron who obviously realized that I was a little out of my depth. Finally, it all came to an end.

"Oh one last question," I suddenly added.

They all looked a little startled until I asked my question.

"How do you guys feel about groupies?"

They all laughed uproariously, Ron included.

"Chad, let me explain the groupie thing to you," said Barry, smiling enigmatically at me. "We don't mind them at all, provided they're prepared to have sex with us."

Another roar of laughter followed. I smiled embarrassedly at having asked the question, and I think Greg noticed my embarrassment.

"Chad, don't let Barry fool you. We're not on this country-wide tour just for sex, although we won't say no to someone we like," said Greg, winking at me.

I wondered what the significance of the wink might be, but as I had got my answer, I thanked each of the guys individually and made my way back to the office to write something? Anything.

Thursday morning my report was in the paper together with a photo of the band that Ron had obviously sent to the office. I read what I had written and thought it not too bad for someone who had spent more time drooling over the guys than listening intently to what they were saying. As I sat reading my article, the phone in my office rang.

"Chad Humphreys speaking."

"Hi, Chad, it's Ron here from the interview yesterday."

"Oh hi, Ron. How are things?"

"Fine thanks. I just phoned to thank you for the good article you wrote on the band."

I smiled to myself, knowing that there must have been comments that I had not taken note of as I was too busy admiring the talent in the Waikiki Room.

"Thanks for the compliment, Ron."

"The boys and I were wondering if you had tickets to the concert and if not whether you'd like a couple as their guest."

I was stunned, but flattered. Although I had originally no intention of going, after having met them I was more interested not so much in their music as them.

"That sounds great," I answered.

"Come to the stadium tomorrow night and just come backstage. I'll be there to meet you."

"Gee, thanks Ron, I really appreciate that," I responded, replacing the telephone.

Friday evening arrived, and I showered, slipped into my jeans and pulled on a T-shirt. I then headed off to the stadium and did as Ron had instructed. When I had passed through security, Ron took me to the guys' dressing room, which was one of the change rooms in the bowels of the stadium.

"Hi there, buddy!" exclaimed Barry when he saw me. "Come on in."

I made my way in and was confronted by four hunky guys, all in leather jeans, leather waistcoats and tattoos. I noticed Greg's bulging biceps extending from under his waistcoat and how snugly his leather jeans fitted his well-defined torso. My attention then moved to Barry and Dave who were in a corner in deep conversation. I saw the back view of Barry and my mouth became dry when I noticed his firmly rounded ass, tightly encased in his leathers. Throughout this, Ron had stood next to me with his hand casually draped on my shoulder, but I had been subconsciously unaware of his presence as I was too busy admiring the leather guys.

It was nearing the start of the concert, so Ron suggested we leave the band and make our way to the side of the stage.

"Would you like to go out front and watch from there or stay here?" enquired Ron.

If I stayed at the side of the stage, I felt I'd have better access to the guys and be closer to them than if I went out front.

"Could I stay here?" I asked.

"Sure thing," replied Ron, "but just stay next to me then you won't get in the way of the technicians."

The band emerged from the bowels of the stadium and having been introduced to the packed, screaming audience, they made their way on stage and began playing.

Wow! I was shocked by their performance. The music, although not what I was expecting or was used to, was tight, loud and frantic. The four guys played their hearts out, and soon they were all sweating from their vigor. Barry and Greg both ripped off their waistcoats to wild screams from the female audience and as they did so, their full masculinity was presented to me. I stared in awe of these two men with their tight abs and broad chests. I felt a tinge of pleasure between my legs, and at the same time, felt Ron push his crotch up behind me. I never moved, but I knew I could feel his hard-on rubbing against my tight little ass.

"Do you like that?" Ron shouted into my ear above the noise of the band.

I wasn't sure whether he was referring to the music or the feel of his hard cock against me. I pretended not to hear him, but still, he remained 'glued' to my ass.

After about five numbers, Dave, the vocalist came off stage to get a drink of water and spotted me with Ron.

"How's it going for you?" asked Dave between gulps of water.

"I think you guys are great," I replied like an excited school girl.

"Well, it gets hotter," he said, rushing back on stage again.

"What's he mean by it gets hotter?" I asked, turning to Ron.

"You'll see."

I returned to watching the band and again felt Ron's solid muscle pushing against my ass, except this time, he stretched an arm around my waist and held me there. I knew that I was also getting hard from the excitement I felt behind me, but I would rather have had one of the band pushing up against me. I also noticed that each of the band members saw Ron holding me as they looked off stage at various moments, but Ron never released his hold.

The concert continued for another hour with the band having a short break of about five minutes while Barry did a drum solo.

"Are you enjoying yourself?" asked Greg as he neared me.

"I'm in awe of you guys," I said, almost gushing. "I think you're brilliant."

"So are you coming back to our hotel after the concert?" asked Greg.

I was somewhat taken aback and didn't know how to respond. No one had invited me back, and in any case, I thought they would be more interested in one of their female groupies whom they could fuck.

"Won't I be in the way … I mean … with your girlfriends?" I asked, now sounding rather stupid.

"Be my guest," said Greg, smiling sweetly at me as sweat glistened on his muscular body and trickled down to the waistband of his tight leather jeans. I wished I could have just licked up that stream of sweat, but I wasn't able to as they hurried back on stage.

As the concert came to an end, amidst the screams and shouts from the many young women and probably a few men, the band members left the stage and headed back to their dressing room. Throughout the concert, Ron had stayed behind me and rhythmically rubbed himself up against my tight ass until I knew that I had been dribbling precum into my briefs. He had aroused me to such an extent that my cock was aching and desperate to fire its load, but standing on the side of the stage was not where I wanted to release. Ron took hold of my arm and led me down to the guys' dressing room.

As we entered, we were met by security guards and a number of screaming young girls who were all over the guys. I watched this behavior for a moment and suddenly felt jealous that I couldn't do what they were doing. Greg and Barry noticed me, and I saw how Greg's eyes went down to the bulge in my jeans. His smile broadened, especially when he also saw the depressed look on my face. I gave a half-hearted smile in return, but it hurt to see the way the girls were kissing them and running their hands over their muscular bodies.

"Let's leave them," said Ron, suggesting we get out of the dressing room.

I turned and followed Ron, but as I closed the door behind me, I gave Greg a last glance and noticed that he was watching me leave. Ron led me down a long tunnel until we reached another change room that had the words VISITOR'S CHANGE ROOM written above the entrance. We entered to silence, and Ron closed the door behind us. We wandered around until we came to the shower area and found a long bench on which Ron sat.

"I'm sure you're hurting inside," he remarked, gently.

I wondered how he knew, but the look I gave him was a sufficient answer to his question.

"Come and sit here, Chad," he said, patting the seat of the bench next to him.

I wandered over and sat down. I could still feel my rock hard cock pushing to escape the confines of my briefs, but that wasn't on my mind at the moment. Ron stretched his hand across and rested it on the bulge in my jeans.

"That feels so good," he whispered.

Gently he began to massage my swollen appendage through the rough denim material. I closed my eyes and thought of Greg. As I did so, I felt Ron slowly begin to unzip my jeans and gently extract my long, hard cock from my briefs. I opened my eyes and looked down as he lowered his face to the cut head of my throbbing cock and took it into his mouth. The warmth of his mouth sent shivers through my body, and I gave a gentle upward thrust as he sank his throat down my shaft.

"Aaagh!" I moaned as his mouth came to rest at the base of my cock.

Slowly he began to rise up to the tip and then once again sank down to the base. I felt his tongue licking some of my precum from the slit as he again reached the tip. The tightness of his mouth around my shaft was driving me crazy. I lifted Ron's head from my glistening cock, stood up and shucked my jeans and briefs to my ankles, then turned my back to him, bent over and displayed my tiny pink rose to him. I felt the tip of his tongue penetrate the opening, and he began to push his tongue tip into my warm hole. As he licked and prodded with both his tongue and fingers, I began working on my cock, sliding my hand effortlessly along its length.

After a while, Ron stopped and stood up. He gently undid my shirt and took it off of me, throwing it onto the bench. Then he undid his trousers and stepped out of them and also took off his shirt while I removed my jeans completely. It was then that I saw how handsome and well-developed Ron was. He had a long, thick cock, waiting to be taken, and I was a willing recipient. I opened my mouth and gulped it down my throat as though I was desperately hungry for something to eat. I could hear Ron's moans and groans as I lubricated his length and ran my tongue ever so lightly over the mushroom-shaped head, inserting the tip of my tongue into the narrow slit at its top.

"Oh yes," gasped Ron, as he held my head, forcing his cock down my throat rather savagely.

I almost gagged as his cock hit the back of my throat, but fought not to. As I continued salivating over his length, I felt his hands wander toward the entrance to my tight little ass. A finger circled my pucker and then slowly began a journey into me. As his finger sank deeper, so my pace increased sucking on his hardened cock. Our gasps and breathing became more intense, and the two of us became lost in our own world of pleasure.

Unbeknown to us, the change room door had been opened, and a voyeur was watching us with passionate interest. Out of our sight, a muscular body played seductively with his heavily-veined, thick cock, spitting into the palm of his hand to lubricate it. Slowly the man's hand slid along the long shaft until it reached the large bulbous head where it rested and massaged it.

"Let me lie down on the bench, and then you can sit on me," suggested Ron, prostrating himself on his back and holding the shaft of his cock so that I could lower my tight ass onto it, and he must have planned this because he pulled a bottle of lube from below the bench, but I didn't care. He slicked up his cock.

Slowly, I lowered my body, allowing the enormity of his shaft to stretch my chute wider. I groaned as I lowered myself until I felt my ass touch his balls then I knew I could relax.

"Fuck! That feels awesome," gasped Ron as he felt the tightness of my chute strangle his shaft.

Our mysterious voyeur, moved closer, removing his jeans as he did so.

I began a slow, rhythmic rise and fall on Ron's cock, and as I did so, so I took hold of his protruding, firm nipples and squeezed. Ron suddenly thrust upwards, impaling me deeply, and letting his cock rub sensuously on my prostate.

Suddenly, as I was enjoying the thrill of having this man fuck me, I felt another hand caress my ass. I turned in fright and saw Greg standing naked behind me, his cock wanting to be part of our action.

My heart leapt with joy when I saw him. Oh how I wanted this man to do to me what Ron was doing. I didn't have long to wait.

Gently Greg pushed me down onto Ron's stomach so that I was almost lying flat on Ron and thereby opening up my ass more. I felt Greg position his cock at my asshole and begin to nudge it toward my entry. There was no way my tight little ass would accommodate two massive cocks at the same time – but I wanted them both.

Greg added some lube from the bottle then holding onto his shaft firmly, pushed ever so slowly and began to sink into my asshole while Ron remained absolutely still. The pain was excruciating, but I was not about to relinquish my position. Instead, I was more than happy to surrender my ass to these two men.

"Oooh yeah!" gasped Greg as he felt his cock come to rest inside my warm, accommodating chute.

Gently, the two men then began to thrust into me and as they did so, so I tried to meet each thrust with my own downward push. There was no longer any pain but just delirium as the three of us let our emotions run.

I could feel the sweat from Greg's body dripping onto my back, and this in itself was turning me on more. Ron, who had already been working me over before Greg's appearance was getting close to shooting, and I could feel his cock throbbing inside me.

"I'm getting close guys," he gasped, in between breaths.

"Me, too," I panted. "Oh fuck! I can't last any longer. I'm coming!"

A stream of warm, white cream shot from the tip of my cock and landed near one of Ron's nipples, followed closely by a couple more shots. As this was happening, I could feel my ass muscles clamping tightly around the double shafts inside me, strangling them. Ron couldn't hold on further, and with a cry, he fired his load into my ass, pumping upward with each load that was shot. Greg, in the meantime had increased his pace in order to shoot together with us, and I felt my body shuddering with his powerful thrusts. As he pounded my ass, Ron tried to pull his cock out, but Greg shouted: "Stay there buddy, I wanna fuck with both of you."

Ron continued to give gentle thrusts while Greg, his face becoming redder, grabbed hold of my nipples and pinched.

"Aaargh!" I yelled as his fingers found their mark.

It was the final thing that he needed to fall over the edge, so to speak.

I felt Greg's body stiffen and then while he groaned with pleasure, I felt the throbs of his cock as it fired his manly seed into me.

Oh what bliss to have this man dominate me and then run his hard hands lovingly over my back and nipples as he emptied his heavy balls of their load.

Ron was the first to withdraw from my ass and as he did so, a sort of emptiness filled me, but I still had Greg with me. I gave a few more thrusts onto his cock as though to say, 'don't go yet.'

"Phew! I could stay like this forever," whispered Greg, as he let his fingers wander near the entrance to my ass and gently insert a couple alongside his thick shaft.

I also thought I could stay like that, but I knew it would all end.

As we cleaned ourselves and dressed, I wondered if I'd ever see them again.

"Thanks guys," I volunteered, "that was awesome, and I wouldn't mind trying that again."

Greg chuckled.

"If you think that was good, wait till you try with Ron, me and Barry."

"But I thought ..." I began to say.

"You thought we were into girls," suggested Greg.

The look on my face suggested that it was what I had thought.

"No way," replied Ron. "We like to keep it in the family."

"I don't understand," I answered.

"Greg and Barry are my step-sons," replied Ron. "So we share everything, and now maybe you'll understand why the band is called The Rams."

All I could do was smile and massage my tight little ass that had just been rammed.

THE SECRET LIFE OF BLADE OAKLEY
By Lew Bull

The hum of the ancient air conditioner was the only sound emanating from the office of Blade Oakley as he sat staring out the window. There wasn't much of a view considering that he was on the twenty-fourth floor, and the only things that he could look at were other sky-scrapers in the distance. His mind seemed to be in a trance, but that was soon broken by the knock on the office door. Coming back to reality, he swiveled his chair from the window to face the opposite door.

"Come in," boomed his manly voice.

"Sorry to bother you, Mr. Oakley," said his glamorously dressed secretary as she entered the office, "but I had a call from a Miss Matthews from Top Media."

"And?"

"She just asked for you to call her; something about an event."

"Thanks Lucy," replied Blade, forcing a smile.

The secretary turned and exited, and Blade's eyes instinctively focused on the young woman's ass, but he never said another word. Instead, he swiveled his chair once more to look out the office window, deep in thought. He sat in this position for what seemed like an eternity and then returned to the mundane world of his office and picked up his telephone. He dialed a number and waited.

"Top Media, good morning," said a sweetly sounding voice at the other end of the line.

"Morning, may I speak to Miss Heather Matthews please?"

"Going through," answered the sweet voice.

Blade waited a moment, and then he heard another woman's voice.

"Heather Matthews speaking, how may I help you?"

"Hi, Heather, it's Blade here. I believe you tried to get hold of me."

"Oh hi, Blade, I've been trying to get hold of you for years," she said, laughing as she said it.

"You and how many other women, hey?"

"Probably hundreds," came the reply.

"So what can I do for you?"

"I heard something on the grapevine that you were doing a gig out of town next week, and I was wondering if we could do a photo shoot with you."

"News travels fast among you people. What did you have in mind?"

"I wanted to send round a photographer to take some pics, if that was OK with you."

Blade's mind went back to his previous state when he was gazing out the office window.

Blade had been in his current job as a financial advisor for a large company for six years, and during that time he had led a double life, known only to very few people. During the day, he had been the epitome of business both in appearance and in attitude, but over weekends and on the occasional evening, he became something different – he became Blake Overton, rock singer and performer. There was nothing out of the ordinary in what he was doing. Many other people did things in their spare time, and singing for a band was nothing out of the ordinary to him. Although he had qualified with an MBA degree in finance, it was his love of music that really tugged at his heart strings, and when he realized that he could sing and could play the guitar, he decided to take a chance in the entertainment field. He had started off slowly, playing pubs and the odd party, but it was when he was noticed by an impresario that his life changed.

Mike Taggart, who was a talent scout, happened to be attending a party at which Blake (Blade) was performing, and found the young man's look and performance appealing, so he introduced himself.

"I think you've got a great deal of talent there. Have you ever thought of taking your music seriously?" enquired Mike.

Blake was a little taken aback by the question, as he thought he was already serious about his music.

"What I mean is with your good looks and pleasant voice, you could be a star one day," continued Mike.

Blake merely laughed at the idea, until Mike invited Blake back to his luxurious apartment to discuss the matter in more detail. It was there that the 'other side' of Blade came to the fore. The two men had settled into the comfort of Mike's plush lounge and were enjoying drinks when Mike said, "I think you are extremely sexy, Blake."

Blake was immediately stunned by the statement as he'd never thought of himself in that light, nor had he shown any interest in guys – he was a ladies' man.

The drinks flowed, and as the evening progressed, so they both became more relaxed until Mike, who was sitting next to Blake, casually laid a hand on Blake's thigh. Blake never objected, so Mike let his hand drift upward toward Blake's crotch. When it reached where he thought Blake's cock would be lying, he gave a gentle squeeze and was amazed to feel something hard in Blake's jeans. Still Blake never objected. Mike took a chance and began to slowly unzip Blake's jeans while keeping his eyes on Blake's face. The two men stared at each other, and soon Mike was able to feel the warm, solid flesh, which he gently extracted from the confines of Blake's jocks. Out came a slightly downward curving, thick circumcised cock just waiting to be enjoyed. Mike held Blake's cock in his equally warm hand for a moment and then lowered his head until his lips caressed the tip of the cut head. Blake's cock throbbed as soon as Mike's mouth touched it, but still the man never objected. Mike opened his mouth wide to engulf the broad girth and then slowly sank his mouth down the long shaft.

According to Blake, that was the first time that a man had done anything sexual to him, but throughout he never objected.

Mike had kept his word and had begun to make Blake a popular musician, but Blade had insisted that he change his name because he thought it better to have two personas and that was how Blake Overton came to be born.

"You do realize," said Mike, "that your life as a performer is going to change; you're going to be inundated with people wanting you, and by that, I mean female groupies wanting to get into your pants because of your good looks. Do you have a problem with that?"

Blade was only too happy to accommodate any woman who wanted him to service them, but having felt the warmth that he had felt when Mike had sucked him off, had made him think that there might be another side to him that would enjoy something different. He also realized that he needed to keep his day persona away from his night persona and that Blade and Blake were not going to be the same. The formality of everyday mundane finance was what Blade existed for, but then after dark, Blake thrived on the freedom of music and what accompanied it. In the office, Blade was happy to be the attraction of the female staff, but at night it became more difficult as there were always hundreds of female groupies who wanted to touch him and get him into bed, yet he missed the touch of a man and would often turn to Mike, who would happily oblige to do whatever Blake wanted. In most cases, Blake would go round to Mike's apartment, and Mike would treat Blake to his hot lips and warm mouth, but Blake never reciprocated.

Soon, Blake's bookings as an entertainer increased, and it meant that to meet the obligations, he would have to take leave from work. Throughout this time, he had managed to keep his two jobs separate and although some staff questioned whether he was Blake, the rock star, he denied it. As to his sex life, whenever he was performing as a singer, he was flooded with offers from young girls, but one evening, Mike introduced him to his friend, Brad.

After the evening's performance, Mike took Blake and Brad back to the hotel in which they were staying. Although Blake was a little disappointed that he never had a young girl for the night, Mike had other plans. Back at the hotel, the usual drinks flowed, and soon the three men were quite relaxed, and Blake had forgotten all about his planned sex for the night. As the night dragged on, Mike said he was going to sleep, so he stripped in front of Blake and Brad and lay on top of one of the beds in their room, which they shared. Brad observed Mike's taut body, but Blake seemed not to notice. Brad and Blake continued to chat casually until Brad decided to make a move and said, "I think I've had too much to drink, do you mind if I stay the night?"

Blake agreed without hesitation and also said he was ready to get some sleep, so both men stripped down to their underwear. Brad noticed how heavily hung Blake looked and soon found himself becoming aroused by the sight. As the two beds had been pushed together, Brad lay on his back in the middle and waited for Blake to climb on the other side. Blake went into the bathroom and Brad could hear him taking a piss, and while this was taking place, Brad casually stroked his already hard cock until he heard the toilet flush and knew that Blake was on his way out of the bathroom. When Blake entered the bedroom, he noticed the erection that Brad had and smiled at what he saw.

"You're quite a big boy, aren't you?" said Blake, bending over and removing his jocks.

Brad immediately looked at Blake and saw the slightly downward curving cock getting harder with each moment.

"You're not so bad yourself," remarked Brad. "That's a pretty awesome cock you've got there, but I suppose that's why the women go crazy for you?"

Blake merely shrugged and grinned to himself. He lowered himself onto the bed next to Brad and just lay there.

After a moment, Brad allowed his hand to drift in the direction of Blake, who had continued to lie there doing and saying nothing, except stare up at the ceiling. Soon Brad felt Blake's thigh and stopped, but before he could do anything else, Blake's hand took hold of Brad's and guided to his already throbbing cock.

"That's what you want, isn't it?" asked Blake sighing softly as Brad's hand slid along the thick shaft.

"I thought you were into women?" whispered Brad, hoping not to disturb Mike, who was silently sleeping alongside of them.

"I've realized I'm bi," said Blake.

"So you're also into guys?"

"I've never fucked a guy, if that's what you mean, but I like a guy to suck my dick – they know how to do it better than a woman does."

"I always thought musicians only fucked chicks and wouldn't admit to being gay."

"I'm not admitting to being gay," replied Blake. "I just told you I was bi, and there's a big difference."

"Yes, you get the best of both worlds," chuckled Brad. "But have you ever thought of fucking a guy before?"

"No, not really."

"Would you like to try?"

"Why are you offering me your ass on a plate?" said Blake smiling at Brad, who was facing him now.

"Well, if you want to, it's either my ass or Mike's, and as he's asleep, you're welcome to invade mine. In any case, I reckon I could handle that big dick of yours, and who knows, if you like it sufficiently, you might be hooked for life and dump the chicks."

Blake took a long, deep look into Brad's eyes, gently raised himself from the bed, went back into the bathroom and soon returned with a condom and some lube. He threw the lube to Brad.

"Get that tight ass of yours ready for me," said Blake as he unrolled the sheer condom along the thick shaft that was eager to rip into Brad's waiting ass.

Brad rolled onto his side with his back to Blake and waited. Soon he felt the sturdy, bulging head nudge against his puckering asshole, and he waited to see if Blake was going to make a gentle, slow entry.

WHAM! Blake plowed right in causing Brad to gasp loudly, waking Mike in the process. Mike opened his eyes to see Brad's pained expression staring at him while Blake began a fast and deep pounding of Brad's ass.

Mike smiled a knowing smile at Brad. He had hoped that something like this might happen and was pleased that he'd been awakened to witness this passionate display. Mike took hold of Brad's hard-on and began stroking it while Blake continued his deep thrusts and gasping as he did so. Mike then scuttled down to wrap his mouth around Brad's stiff cock, lathering it and stabbing at his piss slit with the tip of his tongue. Brad was no longer groaning in pain, but was rather whimpering as he was pounded from behind and sucked dry from Mike in the front.

Every so often, Mike released Brad's wet cock to see the expression on Blake's face – it was a picture of human pleasure. Blake's face showed how determined he was to enjoy the tightness of Brad's chute and how much he wanted to push his thick cock deeper into the warm confines of their young visitor.

It didn't take Brad long to reach his climax as Blake's cock was strumming a merry tune on Brad's prostate.

"Oh fuck, if you keep this up, I'm gonna shoot," cried Brad.

Mike's mouth sank to the base of Brad's cock waiting for the avalanche of salty-sweet cream to escape from the tip of Brad's engorged cock and sucked hard and deep as his tongue tried to caress the slick shaft. With a loud gasp, Brad shot his first load down Mike's throat, followed by more bursts of beautifully tasting cream, which Mike slurped down his throat as though it was the tastiest milkshake he'd ever had. He never removed his mouth, not even when Brad's body began to relax, but continued to clamp tightly around the young man's shaft, draining it of every drop of warm cum.

Blake's intense pounding had increased when he felt Brad's ass muscles clamp tightly around his thick shaft, almost strangling it, and when he knew that Brad was emptying his load in Mike. This felt better than anything he'd enjoyed with any of his groupies, and he wanted to explode in Brad.

The beds were rocking and the bedsprings were squeaking with each thumping thrust that Blake made as he brought himself closer to the edge. Mike watched with anticipation and excitement as his friend reached a high. Mike had taken his own cock in his hand and was stroking it profusely so as to come at the same time as Blake.

"Blake, I'm getting close," groaned Mike.

"Me, too," groaned Blake in between gasps of air.

"Aargh, FUCK!" exclaimed Blake as his body stiffened, and he thrust deeply into Brad's tight ass, impaling the young man with his solid piece of hard muscle, shooting the first of his warm cum.

Blake allowed his cock to fire while he remained impaling Brad, and once he felt that the flow of warm cum was subsiding, he began to pound Brad's ass again as though he wanted every drop to be squeezed from his long shaft.

At the same time, Mike raised himself above Brad and, stroking his cock, fired onto Brad's body. Some of his sticky load fell onto Blake's chest, but that didn't deter the musician who was now enjoying each thrust into Brad as he emptied his heavy balls that had been loaded with seed.

As the three men slowly began to sink back to a state of peacefulness and exhaustion, Mike lay facing Brad and kissed him gently on the lips while Blake stretched an arm across Brad's body and stroked it. Mike noticed that Blake's fingers had some cum on them, so he took Blake's hand and gently sucked the warm goo from his fingers. No sooner had Mike done that, and then he positioned himself over both Blake and Brad and seductively kissed both men while Blake remained fixed to Brad, his cock throbbing gently inside of Brad's warm chute.

Blake had been initiated into the world of man sex and by the satisfied look on his face, had enjoyed it.

"Tell me Heather, this photographer you want to send around, is it male or female?" enquired Blade.

"Oh, come on Blade, I know you too well. If I send one of our young girls around to your place, she'd never be safe with you. No I'm sending a young guy round instead. At least he'll be safe from your clutches."

Blade thanked Heather for the publicity opportunity and replaced the phone in his office. He swiveled his chair to face the outside world again and smiled – maybe Blake could show this photographer a thing or two.

ONE HIT WONDER
By Michael Bracken

Ronnie tours the country under his stage name, playing with pick-up bands at every stop, a one-hit wonder who parlayed a guitar riff accidentally created at seventeen into five albums with four different recording companies and two decades of nonstop touring in the hopes of someday recreating that one summer when he topped the charts, headlined large venues, and opened for stadium-filling super groups.

He picked me up two years ago when the owner of a dive in Springfield wouldn't provide anyone to watch his merchandise table. I'd been standing in the back parking lot holding all five of Ronnie's CDs in my backpack when he arrived and stepped out of a dirty white minivan. Even in faded blue jeans and loose gray sweatshirt, with a pair of dark-framed glasses perched on the end of his nose and his shoulder-length black hair pulled into a loose ponytail, he still looked every bit the rock 'n' roll star he had been twenty years earlier. He graciously signed the CDs, asked if I was planning to attend the show later that night, and then disappeared through the back door.

I was walking away when I heard Ronnie's voice again.

"Hey, kid!"

I was no kid – I had just turned twenty-three – but I was the only person in the parking lot. I turned.

"You want to see the show for free and earn a few bucks?"

I could always use extra money. I lived in my parents' basement and worked part-time selling pretzels at the mall.

Ronnie told me what he needed, and soon we were hauling boxes of CDs and T-shirts into the bar. The owner let us push two small tables together next to the stage, and I unpacked everything while Ronnie worked with the power trio that would be backing him that night, putting a little pop in their power.

That night, the little stage couldn't contain Ronnie. Before the show, he changed into black leather pants that bulged provocatively at the crotch, snakeskin cowboy boots, and a black T-shirt that he peeled off halfway through the night to reveal powerful biceps, broad chest, and washboard abs that I would not have expected on a thirty-seven-year-old man who spent his life driving from city to city in a minivan. I had come to the show because of his one hit, a power pop number about what it's like to be different – a song that had spoken to me in high school when I realized I wasn't like the other boys in my gym class. Watching him perform turned me on. The way he handled the guitar, stroking the long neck, his fingers flying over the strings, made my cock hard, and it pressed uncomfortably against the inside of my jeans.

I know I wasn't the only one turned on by Ronnie's performance. Some of the women – all of them Ronnie's age because people my age don't remember him or his two-week visit to the top of the pop charts – offered themselves to Ronnie during the breaks, not realizing, as I did, his groupie gender preference. They turned out to be his biggest fans, though, buying six T-shirts and almost three-dozen CDs.

"Not bad," Ronnie told me after the bar closed and we were packing to leave. He counted the money, separated out ten percent, and handed it to me.

I stuffed the cash in my pocket, carried his merchandise out to the minivan, grabbed my backpack, and started to walk away.

"Hey, kid," Ronnie said. "Where you headed?"

"Bus stop," I said. "Home."

He opened the minivan's passenger door. "Get in. I'll take you."

I knew from the way he looked at me that he had something else in mind. I also knew when I climbed in the passenger seat and closed the door that I was thinking the same thing.

Ronnie drove to a motel near the highway, a place that had seen better days but was still clean and well maintained, and invited me inside for a drink. He carried his Les Paul in with us, but left everything else in the minivan.

We never had the drink. As soon as the door closed behind us and Ronnie leaned his guitar case against the wall, he pulled me into his arms and covered my lips with his. I opened my mouth, and his tongue slid between my teeth. I sucked on it and sucked hard. Our kiss was long and deep, and when it ended my heart was pounding and my legs were weak, and I had to brace myself against the door to keep from falling over.

"You know why we're here, don't you?" Ronnie asked as he stared deep into my eyes.

I nodded.

"And you're okay with that?"

"I've dreamed about it."

"I'm usually careful," he continued. "I don't invite just anybody back to my room after a show."

Maybe he was telling the truth. Maybe he was lying. I didn't care. I wanted him, and nothing he could say would change that.

I reached out, took his hand, and pulled him to me. Hoarsely, I whispered, "Stop talking."

He kissed me again, harder this time. While he kissed me, I untied the leather thong that held his pants closed, and then I forced my hand inside, finding his thick, erect cock and heavy ball sack.

My own cock was erect, but I was more concerned with pleasing Ronnie than with having my needs met. I grabbed the waistband of his leather pants and pulled them down as I dropped to my knees. To avoid underwear lines, he'd worn nothing beneath the pants, and his erect cock rose majestically between us.

Ronnie still wore his snakeskin boots, and with his leather pants pooled around his ankles and his balls in my mouth, he could hardly move. I had him where I wanted him. I leaned forward and sucked his nuts into my mouth, bathing his hairy sack with my tongue as his thick cock bobbed in front of my face. His nuts tasted of sweat and leather, and his curly hair caught between my teeth.

After thoroughly coating his nut sack with my saliva, I licked the underside of his cock stem from the base to the spongy soft mushroom cap. Then I wrapped my fist around the stiff shaft and took the head of his cock into my mouth. I hooked my teeth behind the glans and teased the pee slit with the tip of my tongue. As I did that, I slowly pumped my fist up and down the length of his cock.

Ronnie was too horny to wait. He grabbed the back of my head, thrust his hips forward, and buried his cock in my mouth. His soggy ball sack slapped my chin as he drew back and thrust forward again and again.

He came quickly, firing a thick glob of hot spunk against the back of my throat. I swallowed, and then swallowed again.

When Ronnie's cock quit spasming in my mouth, he pulled away, stripped off his clothes, and dropped onto the king-size bed. He fell asleep before I had a chance to remove my clothes, and I took care of myself in the bathroom before I climbed into bed beside him.

We hit the road the next morning, on our way to Ronnie's next one-night-stand fronting yet another pick-up band of dubious talent.

All I had in my backpack were the five autographed CDs, a paperback mystery, and a couple of protein bars. At an outlet mall in the middle of nowhere, just after we stopped for breakfast at a Cracker Barrel, Ronnie bought me underwear, socks, and a pair of Levi's. When we returned to the minivan, he opened one of the merchandise boxes and gave me three of his T-shirts. Then he handed me his key ring and told me it was my turn to drive.

Just like that I became Ronnie's driver, roadie, merchandise manager, and lover.

I called my parents when we stopped for lunch, told them I had found a job as a traveling salesman, phoned my old boss and told her I wouldn't be returning to the pretzel stand, and then realized that no one else would care what had happened to me. The life I was leaving behind was no life at all.

During the following months I learned how to take care of Ronnie, and he took care of me. The most important thing I learned is that Ronnie is always horny after a show, so we rocked and fucked our way across America, occasionally stopping at his sister's house in Tulsa to replenish the merchandise from the stash in her garage.

We usually stayed in cheap motels and ate fast food, but Ronnie's booking agent outdid himself a few weeks ago. He arranged a seven-night run at a casino where we stayed in a suite and had our meals comped. Ronnie performed every night on stage and in the bedroom.

When we returned to the suite after the final show on Sunday, Ronnie showered before joining me in the living area wearing nothing but a white hotel robe with a loosely tied sash. The hotel had sent up a chilled bottle of champagne and he uncorked it.

"It's our last night to live like rock stars," Ronnie said as he filled two champagne glasses. "Tomorrow, we hit the road again."

After spending a week in a hotel suite, I wasn't looking forward to motoring from motel to motel in the minivan, and I said so.

"It'll probably never get any better than this," Ronnie said, "and it may be a long time before it gets this good again."

In two years together, this was the first time I'd heard Ronnie admit that he might never again be the big star he had once been. I raised my champagne glass. "To tonight, then."

He lifted his glass in silent toast and then drained it. We drank until we emptied the bottle. When there was no more champagne, Ronnie threw his empty glass at the wall, where it shattered and rained pieces onto the carpet below.

He took my wrist and pulled me to him, slid his hands under my T-shirt, and teased my nipples with his thumbs. After I peeled my shirt off and threw it aside, Ronnie reached for my belt. Half a bottle of champagne wasn't enough to make him drunk, but it certainly caused his motor skills to deteriorate. I helped him with my belt. Then I kicked off my running shoes and peeled off the rest of my clothes.

"You're just as hot as the day I met you, kid," Ronnie said. He shook the robe from his shoulders and let it drop to the carpet at his feet. His cock was half-erect and growing.

The curtains were open, but neither of us considered the possibility that anyone could see us so many floors up.

"Hot?" I asked. "I was just an innocent kid standing in the parking lot hoping to get an autograph." I stepped forward and grabbed his cock. "You gave me a lot more than that."

Ronnie had given me the ticket out of my torpid existence in Springfield, had shown me an America I never would have seen without him, and had taught me more about the bottom end of the music business than anyone should ever have to know. And, all I had to do was be there when he wanted me.

He captured my head between his hands and planted a big kiss on my lips to shut me up. Immediately, our tongues met in a fiery, alcohol-fueled dance of desire.

When the kiss finally ended, Ronnie reached down and dug through the pockets of the robe. When he stood, he held a half-used tube of lube. He spun me around and bent me over the back of the couch, trapping my erect cock against the white leather.

Years of guitar playing had given him powerful fingers, and after he squeezed a thin trail of lube into the crack of my ass, he smeared the lube over the tight pucker of my ass. His fingers were so strong, I couldn't have resisted even if I had wanted to, and he pushed one finger into me. A second finger followed the first, and a moment later his cockhead replaced his fingers.

After he eased the mushroom cap past my sphincter, he grabbed my hips and drove his cock all the way into me. He pulled back and pushed forward, and as he did that, my cock rubbed against the leather couch beneath me.

The friction of my cock against the leather was an unexpected treat, and I found myself enjoying the feeling of my cock against the couch as much as I enjoyed Ronnie rocking my world from behind.

I came first, spewing cum all over the couch. Ronnie came a few strokes later, driving into me one last time and holding my hips tight as he fired his wad deep inside me.

We stood like that for a moment, taking in the view of the city, a view we weren't likely to see again for a long time, until we caught our breath.

Then Ronnie pulled away, retrieved his robe, and called room service for another bottle of champagne, so we could drink ourselves to sleep.

The next day, we returned to the road, to one-night-stands with pick-up bands, to hustling T-shirts and CDs to die-hard fans, and to fucking each other in cheap motels after every show.

Ronnie still has his dream, and I'm living mine.

Thank God for rock 'n' roll.

THE DELICACIES: LUST, LIQUOR, AND CANNABIS By Michael Mandrake

After a fantastic session of hot sex with Bryan and Nicolai, we all needed the rest. Nicolai however wanted to shed the memory of his "moment" with the two of us, so he called his favorite groupie, Renee. He left us the back of the bus to relax in the afterglow of our hot session. After making a few snide comments, he was out of our sight.

That minute, Bryan plunged his tongue into my mouth. When he noticed I was not into it with him, Bryan stopped kissing me. As his browns met mine, "What's wrong gorgeous? Somethin' on your mind or is the marijuana taking over?" He rubbed my bare pale chest while circling my navel.

Bryan leaned upward, rolling on top of me. The second his cock met mine, I felt my groin tighten. He ran one hand through my long stringy locks while the other caressed my cheek.

"Bryan, I ... I'm the happiest I've been in a while man. I know this is turning into some sappy shit dude but ..." I paused when he moved his hand from my cheek to my lips.

"I feel the same, Corey, you don't have to say it. I know it's not love yet, too damn early for that. We both know how we feel for each other, that's good enough." He engulfed my lips inside his own making my dick erect.

"Bryan ... mmmhmmm ..." I cooed as he rubbed his body against mine.

The way I felt right then I did not care that anyone caught us in the act. I had everything that I wanted right here in front of me. Bryan, more liquor in the fridge, smokes, and enough condoms along with lube to fuck all night if we so chose.

# # # # #

The following day when Bryan and I awoke, it was nearly noon.

As we got dressed, we stole kisses and exchanged smiles with each other. Before we could really get into it, we heard Nicolai and Eric's voices. That moment, my mind was racing. Would I continue to kiss Bryan even though Eric was here?

Bryan decided. He pushed me off him. Our eyes met as he lifted a finger to his lip mouthing, "Later."

"Well, well, well, if it isn't Bryan and Corey? How was your night you two little fags?" Eric said with a grin.

Bryan and I looked at each other then at Nicolai. Why did we believe this jerk would not tell Eric? He had probably told the guys from Omerta and Burnt Ash, too.

"Naw, naw, naw, it's OK dudes. Just understand that I don't want any part of what you two have goin' on. Neither do Allen or Nicolai!" Eric quipped.

As much as I wanted to tell Eric that his lead singer was a cocksucker literally and figuratively, I decided not to. The feel of Bryan's hand calmed me down since I wanted to show Nicolai how a faggot could whoop ass.

"It's all good Eric. Bryan and I don't want you, Allen, or Nicolai to play with us. It's safer that way; especially when both of you have had the bi twins and Renee." I smirked while massaging Bryan's shoulder.

Even though I had a thing for Renee myself, I knew talking about her would hurt Nicolai. That statement struck a chord since he stormed over to the fridge and grabbed a beer. Once he had it, he opened the bottle throwing the cap onto the floor. "Listen here, all three of you. No bad words about my girl. You say anything about her then you gotta deal with me. Do I make myself clear?" He took a swig shooting an angry stare at all of us.

"Damn, alright Nic, no prob." Eric walked out the back area.

Still, his pupils were on Bryan and me. "I didn't hear anything from the two of you."

"I'm not afraid of you, Nicolai. I only said that to upset you. I actually like the girl. Since you decided to out us to everybody, I needed to give you some kind of payback," I said while lighting a smoke that I passed to my new lover.

"Ha ha ..." He chuckled. "I didn't out you, fucker! Eric and Allen straggled back here and found you two sleeping on the floor together." He paused while taking another drink from the bottle.

"What you have to learn Corey is that I'm true to my word. Yeah, I'll give you a whole lotta shit, but I told you I wouldn't out you, and I stuck to that. So now, you can apologize. It is accepted!" He lit a joint, inhaled, and stared me down smiling like a Cheshire cat.

Amused, Bryan let out a soft guffaw while combing the back of my hair. However, I was not laughing. I looked at him with disgust as Bryan tried to pull me away.

Pointing my finger at Nicolai, "You are such an asshole. It's a good thing I like being in this band because I swear I wanna beat your ass right now!"

Before he could respond, I trotted out of there with Bryan behind me. Once back by our bunks, we sat on mine and leaned against the wall. Bryan stroked my leg through my pants, making the inside of my thighs stir again. As I closed my eyes, I felt the urge to have sex.

Horny, I knelt down in front of Bryan unzipping his fly. I needed to get my baby primed and ready to fuck me; I could care less who watched. Besides, I was an exhibitionist first.

# # # # #

After Bryan and I fell asleep in each other's arms on the bus, naturally the rest of the band woke us with teases. To make the wound deeper, Wayne from Omerta was there as well. However, he had no crude things to say. Since I knew that being around these homophobic idiots would be a necessity, Bryan and I chatted about growing thicker skin while changing in the bathroom together.

Once done, Bryan and I did sound check alone while the rest of them drank in the balcony. While tuning my bass, I walked in front of Bryan's drum kit puckering up at him as he hit the drumheads. He returned the air kisses as he winked.

# # # # #

Later on as Burnt Ash played, Bryan and I slid out of sight to walk amongst the crowd. During our stroll together, we noticed two gorgeous men in the pit. One of them was more buff than the other, and both were tall. The more muscular man had a Wretched tattoo on his back while the other had the reaper.

Not wanting to move, we stared at these two a bit. One had beautiful blue eyes, the other a caramel tan man with pupils either green or hazel. Bryan tapped me, whispering in my ear. "Like what you see gorgeous? I know I do ..."

Still gazing, I took my hood off pulling my ponytail out my jacket. That moment, I heard whispers and screams of my name and Bryan's as people noticed us.

"Yeah babe. You think they're ..." I stopped quickly as a fan came up shoving a CD and sharpie in my face.

Bryan paid the autograph seeker no attention. "Yes, Corey, most definitely. Why don't you take care of the signing, and I'll round up the entertainment for the evening." As he walked away, I put on my best celebrity act.

Once he came back, we headed to the secured area to spend some time alone. Since we were having company this evening, time alone would not be possible.

# # # # #

While on stage, I peeked at our new friends in the pit. Despite the attempts of the whores in front trying to get my attention, I continued to observe them from a far.

The two of them moshed along with all these seemingly straight fuckers. The muscular white man was taking people out left and right. His partner ran into people, pushing them into others.

I had always felt that the pit was a great means of being able to touch guys without being discovered. Before I was a musician, I loved going out there pushing and shoving dudes especially if they were attractive; it was a great way to cop a feel.

As I played "Fuckin' Amazin," Nicolai walked over slapping me on the back causing me to lunge forward a bit. I swore that if we were not on stage, I would be punching him right now.

He pulled my shoulder down to his level. "I see you eyeing those two dudes. I thought Bryan was the only one for you. Better yet, I thought I was your other man."

I was so shocked by that, I could not answer. Nicolai grinned at me after rubbing my side.

Once he started singing again, I walked back to Bryan's drum kit. I took a swig from the Jaeger he had left for me after giving him an air kiss. Whatever the hell just happened, I would have to deal with it later.

# # # # #

After we went off, Omerta came on whipping the crowd into a frenzy. Although we were the headliners, we had agreed to take turns playing the last slot. Besides, they were our best friends in the business.

Bryan went downstairs to get our new friends to watch Omerta with us. Once he returned with the couple, he introduced them to everyone there. When finished, Bryan brought the hot twosome over my way. Seeing these two up close put an immediate smile on my face.

"Jason, David, this is Corey our bass player." Bryan smiled at me while taking a drag of his joint.

"Hey man, it's a pleasure to meet cha. I'm David." The bigger one extended his hand grinning at me in the process. I accepted it turning my eyes toward his man.

Although David was quite the hot one, I could not help but look at his companion. His hazel eyes were mesmerizing, not to mention the caramel color of his skin.

Wanting to know his name, I reached out my hand toward him. "And you are ..."

"Jason, nice to meet you my man," he said with a smile and a firm handshake.

During Omerta's performance, we were so into it, there was not much room for chat. However, the looks that were exchanged between Jason and me said it all. David did not seem to mind either, which made it even better.

# # # # #

Once we separated ourselves from everyone else, Bryan, Jason, David, and I headed to our bus with liquor I had stolen from the venue. Bryan had gotten some more weed and cigarettes from one of the boys in Burnt Ash with a promise to replace them later on.

Immediately, we went to the back of the bus even though it was Nicolai's domain.

"Have a seat guys. I gotta piss, I'll be back." Bryan sat everything that was in his hands on the table, stole a kiss from me, and ran toward the restroom.

I took a seat between the two of them smacking both their legs. "So gents, how did two hot motha fucka's like you get together?" I reached for the stereo remote turning on some Lamb of God.

David laughed slapping my right hand that was on his knee. "Dunno, it just kind of happened. We are actually part of an open threesome with another man. He's not into this kind of music, more of a fan of the softer stuff. He's kind of a wuss!"

As Jason laughed, I chuckled as well not believing what I just heard. They were part of a threesome? Interested, I had to find out more. "So, you're sayin' there is another man involved in a permanent relationship with you two? Does that actually work?" I got up, getting four beers out the fridge then handing two their way while setting the other on the table for my Bryan.

"Yes it does, for us anyway. We've hung out together since high school. Who better to be with than two other guys you've known for ten plus years?" Jason opened the bottle, tossing the cap on the table.

"True, so true." I took a drag of my joint passing it to David.

Jason stood up and took off his wife beater. "Sorry it's hot in here."

The moment he stripped, I noticed the detailed ink on his arms along with the washboard ab muscles; he was ripped.

I licked my lips as he plopped back next to me. David took his off as well, showing that impressive body that I eyed during the show.

"Whoa …" I whispered as Bryan reappeared. I took another swig of beer after passing the weed to Jason.

"Well alright! Everyone comfortable?" Bryan sat on the couch next to Jason taking the joint out of his hands.

"I would say we are." I said turning up my bottle once again.

# # # # #

After almost an hour of chatting and laughing, I walked to my bunk grabbing lube and condoms to get everything going. When I appeared in front of them with necessities in hand, all of them smiled up at me, knowing exactly what time it was.

The moment I sat back down, David enveloped my lips with his, sending shocks through my body, making my cock instantly erect. I tossed our party favors on the floor, pulling David closer to me. Bryan put his hand in my zipper taking my dick out.

Within minutes, Bryans' mouth had swallowed me fully while his hand worked on my balls.

"Damn, ahh ..." I whispered as David kneaded my neck before engulfing my lips again.

I heard footsteps walk on the bus, but I did not even look to see who was there. Right then, I was in a trance feeling Bryan down below and David on my lips.

Seconds later, I felt another mouth on my nuts. I stretched both my arms out to push both heads further into my crotch. David released my lips before pushing my head a little to the right to kiss my neck. I looked down watching Jason and Bryan suck my dick with reckless abandon.

"Fuck ... ahh ..." I breathed pulling up my shirt, pinching my own nipple. David leaned down taking the other in his mouth, nibbling hard which I loved.

For a moment, I leaned back closing my eyes. Right then, I felt as if we were being observed. Whoever it was, they came on the bus and never left.

Curiosity got the best of me and I opened my eyes searching the room through the drug and sex haze to see whom our observer was. As all three of my lovers for tonight proceeded to ravage my body, my eyes met the beautiful greens of Nicolai.

I nodded and pulled David's head back up to meet mine. Knowing that Nicolai was standing there made this moment even more exciting.

Only a few moments passed before I heard Bryan get up and move the table. Jason took my length in his mouth, licking while grazing it with his teeth. I let my fingers tangle in his brown locks as my other hand had a firm hold on David's neck.

"Shit ..." I mouthed peering into David's gorgeous blue eyes. I looked back over at Nicolai, who was still there out of everyone's sight but mine.

Ready for more, I took my shirt off. Reaching for Jason, I grasped his shoulders as he looked up before joining me for a kiss. His lips were wet with my precum inciting me to force my tongue into his mouth. David united his with ours making this occasion even more mind blowing.

"Damn, that's hot." Bryan said while he stripped his clothes off.

I chuckled as I leaned back watching David and Jason continue to engulf one another. Nothing was hotter to me than seeing two men kiss intimately especially when they were hot like them.

"Ahem, gentlemen, please," said the now undressed, Bryan waving his hand to the blanketed spot he had cleared on the floor.

Chuckling, all of us got up shedding our clothes. I made sure that I stayed in the same spot, so I could view Nicolai hiding behind the curtain.

The minute I sat on the floor, Bryan consumed my lips, while David and Jason were giving me head.

“Isn’t this fun, baby?” Bryan whispered while combing my locks with his fingers.

“Mmm hmmm ...” I groaned as I had one eye peeking at our one-man audience.

Bryan reached for the condom and lube with our mouths still attached. He opened the bottle, squeezing some on his hand.

I smiled as Bryan began priming himself for me. My eyes dropped to his lovely dick, dripping with pre-passion juice. Thirsty, I knelt down taking him into my mouth. David and Jason adjusted themselves, so they could continue devouring me.

As I sucked him, I looked at his eyes roll in the back of his head. “Fuck ...” he yelled as I nuzzled him.

Out the corner of my eye, I saw David get up and grab the bottle. Once he had it, he began preparing his ass for entry. Jason stroked me while grasping his own hard one.

“Ahhh ...” Jason sighed as David knelt in front of him, taking Jason’s meat between his lips.

“Shit, baby I’m ready. Can’t wait any longer, I want you inside me now.” Bryan breathed.

I stopped sucking Bryan, leaning toward Jason giving him a quick kiss. He accepted while removing his hand from between my thighs.

Afterwards, I took a quick look at Nicolai rubbing himself in the shadows. I smirked at him as Bryan bent over in front of me. While putting the latex on, I licked my lips in his direction teasing him.

He returned my look with a wry smile, still grabbing his own hardness. He mouthed, "Your ass is mine later."

Amused, I nodded with a grin as I plunged into Bryan's opening.

"Fuck!" Bryan yelled as I filled him.

I turned my attention from Nicolai to Jason and David who were about to start themselves. Jason was shoulder to shoulder with me on the floor kneeling, arming his dick.

David arched his ass up in front of Jason's crotch, ready for Jason to invade him. In no time, he pierced his bigger lover with all seven or so inches.

"Ugh ... ohh Jas ..." David gasped as Jason started to work that hole.

Seeing him push into David aroused me so much, I lunged into Bryan harder. I also craved Jason's lips. With one hand on Bryans' back, I grabbed him enveloping his with my own.

"Mmmh ... Corey, damn." He said while slowly fucking his lover.

I moved my hand from Jason's neck down to Bryans' ass pulling him into me as he moved back onto my dick.

The feelings of Jason and Bryan created a lot of friction down below. I knew the eruption was not far off. Jason stopped kissing me before grasping onto his lovers biceps, driving himself deeper into him.

"Jason … damn … ahh," David yelled.

"Ooh God!" Bryan reached back for my hands, squeezing them tight.

I moved my hands to Bryans' shoulders as well, shoving into him recklessly. Readying myself for what was inevitable, I tilted my head back. As I inhaled, my chest along with my groin started to burn.

"Oh Goddamn! Shit!" I screamed pulling out, snapping the condom off. Within seconds, puddles of white liquid were on Bryans' backside. While I jerked my cock, Jason put his finger on my bulbous head taking the excess between his lips.

"Mmm …"Jason moaned as he kissed me again. I combed his scalp while my other hand massaged my juice into Bryan's skin.

Bryan rose, uniting his lips with ours. Once we broke, Jason thrust into David harder causing him to squeal. Bryan gave his cock a stroke while crawling in front of David's face.

With one eye on a spent Nicolai, I licked Jason's earlobe. Torturing him gave me so much satisfaction; I had to continue displaying my affection to one of my two new friends.

"Aw fuck …" Bryan breathed as he spurt on David's tongue, which he took in gladly.

"Ahhhh! David …" Jason squealed as he removed his dick from his man's hole. Jagging wildly, he shot blotches onto

David's backside. I rubbed my finger through it, tasting some as he came.

While I watched him, I caressed his neck. He was so pretty. Once he opened his eyes, he took me in, pushing his tongue between my lips.

"Jason ...mmmhh ..." I gasped as he wrapped one arm around my shoulder. I gripped his dick in my hand, smearing his juices onto the fine hairs that surrounded his jewels.

"Corey ... you are fuckin' amazing." He breathed kissing me roughly. Still involved, I smiled at him quoting from one of our hit songs. He did not know how amazing I could be just yet.

"Oh shit ..." David whispered as he sat to my left leaning against the couch.

We stopped, noticing Bryan swallowing David completely causing him to writhe. David's humongous hand pressed Bryan's head down onto his length. Jason moved down to join Bryan on David's crotch. I rubbed David's nipples while encasing his mouth with mine.

"Shi ..." he moaned as I took one of his nubs between my fingers, tugging it until it hardened beneath my touch. "Ooh God!" David screamed as the liquid shot out of his dick.

I looked down observing Jason and Bryan taking squirts from David onto their lips. Longing for a sample, I got some off the tip of his mushroom head for myself while peering into his beautiful blues.

"Mmhmm ..." I smiled at him approvingly. He returned it while pulling my face in for a smooch.

Jason and Bryan rose, diving in, tongues first. All of us shared some of David's natural wine, making this a hot scene that you would only see in a porno.

Collective moans and groans filled the air as we kissed and groped one another. As my three companions continued to partake in our passionate activities, I lifted my eyes searching for Nicolai.

Once I found those piercing pupils that I still loved, he smiled at me puckering up in my direction. Maybe I did not hate Nicolai as much as I had thought. Seeing him enjoy our display turned me on; not only that I felt satisfied knowing that our moment drove him to eruption.

I winked at him as I grabbed my three lovers to savor more of tonight's activities. After all, bus call was not until 5:00 am. There was enough lust along with the delicacies of liquor and weed to last us, including Nicolai, the rest of the night.

MORE THAN AN AUTOGRAPH
By Aiden Lovely

A good song stayed in my head for hours. And a gorgeous face lingered in my heart forever. It had been more than a year since I wasted hours massaging my member between my hands and the computer screen, jerking off at pictures of Sammie Sixx, the rock star. My mind was so vivid. It was easy to imagine his lips curled around my swollen cock and his shaggy blond hair bobbing up and down.

In his earlier days, he was a pornstar, meaning he must screw with skill. And I loved watching every minute of his plump, pale ass bouncing up and down, a huge cock pounding him. But somewhere in the back of my mind, I wished I was the man taking him from behind. I loved his music just as much. I always bought his CDs just to hear his smooth voice, a little raspy from all the alcohol and cigarettes. And whenever he played a guitar solo, my member throbbed and twitched.

As a celebrity reporter for *GMYP Magazine*, I was forced to stalk Sammie, which I didn't mind too much. The job was nerve-wrecking, but my mission was simple: find out why Sammie started his solo career during his tour in Maine.

The cold rain soaked my shoulders. I had been standing outside of his suite for hours. His room displayed the gorgeous view of the seashore – very pretty when it wasn't pouring out. You could actually see the sunlight glisten over the water like little twinkling stars.

My editor was breathing down my neck. He called my cell phone every ten minutes for a progress report, "Did you get any information on Sammie?" or "Look into his suite, you could get a good photo of him."

I stopped answering his calls. But, I was ready, armed with a camera and a pair of binoculars to get a good story. If I didn't get the scoop on him, I'd lose my job – that was not an option. But this hadn't been my first time stalking Sammie either. I had been asked to dig through his garbage before, steal a piece of his mail and so on.

I shimmed up the nearest tree, bending my legs over a branch and hanging upside down. I looked through the binoculars, pointing them toward the window of Sammie's room. I couldn't see anything, not even a piece of his hair.

"This is stupid." I closed my eyes and rested my head, then took a deep breath. I stretched my arms and then held the binoculars to my eyes. "Hey there?" A talented voice said from behind me.

Bang to the face, I crashed out of the tree. My eyes met his patent leather boots. He stood there with slouchy posture. I couldn't take my eyes off him, moving up every inch of his skinny body.

My stomach was twisting in knots silently, the butterfly feeling and the heaviness closing my throat. My spit was stale, washing back and forth, trying to moisten the dryness in my mouth. My legs wobbled like jello and my heartbeat was the only noise I could hear. The sky was gray, and the battering raindrops crowded the ground between us. I stood up, balancing my hands on knees. My cold breath came out in chunks, making little clouds before me – before him – Sammie Sixx. And anything at all that I had planned to say had vanished.

Sammie's hair was blond, bright like the sun, feathered and spiked. Eyeliner traced his eyes, and his silver earrings dangled. His well-hung member hid behind the rough leather, squeezed by the fabric. And his strong thighs supported his bubble butt. His moist tongue wetting his bottom lip, his trail of sexy Chanel Egoiste following every step he took. I stood there, trembling, mesmerized.

"You've been outside here for a long time," he said, crossing his arms. This was it. I was about to lose my job – or even worse, be arrested for stalking.

I batted my eyes and poked my lip out, "I'm waiting for a friend. They have a room in the hotel."

He looked at me, "Bullshit. You carry binoculars on the daily?"

He smirked, "What are you? A crazy fan?" The more he spoke, the more his alcohol breath mixed with his cologne – that was just like him drinking in the middle of the day. I was speechless. I had to cover myself quickly.

"Yeah." I took a quick breath. "I'm so sorry. I'm a really crazy fan. Please understand."

"I'll give you an autograph. Got some paper?"

"Sorry. I don't have any paper. Can we grab a bite to eat instead? Pretty, pretty please. That would make today really special. Please. I'm you're biggest fan." I forced a tear to escape my eye. He snorted and then looked away, then back at me.

"Hmm ... lunch. Ok. I am kinda lonely. Let's go to my suite." And just like that I was climbing his heels up the stairs to his lovely chamber. The door slammed behind me. And already Sammie was sucking on his bottle of liquor.

There was pizza on the table surrounded by empty beer cans and condoms. Even the bed was a mess. He patted the seat next to him on the small couch. He pushed his liquor bottle in my face, "Want some?"

"No thanks," I said, drying myself off with a towel, and then I turned my cell phone off.

"Take off your wet clothes. You might wet up my room." Obedient as a puppy, I removed my shirt and my wet pants, revealing my damp muscular chest, sitting in my boxers. I was embarrassed. I didn't want him to notice my throbbing boner, so hard as if it were made of rock, and having a big cock twitching in your boxers was damn hard to hide. Sammie didn't notice.

"Mr. Sixx, um ..."

"Call me Sammie."

"So sorry," I cleared my throat, "Um, so w-what's been up?"

"What? What do you want to know?" The whisky ran down his chin.

"Um, I mean, why did you go solo? Was it something more than what you told the news reporter?"

Sammie squinted. "Well." he said, "I was dating the drummer of my band. I mean, he was good in bed. Real good. But, every time we changed a position, he tweeted about it. It was embarrassing." Listening to his talking about his sex-life wasn't the best idea. All I could think about was his moist lips wrapped around my cock or pummeling him more than he could bear. I blushed. And then he noticed my cock ready to explode in my boxers. He sized me up. He reached out toward it with his soft hands, gently stroking my cock through the cotton boxers.

"You're pretty big. Bigger than my last boyfriend." His lustful eyes traced my body. "I'm in a good mood. Wanna try your thing out on me?" He gave a flirtatious smile. And there was no way I'd refuse this. He finished his bottle of liquor and then threw his shirt to the floor. The noise from his fingers fiddling with the zipper on his skin-tight leather pants filled the entire room, his pearly flesh before me. I licked my lips, plagued with so much pent-up passion. We moved to the bed.

My muscular arm was draped over Sammie's small shoulders as his hot fingertips scraped against my sweaty chest. Sammie's nipples were erect, looking like rubies. And his saucy smile beamed in the artificial light. My fingers curled in his shaggy mane. And my other hand softly massaged his body. With his hair clutched between my big fingers, I pressed my moist lips against his. I slowly parted his lips with my hot tongue, allowing me to taste him. His hands rested on my throbbing shaft, aching to be released, jutting through the fabric. I didn't know how much longer I could bear without taking Sammie. His small, pale hands cupped my balls, as he sucked and pulled on my bottom lip, his tongue coiling, wrapping around mine. His guilty eyes were tightly closed as he managed to pull himself on top of me. His weak body shuddered at the touch of my hands caressing his plump ass. My fingers aligned with his crack, gliding up and down, back and forth.

He yearned for more, pushing his chest on mine. I felt the vibration of his heart pounding in his chest. I was surprised I couldn't hear his heart beat. Sammie traced the outline of my six-pack, trailing his blazing fingers on my scorching manhood, tightly squeezing, pulling, and rubbing it. He couldn't wait to have his fun with it. Our hot lips remained locked as I rubbed his back. His body was on fire as he fiddled with the elastic rim on my boxers, teasing me.

Sammie's hot breath rested on my nipples, now sucking and kissing them. My rod now exposed in the light, hard and fleshy red. He didn't hesitate, his hands stroking it. His shaggy hair brushing on my chest was enough to make me come at that moment. My cock greeted his lips. Then he engulfed it in his mouth. He could barely keep it in. A thin coat of saliva surrounded the tip, his warm mouth capturing it, his head bobbing up and down. His mouth was twisting it, squeezing it, and his tongue was teasing it. He held it by the base, quickly striking the tip with his tongue like a snake.

I played with his hair, moaning wildly as it tickled my groin. I tried to relax; enjoy the pleasure. His lascivious tongue licked his bottom lip. He looked at me, my precum leaking out of the corners of his mouth. He knew what I wanted.

He sat up, his body begging me to take him. He raised his butt, arched his back. And my cock pushed against the tight entrance. It pressed on his soft pink anus, the naughty rock star dying to be pounded. He sat on my fat shaft, only letting the tip enter and then quickly pulled it out.

Instantly, I pushed him down. My libido crowded my mind. And now all I could do was fuck him. Sammie's hair tickled my nose, his head rocking back and forth, his body eager for me to push inside. I mounted him. My throbbing manhood penetrated his juicy hole. His voice was husky. His skinny arms thrashed about, his teeth biting the sheet, gripping and pulling with his fingers, his face flushed, me; pounding his ass. He cried out. His eyebrows wrinkled and his eyes were closed. His body was writhing under my muscular torso. My strong arms captured him, straddling him around his waist. And then I plunge all the inches of my member up him, stopping at my balls, his moans were mixed with pleasure and pain, hiding his blushed face in the pillow. And being the type of guy I was, even when Sammie's member was swollen – about to burst, my fingers circled the base of his cock, squeezing, holding him back. I wanted us to come together. I gritted my teeth and increased my speed. The bed rocked back and forth. It squeaked as if it were going to break.

My flesh was layered with sweat. I pushed in deeper, gripping Sammie's shoulders, our bodies harmonized. And then, Sammie's body fell limp. I shot my load in him. And his load gushed onto to my fingers.

My chest was heaving. Sammie was out of breath, too. His eyes were kind of open but kind of shut. And then he dozed off. I retreated from his body. I pulled on my pants, watching him sleep. Big, thick globs of sperm rolled from between Sammie's plump ass. His red golf ball-stretched anus was contracting – searching for a fat cock to fill his, now lonely body. The sticky goo spilled from between like icing, drizzling down to his thighs, and his soft voice cooing from the pleasure. His breath rested on the pillow.

The door slammed behind me, and I jogged down to the lobby, my heart racing. I couldn't believe what just happened. Sleeping with a drunken rock star? I couldn't tell my editor that. I didn't know what to tell him. But I wished I could thank Sammie. He did give me more than just an autograph.

POUNDING THE SKINS
By HL Champa

I knew I was in danger of breaking the cardinal rule. You don't fuck your drummer. Band mates and sex just don't mix. Everyone knew that, including me. But, after taking one look at Trevor, I was hooked. Besides, it wasn't as if he was our full-time drummer or anything. He was just sitting in as a replacement, until Derrick's arm healed. In my mind, that made him more than fair game. It made him too big a temptation to ignore. Derrick could tell I was interested from the first moment he walked into the rehearsal studio with Trevor in tow.

I devoured the newbie with my eyes, taking in his lanky frame while he set up his drums, oblivious to my stares. Derrick, however, wasn't. He pulled me aside and told me what I already knew; that I should keep my hands to myself and my dick in my pants.

"I know what you're thinking, Nick. Just forget it."

"What am I thinking, Derrick?"

"Just leave Trevor alone. He's here to drum, not to get you off."

"Okay, okay, Derrick. I won't touch him. Saving him for yourself?"

"Hardly, Nick. He's too innocent for me. That's the type you like."

"Fuck you, Derrick. I think I can manage to stay away."

"See that you do. This tour isn't just an excuse for you bang everyone in sight, Nick. This is important to all of us."

He knew there were some things you just didn't fuck with. But, no groupie or hanger-on had ever piqued my interest like Trevor did. Damn, why did this forbidden fruit have to look so damn sweet?

Derrick had met Trevor years before, while they were both drumming for other bands. When Derrick decided to let his anger over his ex-girlfriend take over and punch a wall two weeks before the second half of our club tour, Trevor seemed like a logical choice to replace him until his broken knuckles healed. He was in between bands and was a quick study, and he could pick up Derrick's moves without too much effort. Or so Derrick said. I honestly didn't care whether he hit all the right beats. All I wanted to know was what his lips would look like wrapped around my cock.

My right mind, my logical mind told me Derrick was right. I should stay away from Trevor. He seemed young, naïve and way too nice. It all added up to trouble. Fucking Trevor, despite its obvious short-term advantages, would end up being a bad move. If nothing else, it could end a friendship that really mattered to Derrick. Now, how could I tell that to my dick? Being in a band, even a crappy band like ours, was supposed to be an open invitation. Rock and roll came with sex and drugs. Staying away from gorgeous, available guys wasn't part of the plan. Hell, meeting guys like Trevor was half the reason I joined the band in the first place.

Trevor turned out to be a great drummer. Derrick was right about his talent, but that was the least of my concerns. Band practices had become a test of my resolve and will. Watching Trevor's arms flex and flail as he drummed was more than a distraction. It was a total turn-on. I missed bass cues on every song because my mind and my eyes were occupied with Trevor and his movements. He sweat a lot, his shirt soaked through by the time we broke for the night. Derrick sat in on our practices, in case Trevor had any questions or problems with the songs. He was also there to make sure I kept my promise to be on my best behavior. Not that Derrick ever gave me a chance to make a move. As soon as practice ended, he would steal Trevor away at the end of the night, so I couldn't get close to him. If Derrick weren't my best friend, I would have kicked his ass for cock blocking me like that.

#####

Finally, Derrick gave up trying to babysit Trevor and me, and we had a few rehearsals without his watchful eye. In order to put Derrick at ease in the beginning, I had been on my best behavior. Trevor was right next to me every day for the last week, and we had barely spoken. Between my hyper-vigilance and Trevor's shy nature, it was the perfect storm to keep us both quiet. But, now that Derrick and the other guys were gone and we had the space all to ourselves, it was clear that Trevor's silence was about more than just being timid. I was sure that Derrick had warned him about me. Every time I would take a step toward him, for any reason, Trevor would move away, trying to maintaining a safe distance.

It wasn't that noticeable at first, but one night, after rehearsal was over, I dropped one of my cords on the ground near his feet; he practically jumped as I bent down to reach for it. When our eyes met, Trevor looked embarrassed at his overreaction. I just smiled, watching the flush rise in his cheeks. He retreated behind the drums and sat on his ratty stool, looking at his watch. I could hear Derrick's voice in my ear telling me to be good, but I ignored it. Stepping closer to Trevor once again, I decided it was time to say something.

"Sorry, Trevor. I didn't mean to startle you before. I know we haven't had much time to talk since you got here, but if you give me a chance, most people think I'm a pretty nice guy."

He shuffled his feet back and forth against the dirty floor, reluctantly meeting my eyes before looking away again.

"You do seem like a nice guy, Nick. But, Derrick said it would be better if I kept my distance from you. So, I don't get distracted. So, we ... don't get distracted."

I laughed, thinking of Derrick talking to Trevor like a concerned father, warning him about the dangers of getting to know me too well. Trevor was still blushing, but I couldn't resist another little push.

"Distracted by what, Trevor?"

He looked adorably confused and stammered as he answered me.

"Well, he didn't say anything, well, specific. But, I'm pretty sure he was talking about, um, you know, physically distracted."

I laughed again at his cuteness. He stood up and walked across the room, pretending to be very interested in the view of the alley out the taped-over window. His fists were opening and closing as he shuffled from one foot to the other. When I reached him, I put my hand on his shoulder, and he surprised me by turning around. He looked at my hand, his eyes wide with a mix of fear and excitement. I stepped a few inches closer, until our faces were only a few inches apart and his back hit the window frame. His chest was rising and falling at a rapid rate, his dilated pupils darting back and forth between my lips and my eyes.

"Are you physically distracted now, Trevor?"

"Yes. Extremely so. But, Derrick is right. This is a mistake, Nick."

I moved my hand from his shoulder to his neck and pulled him right up against me. His hands held onto my back for dear life, gripping my shirt in his fists. My voice hid my nervousness, coming out stronger than I felt inside.

"It doesn't feel like a mistake. In fact, it feels like a great idea to me."

I punctuated my last words by looping my finger into his belt and pulling his hips to mine. He was hard, and as I pressed into him, I could feel his cock twitch against me. A little gasp came out of his mouth, and I smiled, satisfied that I had proved my point.

"Nick, we ... we just can't tell Derrick, okay?"

"Fine with me, Trevor. It can just be our little secret."

He seemed placated by my words, so much so that he leaned closer, letting his lips touch mine for the first time. His tongue had no trouble plunging inside my mouth, his hands now firmly planted on my ass. I thought back to what Derrick said and couldn't suppress a giggle from bubbling up.

"What? What's funny, Nick?"

"Nothing. Just something Derrick said about you being innocent."

Trevor grinded his cock into mine, his teeth nipped at my neck before he responded.

"Derrick doesn't know everything about me, Nick."

"Obviously."

He pushed me back, toward the ratty couch that sat against the wall. I sat down, and he immediately straddled me, his mouth back on mine before I could say another word. Despite his protests, there was a bit of inexperience in his groping hands, his eagerness a welcome change from the jaded hipsters we met on the road. Our shirts and pants were quickly on the floor, the urgency of our desire making things move quicker than they needed to. In an effort to slow Trevor down, I moved him from my lap, just long enough to find the coat I had thrown near the couch at the start of rehearsal. I gave one last fleeting thought to Derrick and his warnings, before digging into my jacket pocket for the condoms and lube I had been planning to use on Trevor for over a week. I figured a little wishful thinking couldn't hurt.

Once I got back to the couch, Trevor was right back onto my lap, our hard cocks rubbing against each other as I pulled him closer and took one of his tiny nipples into my mouth. While he was distracted, I popped open the lube and began smearing the liquid onto his puckered asshole. He started groaning and pushing back against my fingers. I strafed his nipple with my teeth, just as the tip of my index finger slipped inside him. I expected him to pull away, but he grabbed my head, holding my mouth right where it was. He squirmed above me, and managed to work my finger inside him almost all the way. Trevor sat back, licking his lips as he stared down at me.

"Shit, Nick. I'm tired of waiting. Fuck me."

His brazen words shocked me. Shy Trevor was clearly long gone; his lascivious eyes devoured me as I rolled the condom onto my waiting cock. He took me in hand and positioned himself above me, guiding me as the tip spread his asshole open. I closed my eyes, just for a moment as I felt him open up, a little at a time, his tight heat covering my cock.

Trevor was silent above me, and my eyes went from his sweet face to watch the last few inches of his cock disappear into my ass. His hand wrapped around his dick, jerking himself as he adjusted to my cock in his ass.

"You were right, Nick. This was a fucking great idea."

I put my hands on his hips as he started to ride me, his tight ass squeezing my cock with each move. He leaned forward and kissed me slow and sweet, his free hand pressing hard against my chest. Trevor was moving faster than I wanted him to, pushing me too close to the edge. As much as I wanted to keep watching him bounce around on my dick, I knew I would blow my wad too soon if I didn't slow him down. I stayed inside him as I pushed him down on the couch, flat on his back. I held his ankles in my hands and slowly pulled my cock nearly all the way out of his ass. I only stayed still for a few seconds, but Trevor whimpered as if it had been an hour. I smirked at his distress and then thrust back inside him, repeating the same slow torture a few more times. He looked down and watched me fuck him, his eyes transfixed on the place where our bodies met.

"God, Nick. Fuck. I'm so close. Oh fuck."

His hand moved frantically over his cock, jerking hard as I continued to fuck him nice and slow. His eyes were pinched shut, the muscles of his body tensed at once, and I watched him come all over his sweaty stomach and chest. As the last shot filled his navel, I couldn't hold back any longer. Putting his feet on my shoulders, I pounded into him with abandon, days of pent up frustration and lust flowing through me as I looked down into his tranquil brown eyes. I came harder than I had in months, his tight asshole milking every last drop of cum and every last bit of energy out of me.

I could barely move as I pulled away from Trevor, collapsing on the couch in a heap. My eyes felt too heavy to open, my whole body sated and loose. I heard Trevor stirring next to me, felt his lips on my neck as I struggled to stay awake.

"Derrick is full of shit, isn't he, Nick?"

"Absolutely. Completely."

We cleaned up and started to get dressed. The heat of the moment had been replaced by a new comfort; all the tension and awkwardness had disappeared. I couldn't resist pulling him close and kissing those sweet lips one more time.

"So, Nick. I was thinking I could still use some extra practice. How about tomorrow night? We could pick up right where we left off."

"Sounds good. After all, Derrick does want you to be prepared. We wouldn't want to let him down."

He smiled at me one last time before walking out into the night. I picked up my coat and thought about that old cardinal rule. Ah, fuck rules. This was rock and roll.

STORM INSIDE YOU
By Kitty Key

It's raining when they arrive in West Palm Beach. The palm trees dotting the road they're driving along thrash in the wind. John watches a woman in a pink rain slicker and matching high-heels trying to walk into the wind, clutching her purse against her chest with one hand and the baseball cap on her head with the other. Her blonde ponytail is soaked against the back of her, neck and mascara is running down her cheeks. He smirks a little between drags on his cigarette, remembering watching various girlfriends take hours to look like they only did their hair and make-up in minutes, and thinks that this girl must've looked like that before the rain.

When the bus pulls up in front of the hotel, they're staying in for the time being, John stubs out his cigarette and slides out of the booth in the kitchenette, heading toward the front of the bus without bothering to inform his sleeping band-mates that they've arrived. Someone will tell them, eventually. He follows the driver down the steps and waits under the awning on the sidewalk, out of the rain, for someone to hand him his overnight bag. Vaguely, he wonders if anyone bothered to book him a smoking room this time or if he's going to have to wander back down here later. For a moment, he reconsiders quitting, but then the driver is handing him his bag, and he forgets all about that.

Once inside the hotel room, John throws his bag down on the dresser and gives the room a quick once-over. It looks like the last room he spent the night in. Maybe, he thinks, that most of this tour is an illusion; that they haven't really been traveling anywhere all this time, except that the venues all look different, so it can't be true. He glances at the alarm clock and wonders if the hotel bar is open. He's pretty sure that he has enough time before sound-check to grab a drink.

Inside the bar, he sits in a booth at the back with his back to the door, hoping that no one who glances inside will notice him sitting there and come over to talk. When the bartender brings his beer, he wonders why he ordered it. Most children of alcoholics either become fanatically against drinking or alcoholics themselves. John likes to think he's found some kind of middle ground with that, but it's been his experience that most addicts think they're just fine until someone forces them into rehab or they die. So he only takes a sip out of the bottle and then peels off the label instead.

When he hears someone approaching behind him, he doesn't move or look up. Maybe if he pretends hard enough that he's invisible, they'll go away. It doesn't work. A napkin and a pen are set in front of him.

"May I have your autograph?"

The voice sounds vaguely familiar, just slightly off in tone, but John doesn't look up as he scrawls his name on the napkin. It's only when a drop of something, water, maybe, lands on the napkin, that he tilts his head upward. His eyes meet pale green ones, and he immediately smiles as he gestures for the other man to take a seat.

"Nick? What are you doing here?"

"I heard you'd be in town," Nick answers as he slides into the booth across from John.

John tilts his head, noting that Nick is soaked; his white T-shirt sticking to his skin and little rivulets of water are running down his neck. He's mesmerized by the way the water pools in the hollow of Nick's throat before moving downward. It isn't until Nick clears his throat that John realizes he's let the conversation lapse. He looks up and meets Nick's eyes again, noting the start of a beard as his eyes drift upward. Now that he's looking into Nick's eyes for more than five seconds, he notices a change in them. It's subtle, but it's there. He wonders what he's missed since he last saw Nick. Besides the new boyfriend he heard about on the news, Nick's lucky that his audience doesn't care whom he fucks as long as he still shakes his ass on stage. John certainly doesn't have that luxury.

"Earth to John."

Nick waves his hand and John blinks. "You're soaked."

"Well, that's what happens when you decide to walk in the rain instead of taking a taxi," Nick says with a grin.

John laughs softly and shakes his head. "Want to come up to my room and get dried off?"

"If you don't mind."

As always, Nick is gracious, but there's a hint of something in his voice. John can't quite put his finger on it; he almost sounds amused but that's not it. Teasing, that's it, John thinks as he pays for the beer.

They walk across the lobby and into the elevator in silence, both acting as though they don't know the other. It's something they're both used to doing, for various reasons. John doesn't think about his motivations for doing it this time. At the door to his room, he uses the keycard and holds it open for Nick.

"Plenty of towels in the bathroom," John says as he gestures that way.

"Thanks."

Nick smiles at him before kicking off his shoes and then opening the bathroom door. He doesn't close it all the way before stripping out of his T-shirt. John thinks that he probably shouldn't stand there spying on him, but his body has other ideas and isn't quite inclined to move just yet. He watches the drops of water move down Nick's back, mesmerized yet again. Before his mind is able to catch up with his body, John is stepping forward, into the bathroom. His index finger runs down Nick's spine, tracing where the water had gone. Nick looks at him over his shoulder.

"May I help you?"

There's that teasing note again. John opens his mouth and then closes it. He shakes his head. Nick smiles and reaches for a towel. He runs it through his hair roughly before throwing it around his shoulders. With his hair sticking up in all directions, he looks a lot less polished than he usually does. A lot more tempting. John blinks as the thought comes, and Nick grins at him in the mirror.

"Are you going to let me out of here or what?"

The second part of the question almost seems like a challenge. Although, John thinks, he could just be hearing what he wants to hear. Either way, he finds himself dipping his head down to press his lips to Nick's neck. Nick's breath quickens ever so slightly, and John trails his tongue up to his ear, licking away the few remaining droplets of water. Their eyes meet in the mirror.

"I can't. I'm seeing someone ..."

"I won't tell him if you won't," John interrupts.

Nick nods slightly and then tilts his head to the side to give John better access to his neck. John watches him in the mirror, wondering how Nick is going to explain whatever marks John leaves on him to whatever-his-name-is.

"John ..."

There's desperation in Nick's voice, as if John doesn't touch him this second, life as Nick knows it is going to end. John bends his head again, sucking and licking at Nick's neck as his hands lay flat against his stomach. When Nick moans, one of John's palms slide up to Nick's collarbone, the other slides down to cup Nick's cock through his pants. Nick arches up on the balls of his feet, toward John's hands.

Nick's breath is coming out in breathy little gasps now. In comparison to Nick's speaking and singing voice, both deep bass tones, they sound a little strange. John slowly undoes Nick's pants and then slides them and his underwear off his hips. Nick steps out of them, and now he's completely naked except for that towel. John's fingers trace the curve of Nick's ass before his hands move up his back to grab the towel and pull it away before he grabs Nick's wrist and spins him around to face him. Nick's eyes are wide, and his face is flushed. John wants to see him writhing on the not-exactly-pristine white hotel sheets, sweat pooling at the hollow of his throat instead of rain. His thumb caresses Nick's inner wrist before he lets go of him. Without a word, he turns and heads into the bedroom, stripping out of his clothes as he goes before turning down the bedspread.

He's not surprised to find Nick standing right behind him when he turns around. John grabs his wrist again, propelling him into the bed. He watches Nick settle against the pillows, legs spread, fingers trailing down his neck while John finishes undressing himself, tossing clothes across the room. John crawls into the other side of the bed and lies down next to Nick, on his side. He puts the palm of his hand on Nick's flat stomach while he uses the other to prop up his own head. Nick turns slightly and brushes his lips against John's.

It's the smallest, fleeting touch, but it's like a switch gets flipped in John's head. Suddenly, John doesn't just want to admire and study Nick, he wants to possess him and devour him.

His hands, his mouth, his body, they try to be all over Nick, all at once, leaving behind bruises and scrapes and bites. Every motion, causes Nick to writhe and moan, his fingers digging hard enough into the sheets to start to pull them off the bed.

"Oh, God, John, please fuck me."

Over the rush, John doesn't hear Nick at first, but when he does, it's like that flipped switch is put into overdrive. His arm reaches for the shaving kit he dumped on the night stand earlier, and he rifles around for a condom and lube. Meanwhile, Nick sucks on his right nipple while he pinches the left, which is more than a bit distracting. When he's finally found what he needs, John flips Nick over onto his stomach and spreads his ass cheeks, revealing his hole. He sweeps over it with little flicks of his tongue that catch the rim and make Nick arch back against him, forcing him to lick harder, go deeper, until Nick is a writhing, panting mess.

John blindly grabs for the lube and coats two fingers before pushing them inside Nick. He fucks them in and out, getting Nick ready, even though Nick is panting "please, John, now, please," every time John twists his fingers and brushes that sweet spot inside him. Sweat is pooling in the little dip of Nick's lower back, and John can't help but lave his tongue over it before removing his fingers.

He's about to put the condom on, when Nick flips over and grabs it, doing it for him. Instead of flipping back onto his stomach, Nick grabs his legs and pulls them toward his chest. It's a beautiful sight, his cock hard and weeping from the slit, his hole shining and winking at him with every heaving breath Nick takes.

"C'mon, John, want this," Nick practically growls when John gets caught up in admiration.

John grabs Nick's legs, and he slides inside that tight hole, pausing only a moment for the other man to adjust before he's fucking Nick hard and fast. The headboard is hitting the wall, and Nick's head is in danger of hitting the headboard, but he doesn't seem to be aware of that at the moment. His eyes are glazed over with pleasure, his mouth hanging open as little growls escape his throat, and sweat is glistening on his chest and neck as he reaches to stroke his own cock. John isn't sure where to kiss him first. His mouth is hungry against Nick's flesh and lips. He thinks Nick is the best thing he's ever tasted.

When Nick comes, it's without inhibition, with a near scream that almost sounds musical. John can't hold back then, and he buries his face against Nick's neck and let's go, coming so hard, he sees stars behind his eyelids.

Later, when John wakes up, it's stopped raining and Nick is gone without a trace. As John takes a shower, he wonders if Nick was an illusion, much like he's been thinking the whole tour has been. But when he comes out of the shower, he's sees that a message has appeared in the steam, as though someone had written on the mirror with a wet finger.

Thanks for the towel. Love, N.

Below that is the outline of a mouth puckered in a kiss. John grins before wiping the steam away.

ABOUT THE CONTRIBUTORS

AIDEN LOVELY is a freelance writer and poet. Lovely is also a member of the LG Writing Group. He was born in New Hampshire and dreams of moving to France.

DERRICK DELLA GIORGIA was born in Italy and currently lives between Manhattan and Rome. His work has been published in several anthologies and literary magazines: "Courtesy of the Hotel" in *Island Boys* (Alyson Books), "Couch with a View" in *Cruising for Bad Boys* (STARbooks Press), "A Secret Worth Keeping" in *Pretty Boys & Roughnecks* (STARbooks Press), "Pyramids in Rome" in *Best Gay Love Stories 2010* (Alyson Books), "Antimatter Matt" in *Unmasked II: More Erotic Tales of Gay Superheroes* (STARbooks Press), "Santa's Red Furry Briefs" in *Unwrapped: Erotic Holiday Tales* (STARbooks Press), "Panoply" on *Six Sentences*, "Heart Tartare" on *writers'DOJO*, "Connecting my Camera 2" in *Video Boys* (STARbooks Press), "How Did You Meet Philippe Hcnirt?" in *Boys Getting Ahead* (STARbooks Press), "Like a Green Olive on a Toothpick" in *Teammates* (STARbooks Press), "Number 023 of the 200 Made" in *Biker Boys: Gay Erotic Stories* (Cleis Press). Visit him at www.derrickdellagiorgia.com.

FOX LEE is an erotic fiction writer living in the Midwest. Fox has written several short stories and is currently at work on an erotic novel. When not writing, Lee enjoys large amounts of coffee and learning Cantonese swear words.

HL CHAMPA has stories in numerous anthologies including *Men at Noon, Monsters at Midnight*, *Video Boys*, *Tight Ends* and *College Boys*. If you prefer your erotica in electronic form, shorts stories can be found at Dreamspinner

Press, Ravenous Romance and Torquere Press. Find more online at heidichampa.blogspot.com.

Published in dozens of gay erotic anthologies, **JAY STARRE** pumps out fiction from his home in Vancouver, Canada. His short stories can be found in STARbooks titles such as *Love in a Lock-Up*, *Don't Ask, Don't Tie Me Up*, *Unmasked I* and *II*, *Boys Caught in the Act*, *Pretty Boys & Roughnecks*, *Unwrapped*, *Service with a Smile*, *Men at Noon, Monsters at Midnight*, *Boys Getting Ahead*, *Nerdvana*, *SexTime*, *Cruising for Bad Boys*, *Boys Will Be Boys*, *Ride Me Cowboy*, *Muscle Worshipers*, and *Daddy's Boyz*. His steamy gay historical novels *Erotic Tales of the Knights Templar* and *Lusty Adventures of the Knossos Prince* are also published by STARbooks Press.

KITTY KEY shares a condo with two adorable rescue dogs. When she's not taking them for long walks on the beach, she works for an international marketing firm. She loves Indian food and punk rock and can't get enough of seeing the cute gay couples with dogs in her neighborhood.

South African, **LEW BULL,** recently had his fifth novel published, titled *Shadows*. This novel adds to his collection of mystery stories titled, *Power Buddies*; *Wet, Wild & Willing*; *The Bonds of Friendship*; and *Caribbean Cruising*. Added to these are his two recently published anthologies, one of exotic cocktail recipes accompanied by equally erotic stories entitled, *Cocktales*, and the other titled *Mystique*. Other recent anthologies that contain his work include, *Taken by Force*; *Boys Will Be Boys*; *Don't Ask, Don't Tie Me Up*; *Service with a Smile*; *Pretty Boys & Roughnecks*; *Special Forces*; and *SexTime*.

MARTHA J ALLARD lives and writes in Flint, Michigan, despite all the warnings. Her short fiction has been published in places like *Talebones* and *Not One of Us*. She is currently working on a novel about the spaces between Heaven and Hell.

MICHAEL BRACKEN's short fiction has been published or is forthcoming in *Best Gay Romance 2010*, *Biker Boys*, *Black Fire*, *Country Boys*, *Freshmen*, *Hot Blood: Strange Bedfellows*, *The Mammoth Book of Best New Erotica 4*, *Men*, *Muscle Men*, *Teammates*, *Ultimate Gay Erotica 2006*, and many other anthologies and periodicals.

MICHAEL MANDRAKE is a happily married parent of two in Chicago. He freelances for www.fourteeng.net, the metal music site.

R. TALENT is the bastard seed that STARbooks Press thought they wiped away on the cum towel. He has been published in such anthologies as *Love in a Lock-Up*, *Don't Ask, Don't Tie Me Up*, *Ride Me Cowboy*, *Teammates*, and *Video Boys*. He is still driving his big-rig, still playing poker, and still working on his novella.

R. W. CLINGER travels between Pittsburgh and Florida. His hobbies include men-watching, boy-bar hopping and beachcombing. His recent works have appeared in STARbooks Press's *Unwrapped* and *Pretty Boys & Roughnecks*. R. W. is currently at work on a string of new gay erotic stories, which you can enjoy soon.

ROB ROSEN, author of the novels *Sparkle: The Queerest Book You'll Ever Love* and *Divas Las Vegas*, has been published to date in more than 100 anthologies, most notably the STARbooks Press collections: *Ride Me Cowboy*, *Service with A Smile*, *Unmasked II: More Erotic Tales of Gay Superheroes*, *Cruising for Bad Boys*, *SexTime: Erotic Stories of Time Travel*, *Pretty Boys & Roughnecks*, *Teammates*, *Boys Getting Ahead*, *Unwrapped – Erotic Holiday Tales*, *Video Boys*, *Big Holiday Packages*, *Who's Your Daddy?*, and *Gym Buddies & Buff Boys*. Visit him at www.therobrosen.com.

Award-winning, multi-published author of erotic romance, **SEDONIA GUILLONE**, spends her days writing deliciously naughty romances – when she's not cuddling with the man she loves or watching Kung Fu and Samurai films and eating chocolate. Sedonia welcomes comments from readers. You can find her Website and email address on her author bio page at www.sedoniaguillone.com.

STEPHEN OSBORNE has had stories published in many anthologies, including *Unmasked I* and *II*, *Boys Caught in the Act*, *Best Gay Love Stories 2010*, *Queer Wolf*, and *Hard Hats*. He is also the author of *South Bend Ghosts and Other Northern Indiana Haunts*. He and Jadzia the Wonder Dog can be followed on Twitter under the moniker southbendghosts.

THE EDITOR

ERIC SUMMERS resides in West Palm Beach with his partner, Mickey Erlach. This is his twelfth anthology for STARbooks Press. He used to sing in musicals, but don't get too excited; it was community theatre.